MY LADY, MY LOVE

Recent Titles by Anne Herries

CAPTIVE OF THE HAREM
THE COUNTERFEIT EARL
A DAMNABLE ROGUE
THE REGENCY RAKES
THE SHEIKH
A WICKED WENCH *
MILADY'S REVENGE *

Writing as Linda Sole

THE TIES THAT BIND *
THE BONDS THAT BREAK *
THE HEARTS THAT HOLD *

THE ROSE ARCH *
A CORNISH ROSE *
A ROSE IN WINTER *

BRIDGET *
KATHY *
AMY *

FLAME CHILD *
A SONG FOR ATHENA *

* available from Severn House

MY LADY, MY LOVE

Anne Herries

This first world edition published in Great Britain 2005 by
SEVERN HOUSE PUBLISHERS LTD of
9–15 High Street, Sutton, Surrey SM1 1DF.
This first world edition published in the USA 2005 by
SEVERN HOUSE PUBLISHERS INC of
595 Madison Avenue, New York, N.Y. 10022.

British Library Cataloguing in Publication Data

Herries, Anne
    My lady, my love
    1.   Love stories
    I.   Title
    823.9'14 [F]

    ISBN 0-7278-6183-2

Typeset by Palimpsest Book Production Ltd.,
Polmont, Stirlingshire, Scotland.
Printed and bound in Great Britain by
MPG Books Ltd., Bodmin, Cornwall.

One

The man being rowed ashore looked thoughtful, his dark eyes focused on the waterfront, his thoughts far away, expression stern, forbidding. His ship was anchored further out in the bay, because the port of New Orleans was crowded with vessels of all kinds. Since the Louisiana Purchase of 1803 by the Americans, the Mississippi River had been freed up to allow an ever-increasing flow of traffic, bringing with it a flood of hard-talking, hard-fighting men. These men haunted the brothels, taverns and gambling houses that clustered the banks of this part of the river, causing disruption and sometimes terror to the law-abiding residents of New Orleans.

Justin St Arnaud, the bastard child of Madame St Arnaud and the English Marquis of Blechingfield, had no liking for such places. He was here only to honour a promise to a friend. As Robbie Marshall lay dying of his wounds, gained in pursuit of his business as a merchant adventurer and sometime privateer, he had begged Justin to find the woman he loved and his son.

'Petra was so beautiful when I first saw her,' he'd told Justin as the life drained out of him. 'She was working in a whorehouse frequented by the sons of French Creole gentleman, but she hated them and all they stood for. I fell in love with her, and I took her away from that place. I found her a small house and she was always there for me when I came back from a voyage. She gave me a son. He's a fine lad, nearly grown to a man now but . . .' He sighed. 'It's more than two years since I saw them. Find them for me, Justin. Promise me you will find them?'

'Yes. I give you my word. I shall find them. Rest now, my friend.'

Robbie's hand moved restlessly on the coverlet. 'The *Dark*

1

Angel is your ship now, for you've been as a son to me, but the money is for them.'

'I swear I shall find them and they shall be cared for as you would wish.'

'God smiled on me the day you were shanghaied aboard my ship.'

Robbie clasped Justin's hand, holding it until he breathed his last, trusting in the man he had come to love to do right by him. Justin St Arnaud was a man of his word, and in the ten years they'd known each other their friendship had become a deep and abiding thing.

Justin had buried his friend at sea, turning his ship homeward towards the Gulf of Mexico where lay the now thriving port of New Orleans.

It had not always been thus. When the Sieur De Bienville first persuaded his French masters to settle the area the colony had been beset with problems. Fever, flooding, shortages, frogs and other more dangerous reptiles that hid in small banks of grass in the streets and crept into houses, and the scum of French prisons dumped on the settlers by the French government, all added to the settlers' troubles. After the territory was ceded to the Spanish in 1769 some improvements were made both in the moral behaviour of its citizens and to its development. Then, when two fires swept away many of the old, crude wooden buildings, a beautiful Spanish town was built to take their place. Yet the Spanish government guarded their territory jealously and had tried to forbid trade with the interior. Under the Americans it had flourished, trading posts and small settlements springing up along the banks of the rivers and spreading their tentacles over the fertile land of Louisiana.

Gangs of river pirates flourished too, often attacking the flat-bottomed boats that had to be propelled down river by means of men with long poles, who walked from the front to the back of the boat in turn, moving the cumbersome craft by sheer strength. These boats were vulnerable to attack by the gangs who flourished on the banks of the river, and it took a certain kind of man to brave the journey. Little wonder then that when they were in port they indulged in heavy drinking to relieve their tension.

Justin listened to the voices around him as he stepped ashore

2

and made his way through the crowded walkways. Cultivated French and Spanish voices mingled with American, Cajun and Negro in a rich mixture. Some of the Negroes moving about the waterfront might have been slaves on business for their masters, but many were free people of colour and able to trace their ancestry back as far as any French Creole.

The air was redolent with the scents of spices and molasses, which were being unloaded from two ships in the bay, blending with the enticing smell of gumbo cooking at little stalls or eating-houses. And, wafting on the breeze, the perfume of some exotic bloom from a secret garden hidden behind high walls.

Justin stopped to inquire after the woman he sought. Some passers-by intent on business ignored him, others shook their heads and hurried on, slightly afraid of the tall dark man with the brooding look and deep scar on his left cheek. He had the look of an adventurer, a strong, dangerous man, perhaps one of Jean Lafitte's band of cut-throats or another of that ilk, and it was best for ordinary folk to steer clear of such men. It was not for several minutes that someone pointed out the way to Petra's house.

It was a fair walk, the area better than that immediately on the waterfront, though not a part of the beautiful Spanish town that was still called the French Quarter. The wooden-boarded houses, some still built on stilts against invasion by water or inquisitive reptiles, despite the levees that had been built to protect them, were well kept and the people who lived here respectable. Justin was pleased to see that the windows of the house he had come to find were open and a woman's voice was raised in song somewhere within. However, when she answered his knock, the news was disappointing.

'She doesn't live here. My husband took the house on when the owner put it up for sale.'

'Do you know where Petra went?' Justin asked with a frown.

'We only moved here three months ago.' The woman hesitated, then, 'Try Marietta. She knows everyone.'

'Can you direct me to her house?'

'Across the street, the one with pots of flowers on the windowsill. She's old and doesn't come out much these days, but many people visit her and she will know if anyone does.

Sometimes the girls from the House of Pearls visit her. They bring her food I think.'

The House of Pearls was a brothel, rather better than many in the area, and frequented mostly by gentlemen and officers rather than the rivermen who preferred the cheap dives nearer the waterfront.

Justin thanked his informant and began to cross the road. A thin mangy dog was nosing hopefully in a pile of rubbish in the street. At one period a plague of rabid dogs had terrorised the settlement but this dog was merely hungry and ignored Justin as he passed.

The boarded house he was heading for looked in need of a coat of paint and a few well-placed nails, its roof lacking the repairs wanted to keep out the rain, which could be torrential at times. However, the garden seemed well tended, the flowering pots lovingly cared for and the curtains billowing at the open window of a soft creamy lace. Clearly someone cared for the old woman that lived there.

As he hesitated, a girl came out of the house. She was wearing a dark blue gown of stylish cut and good cloth, her long bluish-black hair tumbling over her shoulders in a profusion of silky waves and curls, a basket over her arm.

She was beautiful! Justin was struck by the way she held herself, pride and fire in every movement, every line of her shapely body. Her skin was a beautiful creamy colour, and as she approached him her eyes looked straight at him and he saw that they were very dark but seemed to glow with silver in their depths. He thought that he had never seen a girl to match her.

She must be one of the girls from the brothel, he thought, for surely no girl of good family as lovely as she would dare to venture this close to the waterfront. Besides, she was no shrinking flower, for there was a boldness about her as she met his look with a slight toss of her head that confirmed his opinion that she was no stranger to men.

'Whither so fast, sweet lady?' Justin asked, moving to cut off her escape as she would have passed him. 'I believe you have been visiting the house of the person I seek.'

'What business have you with Marietta?' The girl's magnificent eyes narrowed, a hint of temper in their lucent depths.

'If you mean her harm you should know that she has friends who will protect her.'

'No harm in asking a few questions I believe?' Justin feasted his eyes on the girl. He had been at sea for long months and had the natural appetite of a man, and this girl was arousing a deep, burning need. He had always been particular in such matters, choosing discreetly, often the wives of respectable men who were too old to satisfy their ladies' desires, and seldom visited a whorehouse. But this girl was different, and he could feel the strain of his breeches as his desire manifested itself strongly. 'You are sweet fare for the eyes of a man fresh from months at sea, lady. Tell me, are you to be found at the House of Pearls? And do you go there now, for if you do I bid you prepare for a visit as soon as my business here is done.'

A hot stinging flush crept into the girl's cheeks, a look of fury springing up in those wondrous eyes. 'How dare you?' she cried. 'You insult me, sir. I am not what you think me, but the daughter of a gentleman. If my father learned of your insult he would demand satisfaction.' Her hand snaked out suddenly, catching Justin unawares as she slapped him across the face.

Few other women would have dared, and had they done so would have met with retribution, but for some reason he felt no desire to punish her. Yet the throbbing need in his loins became uncomfortable, and he knew a primitive desire to carry her off to a secret place and have his pleasure with her. Yet even as he wrestled with his urgent need, he was amused for she looked so indignant, so furious as she swept by him.

Other women had pretended to outrage at a bold suggestion from Justin, but most melted in his arms at the end. He had no illusions concerning fine ladies, for in his experience they had no more morals than the girls who lived and served in the brothels, and indeed were often less honest. He had believed otherwise once and learned the treachery that lay behind a pretty face to his cost; he would not be deceived again. But he would have enjoyed dalliance with the fiery beauty for an hour or so, he thought, knowing a moment of regret as he walked up to the door of the house just ahead of him.

His knock brought no response, so after some hesitation,

he opened the door and went in. The parlour was furnished with relics of some sea captain's voyages, carved pieces that came from the east, jostling with a couple of solid English oak chests, and a painted cabinet of French origin filled with curios. The door to the next room was slightly open.

'Is anyone here?' Justin called, for the front parlour had a disused air and smelled musty. 'I seek Marietta's help if she will receive me.'

'Who are you and what do you want?'

The voice belonged to an old woman and came from the room behind the parlour. Justin opened the door further and went in. In a spindle chair by the stove a woman sat, apparently half dozing in the sunlight that flooded in through the back door, which stood open. A tabby cat was lying on her lap, and she stroked it with fingers that were curled and gnarled with age, the nails yellowed and long. Her face was so lined that she looked very ancient and wizened, her skin a dirty grey, and yet her eyes were bright and knowing as they focused on his face.

'Why have you come to see me? I shall not sell my house to you no matter how you threaten me.'

'I do not want to buy your house,' Justin told her. 'Nor would I threaten you if I did; you are safe from me, Marietta. I come only to ask if you can tell me where Petra has gone and her son Piers.'

'Why do you wish to know?'

'I have news for them, both good and bad.'

'How do I know I can trust you?'

Her look was so suspicious that Justin laughed. 'In truth you cannot know, madame, but if you do not tell me then Petra will lose what is rightfully hers.'

'You bring news of her man? He was a sea captain . . .'

'Robbie is dead, God rest his soul,' Justin said and his dark eyes clouded with sorrow. 'He wants to make sure that his legacy goes to Petra and his son.'

'Petra has no need of it now. She died of a fever six months past. After she died, the boy ran off. I'm not sure where he went but he had a friend – Joshua Renger. He was once a seaman and you'll find him in a tavern down by the port if you look hard enough. The boy may be with him.'

6

'Petra is dead?' Justin had not expected this and it shocked him for he felt that in part he had failed his friend. 'I am sorry to hear that, madame. But I shall search for the boy. Can you tell me what he looks like? Give me some clue that will make my search easier?'

'Piers is a big boy, of your own build I should say, or will be when a man grown. He has dark curling hair and blue eyes – and a temper on him that used to drive his poor mother wild.'

'Thank you, you have been very kind.' Justin took some gold coins from his pocket and laid them on the table for her to see. 'Now, there is one more thing I would ask, concerning the girl I saw leaving here just now.'

'What girl?' Her eyes narrowed and he knew that her suspicions had been aroused once more.

'The beautiful girl with black hair and eyes like . . . none other I have ever seen,' he ended for lack of words to best describe her. 'She had been here for she demanded to know what I wanted of you.'

Marietta gave a harsh crack of laughter. 'Aye, she would – that is my Estelle. Such pride . . . such pride . . .' Her laughter faded and she looked anxious, even frightened for a moment. 'Sometimes I fear for her, my beloved child.'

'She is your daughter?'

'No, though I nursed her after her mother died giving birth to her. My own child was weaned and it was my milk that reared her, my hands that tended her until she grew beyond childhood and her father sent me away for fear . . .' Marietta shook her head, her eyes narrowing once more. 'Why do you ask? If you mean her harm I shall kill you, strong and fearless as you are, you shall die.'

'Shall you work your magic spells on me, Marietta?' Justin asked with a wry smile, for he had met other women who claimed the power of strong magic. 'I pray you will not for I mean your darling no harm. I thought her from the House of Pearls and offended her by asking that I might attend her there, and I want only to apologise.'

'Her name is Estelle Lebrun,' Marietta told him, and the look in her eyes was speculative. 'Her father is rich and powerful and lives by the code of the French Creole gentlemen.

If you pursue her he would consider it an insult and expect satisfaction. Once he would have killed you in a duel, but now . . . he is more likely to seek reparation in other ways for he is not a well man. Estelle knows it not, but her father has a sickness that will not grant him many years.'

Justin looked at her with sudden intent for he had business with a certain Henri Lebrun. 'This gentleman – is he Monsieur Henri Lebrun? He had a banking and investment house I believe?'

'That is so, though he has been retired for some months now,' Marietta said, 'for reasons of his health they say . . .'

'You have heard rumours?'

Marietta considered and then shook her head. 'I have answered enough questions. Be gone, and take your gold with you. I have no need of it.'

Justin thought of the repairs needed to the house. 'It would fix your roof, madame, and you have done me service.'

'Then do me service in return,' Marietta said and her mouth crooked in wry amusement. 'You are young and strong and not afraid to climb to the roof I daresay – mend it and I shall bless you, but I'll not take your money.'

Justin laughed as he saw the old woman's expression. He discovered that he liked and respected her, and nodded as he gathered the gold and returned it to his jerkin pocket.

'You drive a hard bargain, Marietta, but I enjoy a challenge. I shall mend your roof.'

'And treat my Estelle well or you shall suffer the torments of hell for it, sir.'

Justin bowed to her. 'I give you my word that your child will come to no harm at the hands of Justin St Arnaud, madame. I wish merely to apologise, that is all.'

'In that you lie, sir, for I can read your mind. I know what you want of my girl, but I also know you will be her salvation – aye, though it will be after storm and tempest, she shall come to a safe harbour.'

Her eyes closed as she spoke and Justin felt the chill trickle down his spine. There was a kind of aura about the old woman at that moment, and her talk of spells and retribution made him think that she had dabbled in the magic that some called Voodoo. It was the old, dark magic of Africa and flourished amongst the people of Haiti and the islands of the West Indies. He smiled to himself as he left. He was not a stranger to such practices and knew that many believed and feared such women, believing them capable of working terrible spells. Justin neither feared nor ridiculed the idea, for on his travels around the world, he had seen men die after being cursed, though whether they had died from fear or an illness already harboured inside them he could not say.

He thought for a moment of Sinita, a woman of free colour from Haiti who lived on Grand Terre near the house that Jean Lafitte had built for himself. She was lovely in her own way, a hot-tempered woman who chose her lovers and sailed her own ship, mixing without fear with the pirates, cut-throats and murderers who frequented the island. On his last visit to trade with Lafitte, she had made it plain that she wanted Justin as her lover, but he had laughingly refused her offer and the look in her dark eyes had been one of hatred.

Sinita had vowed revenge on him, and he knew that she too claimed to have the powers that Marietta had spoken of. It was possible that Sinita had formed an image of him and was sticking her pins of hate into it at this moment, but as yet he had met with no ill fortune. In Justin's mind a man made his own fate, and life was there for the taking, worth the risks that had come his way as he worked before the mast, and in the battles that he had fought by Robbie's side.

As a youth of seventeen, he had been tricked, kidnapped and taken aboard the ship of a merchant adventurer, a man who lived by his wits and did not turn away from the chance of rich pickings in the form of a Spanish ship. Robbie had called himself a privateer for he attacked only Spanish ships, and considered them his enemy. He hated the Inquisition and the history of such men, and since, as he said, England, the country of his birth, was more often at war with Spain than not, Robbie considered that justification enough for helping himself to the merchandise that they carried.

In his attitude he was very like Jean Lafitte, who sought to justify his own piracy with such claims, but in truth they were pirates, as Justin himself had been while he sailed with Robbie. It was his intention now to turn away from piracy towards legitimate trade, for he believed that more money was to be made from rich cargoes. Besides, he had not chosen the life he had been given, and there was within him a sense of decency, a code that came from his early upbringing. Already in possession of sufficient money to buy a plantation and live like a gentleman if he wished, Justin had no such desire.

He had known another kind of life once, and his memories were bitter. He had trusted and believed in his heritage, in the love of his mother and her honesty, but on the day of her death he had learned that she had betrayed her husband with a lover.

The fact that he was a bastard had been flung at him by the man he had believed his father. The Chevalier St Arnaud had kept his silence while his wife lived, for he had loved her despite her betrayal, and his anger was reserved for the son of the man who had stolen what was rightfully his. For after the birth of her son, Juliette St Arnaud could never bear another, and the Chevalier could never have a true heir. Determined that a bastard should not inherit his lands and fortune, he had cast Justin out to seek his fortune where he might.

Justin had travelled to England to seek his father ... A frown creased his brow, for the memory was one that he seldom admitted into his conscious mind. He dismissed it now. He had met with a cruel betrayal but it had been his good fortune in the end, and he would not allow bitterness to sour his life. He had more important things on his mind for the moment.

Estelle Lebrun entered her father's house by the back entrance, giving her empty basket to her faithful maid Jessie. 'Has my father asked for me while I was gone?'

'Your Papa he bin working in his office all morning, honey chile,' the woman replied in her singsong voice, her eyes crinkling at the corners. Her skin was the colour of ebony, and she was large and plump, a white turban wrapped around her head, her dress blue and white cotton. 'Ah'se kept out of his way; if'n he don't ask no questions, Ah don't tell no lies.'

'I do not want to lie to him,' Estelle said, a little frown creasing her smooth brow. 'But he would not like me to visit Marietta and I cannot desert her. She was like a mother to me for I had no other, and I love her dearly.'

'You'se a lovin' chile,' Jessie crooned and smiled at her.

'Go on into your father now and tell him you'se been visitin' with a friend. He ain't likely to worry his head over that none.'

Estelle nodded, then sighed. 'Marietta is so brave but I am afraid she is far from well, Jessie. I wish I could do more for her.'

'Don't you worry your head none over that ole gal,' Jessie said in a scolding tone, her chins wobbling as she shook her head. 'She got all them gals from that *place* to run after her.'

'The House of Pearls you mean?' Jessie's words and look of disapproval brought back the memory of her encounter with that man – the large, dark man with intense eyes and a scar on his face. 'I've met some of them at Marietta's from time to time and they seem pleasant, friendly girls to me.'

'Lord have mercy!' Jessie exclaimed, her face stern with disapproval. 'If'n your Papa hears you say that he'll take a blue fit. Certain sure he'll forbid you to go there again, and a good thing too if'n you'se meeting them gals.'

'I cannot be rude to them when they have been so good to Marietta,' Estelle said. 'Don't look at me like that, dear Jessie, for I cannot bear it if you are cross with me.'

'Ain't cross with you, chile,' Jessie said. She worried about her beloved girl for reasons that she could never reveal to a living soul, for there were things she knew that she had no right to know. 'Go on into your Papa now, and tell him Ah'se ready to serve your dinner when you'se ready.'

Estelle smiled at her as she left the kitchen and went through the house to her father's office, which was at the front of the house and looked out on the street of beautiful stone Spanish-style houses. Shady trees lined the quadrangle, which had been formed when the settlement had first begun, though fires had swept away the old wooden houses some years ago. Not far away was the Place d'Armes and many important Government buildings, for they lived in the heart of the French Quarter and her father's family had owned property here for almost a century. His great, great grandfather had been one of the first to settle here, the younger son of an ancient French family, rich in culture and breeding but poor financially. The family had grown prosperous over the years, her father's business of lending and investing money for others one that paid hand-somely for her beautiful gowns and the luxury of her home.

11

Estelle knew that she was fortunate to have such an indulgent, loving father. Henri Lebrun spoiled his only child, giving her everything she could want, his pleasure to see her eyes light up over some new treasure.

'You are all I have to live for, my child,' Henri had told her many times. 'I wish only for your happiness, and I shall do all that I can to make you secure.'

Sometimes Estelle wondered why her father seemed to worry over her so much. She was barely eighteen but already she had admirers, in particular the son of one of her father's close friends – André de Varennes – a young man who made her heart beat faster when he smiled at her. As yet she had scarcely thought of marriage, but, when the time came, she hoped that André would speak to her father. It would be a good match, and fitting for both families were French Creole and wealthy. André's father was an importer of goods, luxuries that came from France or the East, and the two businesses should blend easily. So why should her father worry for her future? Surely he must see how easily it could all be arranged.

He was sitting in a chair by the window when she entered his office, his eyes closed and his head resting against the back of his comfortable armchair, which was of the English Georgian style, with front legs carved in the shape of a lion's paw and covered in tapestry. The desk in front of him was a magnificent partners desk with a leather top tooled with gold, and that too had come from England, one of the few British imports that had managed to slip through the Spanish embargo.

Things were different now, of course, for trade flourished with many countries, and New Orleans thrived in the thrusting climate the Americans had brought to the port. It was perhaps the new wealth that had caused England to cast jealous eyes over the territory. In the past two years there had been bloody battles between the British and the Americans, and Estelle's father believed there were more to come.

'Depend upon it, the British will try to take back as much of what they lost in the War of Independence as they can. They are a greedy, grasping nation, as France has known to its cost in the past. We grow too prosperous here, and they will take what they can of it.'

Estelle found such sentiments disturbing for she knew that

her father worried about his business interests if New Orleans were to be invaded. He had ceased to invest so actively this past year or so, because his doctors had told him he was working too hard and must rest more. His daughter knew little of her father's affairs, for if she asked he merely smiled and told her not to bother her pretty head over such trifles.

It seemed that there was always money for her, though she had noticed that her father did not give the lavish receptions he once had, limiting himself to close friends for informal dinners and al fresco breakfasts in the gardens when the weather was warm and pleasant. Yet he had never expressed any real concerns and it was a shock to her to see how grey his skin looked, and how tired and worn down he appeared sitting there with his eyes closed.

'Papa,' she said softly. 'Are you unwell?'

He opened his eyes and looked at her. He was still a handsome man, with silvered hair, slate grey eyes and a full, generous mouth. Yet his eyes had a wearied look and his skin an unnatural pallor.

'Estelle, my dearest,' he said, and smiled at her, though nothing could hide the tiredness. 'I was just thinking of you – of your future. I have been remiss in my care of you for you are eighteen and as yet un-promised. I have not wanted to part with you, my love, but it is time something was done about your marriage.'

'Surely there is no hurry, Papa? I am happy with you and do not mind if I am not married for another year or so.'

'Another year . . .' Henri sighed for he knew that by the time a year had passed he might not be here to take care of his precious child. What would happen to her then? It worried him that she might be at the mercy of unscrupulous men, especially if his secret – his sin – were ever exposed. He ought to have sought an alliance for her before this, but he had selfishly kept her with him, and now . . . now it might be too late. 'We have been invited to a grand ball given by Mrs Philip Spencer, who is the sister of Mr Frank Erskine, a wealthy American with whom I have conducted business in the past. It will be an opportunity for you to meet gentlemen and perhaps something can be arranged.'

Henri did not tell her that he already had an offer for her

hand in marriage or that Frank Erskine had called on him earlier that day for the express purpose of making his intentions known. The American was rich and traded with the men who brought their cargoes down from the interior as well as some of the sea captains, his business interests thriving and growing at an alarming rate. He was already an important man in the state and would become more so, for he had ambitions that went beyond his business.

It would be a good match for Estelle, more than he could hope for in truth, though it was not what he wanted for his darling girl. He would have preferred a gentleman, but there was no hope of that now – if in reality there had ever been. For though Estelle herself had no notion of it, she was the child of his mistress not his wife.

Leah had been the most beautiful girl he had ever seen when he first met her at a Quadroon Ball, and he had fallen instantly in love with her. Their liaison had lasted many years, until in fact the day Leah died giving birth to her daughter, their love continuing despite Henri's decision to take a wife for the sake of an heir. In that fate had played a cruel trick on him for his wife gave birth on the same day as his mistress, and both she and her daughter had died soon after.

Henri had seen the soft creamy complexion of his surviving child and known that it would be easy to pass her off as the child of his wife. So he had taken her home with him, swearing her nurse Marietta to silence on pain of dire punishment should she betray his secret.

Estelle had given Henri's life new meaning. He adored her as he had adored her mother, spoiling and delighting in her as she grew to girlhood and then to become a beautiful woman. But the problem of her marriage had exercised his thoughts for some while now, and he had hesitated to arrange a match with the son of his friends.

It was forbidden to marry a person of colour, and no matter that Estelle's skin was as creamy and fair as any woman of French Creole descent, in law she was deemed to be of coloured blood. Even Henri had not defied the law, which Bienville had signed when the colony was formed, despite his love for Leah.

Henri knew that his friends would despise Estelle if they learned the truth, but Erskine was an unknown quantity. He came from the north where such traditions were not so deeply entrenched, and perhaps would not care if he learned subsequently that his wife had mixed ancestry. He was also wealthy, well able to keep his wife in the manner to which she had been accustomed. Yet still Henri hesitated for there was something about the man that gave him pause, faint whispers had reached his ears only recently and he was uncertain what to do for the best for his beloved child. Nothing mattered now other than that she should be safe.

He smiled at her lovingly. 'Well, we shall see,' he said. 'As you say, there is no hurry. We have time enough, my love. But we shall go to this ball for it is our duty. Mrs Spencer is raising funds. We need to strengthen our defences and raise more militia in case the British attack us.'

'Oh, Papa,' Estelle cried. 'Surely it will not happen?'

'Last year the British attacked Michigan and captured an American fort,' her father said with a frown. 'Earlier this year, the British repelled troops from Kentucky at the battle of Frenchtown. Though that does not affect us here it is a sign that there could be an attack at any time. They covet our position, child, for we are the gateway to the interior and its wealth. We must be prepared for the worst.' He sighed deeply. 'But you will enjoy the ball and perhaps you will meet someone who could make you happy.'

'I am happy,' Estelle said and kissed his cheek. How soft and dry his skin felt against her lips, and she was aware of his frailty as never before. 'If you will excuse me, dearest Papa, I shall go up and change my gown before we dine.'

She was frowning as she left him for such talk disturbed her, because she knew it worried her father. She would not think of war, she decided, her thoughts returning once more to the man she had met as she left Marietta's house.

How could he have thought her a girl from the House of Pearls? She had been so angry with him, but her anger had cooled now. It had been reckless of her to slap him for he might have retaliated with violence. He was a strong man and might have punished her in any way he chose. Yet she believed she had caught a look of amusement in his eyes as she walked past him, as though her show of temper had amused him.

What did he want of Marietta and who was he? Estelle

15

wondered as she went upstairs to change, and then put the incident from her mind. It did not matter. She was unlikely to see him again.

Two

Justin stood looking at the elegant façade of the imposing house; its fancy iron grills at the windows were very Spanish and somehow forbidding, as if warning potential intruders to beware. But he was not a man to be intimidated and he had no time to waste on this business. He had spent the previous evening searching for Robbie's son, but had found nothing to help him discover the boy or yet the sea captain of whom Marietta had spoken.

Some of the men he'd questioned had known of Joshua Renger, remembering him as an old man who had retired from the sea and spent his days nodding in the sun by the water-front, but apparently he had not been seen for some months. No one seemed to know anything of Piers, for who would notice a lad amongst so many? There were always boys on the waterfront trying to earn a few coins doing any odd jobs that came to hand. Justin knew that it could take months to find the lad, perhaps years. He would not give up his search, though he might be forced to employ others when he returned to sea. If Piers had left New Orleans he might be anywhere.

Should Justin turn his search inland? Without friends, possibly penniless and grieving, Piers must have felt lost and alone. Had he gone in search of a living somewhere in the interior? Or perhaps the sea . . . the sea was in his blood for he was Robbie's son. Marietta had spoken of him having made a friend of Renger, which all pointed towards a feeling for the sea. It was quite possible that the boy had gone to sea as a cabin boy. If that were the case it might be years before he returned to New Orleans.

16

Justin frowned, bringing his thoughts back to the matter in hand. Some of Robbie's money had been invested in the cargo he had recently sold, now safely lodged with bankers Justin trusted. Robbie had also told him of a large investment he had made with Henri Lebrun.

'I lodged five thousand English gold sovereigns with Lebrun. There was to be interest of five percent a year and he has had the money for five years. It should be a sizeable sum by now, and I want my son to have that money, Justin. You will find the papers in my sea chest. Lebrun will repay you if you present the papers.'

Five thousand sovereigns was a large sum of money, Justin thought as he approached the house, and five years a long time. Anything could have happened. Lebrun was not a bank but an investment broker and, as such, more vulnerable to the vagaries of fate.

He was admitted to the house by an elderly Negro who spoke gravely and asked Justin to wait while he inquired if his master were at home. However, he was not kept waiting many minutes and soon found himself admitted to the gentleman's office.

Marietta had not been wrong about Lebrun's health, Justin thought as he measured the cut of the man. Undoubtedly a gentleman, distinguished, wealthy by the look of his home . . . and yet there was something that did not fit. A slight hesitation, a quick frown as Justin named his purpose, and something in the eyes – a flash of fear perhaps? He could not be certain.

'Ah, yes, Mr Robert Marshall, I recall the gentleman,' Lebrun said looking at his hands as if he needed some point of concentration. 'It was a long time ago. I cannot lay my hands on the file just like that. I shall have to see where the money was invested.'

'I have Robbie's papers here,' Justin said. 'He asked me to seek repayment on his son's behalf.'

'Yes, yes, I am sure it can be arranged, but I must look into it further. Some investments do not prosper as much as others. There may be more or less in the account.'

'I fail to understand you, sir,' Justin said giving him a hard look. 'Robbie said that there was to be interest of five percent a year, he did not mention the risk of loss to his capital.'

'I am not a bank, sir.' Lebrun's hand shook slightly and he was a little grey in the face as he shuffled a pile of papers. 'I invest on behalf of others and when a figure of profit is mentioned it is purely speculative. It may be three or five percent – or nothing at all if the investment was disappointing.'

'That was not Robbie's understanding of the transaction between you. Nor do I see any mention of such a loss within the document.'

'I assure you it is perfectly proper,' Lebrun told him. 'The nature of investment is precarious, sir. I did explain that to Mr Marshall, as I do to all my clients.'

'Are you telling me that the investment failed?'

Lebrun's face went a shade whiter as he caught the note of menace in Justin's voice. 'I cannot say for sure until I look through my papers. I have suffered some reverses myself. You must give me time to investigate the matter further.'

'How much time?' Justin's eyes narrowed dangerously. He sensed something false here, and suspected that an attempt to cheat Robbie's son would be made if he were not alert. 'I shall not allow my friend to be cheated, sir.'

'You insult me,' Lebrun said, a note of outrage in his voice. 'I have never defrauded a client in my life – but sometimes the capital invested cannot be returned in full. It is the nature of the business.'

'If that had been the arrangement I would accept your word, sir, but I suggest you look very carefully at your accounts. Robbie expected a return of his gold with interest and I know him too well to believe that he would hazard his money in a risky venture. Nor is there any mention of risk in these papers. I shall return in one week and I shall expect the money to be ready for me.'

'But . . .' Lebrun sat down, looking shaken, a flash of something that might have been fear in his eyes. 'I shall see what can be done, but I can make no promises.'

'I am sure I shall not be disappointed.'

Justin turned and went out. Clearly something was wrong here. He was not sure whether Lebrun was trying to avoid repaying the money or if . . . His thoughts came to an abrupt halt as a girl entered the hall. He saw at once that she was the one he had met coming from Marietta's house and caught his breath. He had thought her beautiful then but today she looked even lovelier.

'Mademoiselle Lebrun.' He inclined his head. 'We meet again.'

'You!' Her eyes flashed with temper. 'How dare you come to my home? If you persist with your insults I shall speak to my father. He will be very angry.'

'I wish to apologise for my mistake yesterday, mademoiselle,' Justin said, feeling amused by her spirited attack. 'I had heard that girls from the House of Pearls visited Marietta and thought you one of them – for it is a dangerous area for a girl as lovely as you and I did not imagine a girl of good family would venture there alone.'

'Marietta's friends know me. None of them would lay a finger on me – nor permit others to do so.'

Her head was up but she knew that he spoke only the truth, and it was exactly what her father would say if he knew that she had been to visit her old nurse.

'But there are men on the waterfront that care nothing for Marietta's friends nor yet your father's anger, mademoiselle. In future I should take a servant with you for your own safety.'

Estelle's cheeks were warm but she gave a defiant toss of her head. 'It is not your business what I choose to do with my time, sir. I do not know you nor do I care to. Why are you in my father's house?'

'I have business with your father,' Justin said, his mouth thinning. The girl amused him, but it was typical of her class to behave so. Her father imagined he could cheat Robbie of a small fortune, and she . . . believed men such as he beneath her. 'I must take my leave of you, mademoiselle. I have more important things to do with *my* time.'

Estelle felt the sting of his words, knowing that she had been less than polite to one of her father's clients. Henri would not be pleased if he knew.

'I thought . . .' she broke off as she realised how it would sound if she admitted that she thought he had come in pursuit of her. 'I bid you good day, sir. I must speak with my father.'

Justin inclined his head, passing her to let himself out of the front door. There was no sign of the servant who had let him in, which was a little strange for such houses as these usually had a surfeit of servants to wait on clients and visitors.

He was frowning as he walked away from the house. Was it possible that Lebrun was in financial difficulty? Was that why he needed more time to settle the debt to Robbie, because he did not have ready cash available to him? He had clearly been a wealthy man in the past, for his house and rich furnishings were signs of prosperity, but the investment business could be precarious, and men might lose money as easily as make it.

Robbie had been foolish to invest such a large sum and to leave it so long if it was on the terms Lebrun suggested. It did not sound like the man he knew, nor was he inclined to believe it. Lebrun might well have invested the money however, perhaps in a risky venture that had come unstuck.

If that were the case, Justin would have to think carefully about his next step. In the meantime, however, he had promised Marietta he would mend her roof. He was a man of his word, and the sooner it was finished the better for he needed to be free to search for Piers, and he intended to put to sea again within a week or two.

Estelle hesitated outside her father's office, knocking uncertainly. Would the stranger have told her father that he had seen her near the waterfront? He would be angry with her for disobeying him, but perhaps it had not been mentioned. Plucking up her courage, she went in and then caught her breath in dismay. Her father sat with his arms on the desk, his head in his hands. Clearly he had not heard her knock.

'Is something wrong, Father?' she asked in concern. 'Are you unwell?'

Henri looked up at her, his face grey and anxious. 'No, I am not ill, child,' he said and sighed, knowing that he would have to tell her, that it was unfair not to give her some warning. 'But I have a problem. My business has not done as well of late as it once did – and I have been asked to repay a large loan. It will be difficult to find the money immediately.'

'Oh, Papa,' Estelle said, thinking guiltily of the new gowns she had bought recently. 'I am so sorry. I did not know – and I have spent so much money on my dresses this year.'

'You have not overspent your allowance I hope?' It was said with an indulgent smile but she sensed that he meant it this time.

'No, of course not, Papa. I still have some twenty American dollars, which you may have to help you pay the loan if you wish.'

Henri smiled oddly. 'No, no, child, keep your money. I must find near six thousand English gold sovereigns in a week – if it may be done.'

'Oh, Papa,' she said, feeling dismayed for it seemed a very great sum of money to her. 'Will it be very difficult for you?'

'It will not be easy,' he admitted. 'There are certain bonds I may sell, but that will . . .' He broke off with a sigh. The bonds were in truth next to worthless, for it was an investment in a French company that had failed and near ruined him. He had had to sell most of his assets in New Orleans to pay the clients from whom he had borrowed money, some without their knowledge, to make his investment. Most had been paid, but he had hoped for more time before Robert Marshall's loan need be repaid. 'I fear there will be little left for your inheritance, Estelle.'

'Has all your money gone, Papa?'

'Most of it,' her father said. 'If it had not been for this repayment I might have recovered but as it is . . .' His hands were trembling and he looked ill. 'I think I may have to . . .' He gave a little cry and slumped forward across his desk.

'Papa!' Estelle was alarmed. She rushed to his side, bending over him to discover that his face looked a strange colour and he was breathing heavily. 'You are ill! I must send for the doctor at once.'

She went to the door and called for Erle, her father's manservant, who came running to see what was wrong. He took charge at once, summoning other servants to help him carry the master to his bedchamber and go for the doctor.

Estelle watched with a sense of helplessness, knowing that her father was suffering from an illness she had suspected for a while, though he had always pretended to be perfectly well. The news that he must repay his loan more quickly than he had hoped had brought on this attack, though she now suspected that he must have been under a strain for a long time.

She ought to have known that things were not as they should be when her father gave up his business and started to see the few clients he still dealt with at home, Estelle thought. She had believed he was selling his assets because he needed to rest more, but now she understood that he had been in financial trouble for some time.

It seemed an age before the doctor arrived. He spent half an hour closeted with her father, but when he came out he gave her a reassuring smile.

'Your father has had a mild heart attack, Estelle. He will recover with rest and the loving care I know he will receive at your hands. He is not an invalid, but he must rest and there must be no worry. Another attack like this could be more severe, and then I could not vouch for his recovery. So, peace and quiet for the moment, my dear.'

'Yes, of course, sir,' Estelle said. 'May I go in to him now please?'

'Yes, of course. The sight of your lovely face will, I dare say, do Henri more good than any of my potions.'

Estelle smiled and went into her father's bedchamber. He was lying with his head on a pile of snowy pillows, his eyes closed, but he opened them as she approached and gave her an apologetic look.

'Forgive me for distressing you, my dearest child. It was foolish of me to allow myself to be so upset by that gentleman's visit. I shall simply have to sell something to raise the money.'

'Hush, Papa,' Estelle said, sitting on the side of his bed and taking his hand into hers. 'The doctor said that you are not to worry. It is not good for you.'

'Business has to be attended to no matter what,' her father said. 'But I shall ask for more time. He must grant it to me for I cannot make the necessary arrangements from my bed.'

'Could I not do something to help you, Papa?'

'I suppose you might take a letter to a friend of mine,' Henri said. 'Monsieur Jean de Varennes – I have done him enough favours in the past. Yes, I shall dictate a letter and you may take it to him, Estelle.'

'Yes, of course, Papa.' She fetched his writing slope from where it stood on his chest of drawers and sat with it opened before her on the bed. 'What do you wish me to say, Papa?'

'Begin, My Dear Varennes. Finding myself unwell and unable to attend my business, there is a matter on which I would seek your advice and help. If you could call on me at your convenience I would appreciate the favour of your time. There, that will do, child,' Henri said. 'Give it to me and I shall sign it.'

The letter was duly signed and sealed, and with that done, Henri seemed prepared to settle back for sleep.

'I shall take your letter now, Papa.'

'Yes, yes, child. Go now for I shall sleep easier once I know things are in a way to be settled.'

His eyes were closing and it was obvious that he was very tired. She left the room quietly, taking the letter with her. It was no hardship for her to deliver the letter for Monsieur de Varennes lived only a few streets away, and if she were lucky she might see André.

'So, you have come back,' Marietta said, fixing Justin with a baleful stare. 'If you seek more answers I have none for you. The answer lies in your heart, look there and you will find what you most desire.'

'Speak not to me in riddles,' Justin said. 'I come to repay a debt not to ask more questions. I shall fix your roof, old woman, for if not it will let in the rain.'

Marietta nodded, her eyes narrowed and crafty. 'That front window needs fixin', and there's a loose board on the back porch. That window drives me crazy when the wind blows of times.'

'And you were not born yesterday,' Justin replied with a wry twist of his mouth. 'Very well, I shall mend the window and the porch, and then the roof.'

Marietta nodded, her dark eyes gleaming. 'What did old man Lebrun tell you? Will he pay you the money he owes?'

'How did you know I went there to seek repayment of a loan?'

'Petra told me her man had lodged money with Lebrun. She needed money for her man was away a long time and she had none left after she became ill. She approached Lebrun once but he would not give her anything, though she told me that Robbie had left instructions for her to draw on his money if she needed it.'

23

'I think the man may be a rogue,' Justin said, eyes narrowed. 'Tell me, Marietta, was it for lack of money that Petra died?'

'It made things hard for her, but she would have died of the fever no matter what. I saw that she had what she needed to keep body and soul together.'

'But no thanks to Lebrun,' Justin said. 'Had he shown mercy I might also have done so, but I think he deserves nothing from me.'

'Yet there is Estelle to consider,' Marietta reminded him. 'You have promised no harm to her.'

Justin's eyes flashed with anger, but then his mouth twisted into a smile once more. 'I have work to do, old woman, and you waste my time in idle talk.'

Marietta made no reply but he thought he saw a gleam of mockery in her eyes as he went outside to make a start on the work of making her house proof against the weather. She was right, of course. Lebrun deserved no sympathy if he had tried to cheat Robbie's woman of her rights, but the girl was innocent and must somehow be protected from the worst of her father's misdeeds.

Estelle knew that she would find Monsieur de Varennes at his house since it was now midday and he usually visited his office early in the mornings. She was admitted into the house by a Negro servant, and asked to wait in the front parlour while he inquired if his master was at home.

She contented herself by staring at a cabinet filled with French porcelain from the Sèvres factory near Paris, for like her father Monsieur de Varennes still considered himself French despite having been born here in New Orleans. She was engrossed in her study and not immediately aware of someone behind her until the voice spoke softly.

'And what brings you here today, Estelle?'

'André?' Estelle turned, her heart racing as she saw the young man. How handsome he was with his pale blond hair and bluish-green eyes. 'You startled me, for I did not hear you.'

'You were looking at my father's collection,' André said. 'Some of the porcelain is beautiful, no?'

'Yes, very,' she said and blushed because the hot look in

24

his eyes sent shivers up and down her spine. 'My father has some pieces but not as many or as fine as these examples.'

'My father visited Paris as a young man. He fell in love with the porcelain then, as well as with my mother, who he persuaded to marry him and make her home here. I think she pined for her beloved Paris until she died. That is sad, yes?'

'Yes, very sad,' Estelle said. 'Yet she had your father and you. I do not think I should pine if those I loved were about me.'

André shrugged. 'Well, it was a long time ago. I am sorry but my father is not here today, Estelle. He had to meet with one of the captains he trades with and examine a cargo. Is there anything I can do to help?'

'I came to bring a letter from my father,' Estelle said and held it out to him. 'Papa is not well and he has some business that will not wait. He asks that your father call on him as soon as possible.'

'I shall give it to him as soon as I see him,' André promised. 'I am sorry that your father is unwell, Estelle. You know that our fathers have been friends for many years – and that I have a warm regard for you.'

His eyes and his voice seemed to caress her. Estelle gazed up at him, feeling she might drown in those eyes that reminded her of the restless sea. They changed colour with his moods as did the sea with the tides, and were just as mysterious. What did he truly mean when he spoke of a warm regard for her?

She had been waiting for him to speak to her father for months, but he had said nothing to her, and she wondered if André felt merely friendship. She had always liked him for he was the most handsome man of her acquaintance, and she knew that several girls, with whom she sometimes took tea, were attracted to him. Would he choose a wife from amongst them or would he visit Paris, as his father had at his age, and bring back his true love?

'You look very thoughtful,' André said. 'Will you stay for some refreshments?'

Estelle would have liked to stay but that would mean summoning his Tante Rosemarie, for she could not take tea alone with him, and the woman was such a gossip that meant she would be here another two hours.

'I should have liked that,' she admitted. 'But I must go home. I am worried for my father.'

'Yes, of course,' André agreed with a little nod of his head. 'Perhaps you will allow me to walk with you for a part of the way. I must visit my father's offices, and I shall give him your letter.' He put it away inside his coat, offering her his arm. 'Shall we go?'

Estelle took his arm with a feeling of pleasure. It would be nice to have his company a little longer, and the afternoon was pleasant, warm and still, perfect for a stroll.

Justin had more business in New Orleans than the matter of Lebrun. After he had spent two hours working on Marietta's roof, and discovering that there were many more jobs crying out for attention, he stripped to the waist in her yard and washed away the sweat under the pump. His skin had a golden colour earned during his years before the mast, when he had worked as hard as any crewman, his muscles hard and toned to perfection.

Leaving Marietta, he made his way to the French Quarter, where he spent some time doing business with an importer of silks and fancy goods, then left to visit several others with whom he hoped to be trading in the future.

He had just come from a store that he had used to provision the ship in the past, and had struck a good bargain with the owner for all the dry goods he would need on his next voyage. He had also inquired for an agent who might help him search for Piers and was on his way to see the person recommended to him, when he caught sight of Estelle walking with a young man.

It was clear that they were enjoying one another's company for she laughed and looked up at him, her eyes sparkling with amusement, and he was smiling. There was an air of satisfaction about the young man, who clearly came from a good family and was sure of himself and his place in the world.

Estelle glanced Justin's way for a moment, saw him, her face registering displeasure before she turned away, her cheeks slightly coloured. Her companion had not noticed anything untoward, and Justin grimaced to himself as they passed on. It was better that she had friends, he thought, better that her affections were engaged. He was not interested in marriage, nor did he wish for a wife from that class. She was too proud, too haughty, to look at a man like him, and that was as well for both of them, even if she did make his pulses throb when he looked at her. It was mere lust and he could satisfy that in other arms.

Now that his business was done in New Orleans, he would visit Lafitte's kingdom on Grand Terre. It suited him to keep on terms with the pirate king, even if he intended to trade within the bounds of legality in future. A tithe would still have to be paid to Lafitte if his ship were to pass unmolested in these waters.

But before that he must find the agent he needed to continue to make inquiries for Piers in his absence. His own search had so far come to nothing, though he intended to spend that evening making inquiries along another part of the waterfront.

As he lengthened his stride, aware that he had much to do and little enough time to do it, Justin put the thought of Estelle from his mind. She was beautiful and he desired her, but he had no mind to become involved with a woman like that.

For a moment he recalled the woman who had soured him for others. A pale English beauty, she had led the young man he then was on to believe that she loved him, that she desired him in her bed, and then, when he had tried to make love to her, she had laughed at him. Her lover had come from behind the screen in her boudoir where he had hidden during Justin's passionate wooing, and they had mocked him together. It was after that, that he had ridden away, angry and humiliated, to be set upon by rogues, who had shanghaied him aboard a ship bound for the West Indies.

Justin had never known for sure who had ordered that he should be abducted, though he suspected his uncle might have had a hand in it. Yet why should he have acted so basely towards the son of his late brother? Justin was surely no threat to him. Born of an illicit relationship between Madame St Arnaud and the Marquis of Blechingfield, Justin had no claim to his father's title or fortune – so why should his uncle want to be rid of him?

He had vowed that one day he would return to England and demand the truth of his uncle, but somehow he never had. The sting of his humiliation at the hands of that English milady and her lover, and anger over his abduction, had faded as he found his niche aboard Robbie's ship. After a storm, during which Robbie had saved his life, they had become friends, and through the succeeding years that friendship strengthened. And Justin had repaid the favour by saving his friend's life during a fierce fight for possession of a Spanish vessel.

In Robbie he had found the father he had never truly known, for St Arnaud had been always a distant, cool figure, not actively unkind during his wife's lifetime, but distant, spending little time at home. It irked Justin that he could not carry out his friend's wishes in full, for Petra's death was unfortunate. He had visited her resting place and had a memorial erected to hold the casket, for the ground would become too water-logged in winter for it to be buried, and it had been placed with others in a vault awaiting proper disposal. At least he had been able to do that for Petra, he thought, but until he could find Piers he would consider that he had failed.

He walked into the building where he hoped to find his agent, taking the stairs two at a time in his haste. There was much to do and no time to waste in thinking of the past. In the morning he must visit Lafitte on Grand Terre and renew their understanding, though he had been given the freedom of the retreat since he had saved Jean's brother Pierre from death. It had been a mere accident, a runaway horse in the street, a moment's hesitation on Pierre's part, and action on Justin's. For that he had been an honoured guest on Grand Terre when-ever he chose to visit.

He had stayed clear of the pirate stronghold for as long as he could, because of Sinita, but there was no help for it. Unless he wished to offend Lafitte, he must visit without more delay.

Monsieur de Varennes visited with her father for more than an hour that evening. Estelle could only be glad that he had come so promptly to her father's aid, but when she went in to see him later, he did not look as if his problems had been solved.

'I have brought you a tisane to help you rest,' she told him, feeling anxious as she saw the way his eyes watched her. 'Did Monsieur de Varennes promise to help you, Papa?'

'He will see if a loan can be raised on this house,' Henri said. 'I have hesitated to do it before this, Estelle, because if we could not meet the repayments we would lose our home.'

'Oh, Papa,' she said, her heart catching with fright. She had not realised things were so very bad. 'Would it not be better to sell the house and find a smaller one where we could live without debt?'

'Perhaps . . .' Her father looked at her oddly. 'If we did that it might spoil any chance you have of making a good marriage. If I can keep afloat for a while longer I might come about – or you might marry. For myself I do not mind the disgrace but for you . . .' A little shiver went through him and he placed a hand to his eyes. 'I am a fool, Estelle. I should never have invested so much in one company. It was my policy always to spread the load, but I thought it was a chance to make riches beyond my dreams and it went awry.'

'Oh, Papa,' Estelle said, catching his hand and holding it to her cheek as she sat on the edge of his bed. 'Do not distress yourself for my sake. I beg you not to make yourself ill. I shall be quite happy living with you and Jessie in a little house somewhere.'

'But it is not what I wanted for you. All my planning, all my scheming – and it has come to this.'

'Surely Monsieur de Varennes would lend you some money himself?'

'Ah no, daughter.' Her father shook his head. 'A gentleman does not borrow from his friends, it is a matter of honour. I must hope for a loan from the bank but if none is forthcoming then we shall have to sell the house – unless you make a good marriage.'

'But who shall I marry?' Estelle asked, and in her mind was the young man who had escorted her home that afternoon. 'Has anyone spoken to you of marriage?'

'Yes, one gentleman I might consider,' her father replied, frowning slightly. He had hoped that some other avenue might open to him, that he might be able to leave Estelle enough money to keep her in comfort for her lifetime, and that she need never marry. Now he knew that it was a forlorn hope. He would have little left to leave her once he had repaid the debt to Robert Marshall, and he had no doubt that St Arnaud would not go away without the money owed him. 'He is an American and his name is Frank Erskine. His sister is Mrs Philip Spencer, and it is to her that we are engaged next week.'

'Mr Erskine has spoken to you?'

Estelle felt a cold chill trickle down her spine as she looked at her father and saw the faint flicker of hope in his eyes. He wanted her to marry this man! How could she marry a man she had hardly met when it was another that she had set her heart on?

Besides, if the whispers she had heard when visiting Marietta were true, Mr Erskine was not a man she could like and she would certainly never wish to marry him. It was said that he owned the House of Pearls, and that sometimes he lay with the girls who worked there. They said he was cruel and that he hurt them, and most of them disliked him. Some said that they would leave his house if they dared, but they were afraid of him.

Estelle knew that he was a very rich man, and that he appeared to be an upstanding member of the community, but underneath he was very different. How could her father wish her to marry such a man? Surely he could not know the truth?

'But I do not know Mr Erskine, Father.'

'No, I know that you have met him but twice on his visits to the house,' her father said. 'But he brought me some business this past year and without it . . .' He sighed. 'It has kept us in food and paid for your allowance, Estelle, and the man seems honest enough, though he is not French and does not live by our code. I dare say you might think him a little rough, but he likes you very much and I believe he would treat you kindly. He would settle several thousand dollars on you as a wedding gift, child, and that means you will always be secure. I think also that he might allow me to live in your home for the time left to me – and then I might be settled with no more financial worries.'

Estelle stood up and went over to the window to look out. The sun was beginning to fade from the sky and it would be dark very soon now. It had been a long, disturbing day, and she knew that her irritation of nerves was a combination of all the things that had happened to her.

If her father approved of Mr Erskine, he must be a gentleman, even if his manners were a little brusque. The stories she had heard of his owning the House of Pearls and of treating the girls who worked there badly were surely lies. Her father loved her and would never allow her to marry a man who might harm her.

She turned back to the bed, forcing herself to smile and speak lightly. 'You will give me time to get to know this gentleman, Papa? I shall not be forced to marry him if I cannot like him?'

'You know I would never hurt you,' her father said. 'But I must provide for when I am not here to take care of you, Estelle. It would please me if you would try to like him, for if you do not take him I am not sure what we shall do . . .'

Three

Justin felt the girl's dark eyes boring into his back as he walked away from the camp fire, where he had spent some time talking to the men sitting about it. They were drinking, laughing, sometimes quarrelling in a lazy way amongst themselves as they feasted on roast sucking pig and wild turkey cooked slowly on a spit over the fire.

His meeting with Lafitte had gone well as it usually did, for the men had a kind of wary respect for each other, and providing Justin paid his homage he was free to trade as he would within the sphere of Lafitte's influence. He had asked Lafitte if any word of Robbie's son had reached him, but received a negative shake of the head in return, though it was known that he had disappeared after his mother's death.

'She should have sent word to me if she was in need,' Lafitte growled. 'We take care of our own.'

'I think Petra had friends to care for her,' Justin said with a frown. 'But Robbie made provision for her to draw on his funds and it was refused. I shall have something to say to Lebrun when we meet again.'

Lafitte nodded and spat yellow bile into a spittoon. 'I have heard the man is finished,' he said. 'Foolish investments have ruined him. You will be lucky to recover the money, St Arnaud.'

'He has a fine house,' Justin said, eyes narrowed. 'He can find some means of repaying if he chooses.'

'I daresay you'll put the fear into him,' Lafitte said with a harsh laugh. 'Go now and make merry, take a woman if you choose. There are plenty here if you have a mind for it.' But there were none that interested Justin for his mind was on other things, another woman.

'Why do you avoid me?' Sinita's dark eyes flashed with temper as she suddenly pulled at his arm. 'What have I done that you should scorn me?'

Justin controlled his desire to laugh as he saw the frustration in her eyes. She was used to having her way, much as that other woman he had met recently, but *she* had stirred his senses, this one did not. There was something cold, almost evil, about Sinita that chilled his blood, and he knew that she dabbled in the black arts of the old magic, that she would use her skill to harm or kill if she could.

'I do not scorn you,' he said now, his eyes meeting hers. 'I choose my own women, Sinita, and I have no desire to lie with you.'

She thrust herself closer so that he could smell the hot, tangy musk of her body that had been oiled with something pungent and powerful. It made his blood race and he knew it was meant to inflame him, but his mind remained cool, aloof despite a sudden urgent throbbing in his loins.

'So there is another woman,' Sinita spat angrily at him. 'Go to her then, fool that you are, for she will bring you nothing but trouble. You should have looked at me with your heart, for I shall remember your scorn and one day I shall punish you.'

'I do not fear your magic,' Justin said, meeting her eyes steadily. 'Be careful what you do or say, Sinita. I do not forgive easily.'

Sinita dropped her hot eyes, feeling a chill of fear. She could dominate most men either by her body or her magic, but this one seemed too strong for her. Yet every man had his weakness and it might be that she would find his one day.

* * *

32

'Are you sure you are well enough to attend the ball this evening?' Estelle looked at her father anxiously for he seemed frail still and she was afraid that he might tire himself. 'We need not stay long, Papa. You must tell me if you are tired.'

'Do not worry your head over me,' Henri said, and smiled lovingly at her. 'I shall sit quietly with a few friends until you have danced your fill, Estelle.'

Estelle nodded, kissing his cheek as she went upstairs to get ready for the evening. She was apprehensive about what might happen that night, for she knew that her father was expecting her to make an effort to charm Mr Erskine. He had said no more of it to her, but she understood that he was still worried about his debt to *that* man!

She felt so angry with *him* for upsetting her dearest father. It seemed to her that Henri's illness had become suddenly worse after *he* had visited their house – the man with the dark, shivery eyes and the scar on his cheek. He had made her tremble inside as he looked at her but she was not afraid of him, just angry that he had first insulted her and then upset her father so much that he had become ill.

Would her marriage to Mr Erskine solve all her father's problems? If it were the only way then she would have to marry him, despite her reluctance.

Estelle twisted and turned before the mirror in her gown of dark green silk. It was embellished with a crusting of heavy bead embroidery on the hem and flirted about her ankles prettily. The sash was of cream, pleated and embroidered with green silk to match the hem, and the sleeves were tiny puffballs of froth that showed off her lovely arms to perfection. Around her throat she wore a collar of milk white pearls with an emerald and diamond clasp, and on her arm was a bangle of pearls and diamonds that had been a recent gift from her father.

She looked at it guiltily as she fastened it with a little snap. He had always spoiled her and she must not fail him now, when he needed her help. Surely it was not too much to ask that she should be nice to Mr Erskine?

It was a brilliant occasion, for all the cream of New Orleans society were present that night, the ladies resplendent in finery imported from France, jewels sparkling beneath the chandeliers, the gentlemen elegant, mostly wealthy, assured men of importance. Estelle's hand trembled on her father's arm as she was introduced to various gentlemen she had not previously met, some married, and some eligible bachelors. Most were older than she by several years, and Mr Erskine proved to be so when they met.

She had met him before of course at her father's house, but had barely noticed him. He was tall, heavily built with a ruddy complexion and a small beard. She thought him a few years younger than her father, but still well into his middle years. He was dressed in the fashion of the day in a dark-blue cloth coat and paler grey breeches, which clung to his tree trunk legs like a second skin. His shoulders strained against his coat and he had the beginnings of a paunch. His waistcoat was striped silk and hung with an expensive chain and watch. On the little finger of his left hand he wore a diamond ring, his nails cut short and scrupulously clean.

As Estelle looked up into his face, she noticed fine red lines about his nose and eyes, as if he drank more wine and port than perhaps was good for him. But his eyes were dark and oddly remote as he met her gaze, as if hiding his thoughts behind the smile of welcome he gave her when he took her proffered hand.

'You look beautiful this evening, Miss Estelle,' he told her and his voice had the stickiness of molasses and treacle, making her shiver inwardly. She felt as if he were undressing her in his mind, and a flicker of revulsion went through her as she imagined him actually doing that on their wedding night. 'May I have the honour of the first dance with you?'

'Yes, of course, thank you,' Estelle said in a voice little above a whisper. She wanted to deny him, to run from the room and never see or speak to him again, but knew she could not. She must do her best to overcome this initial reluctance, for her father's sake. 'Your sister's ball is well attended, sir.'

'As I expected,' Frank Erskine replied in a booming voice that grated against her ears. 'We must rally to the cause, Estelle. We need to provide ourselves with better defences if we are to hold off the British.'

'Do you truly think they will attack us, sir?' she asked as

he led her on to the dance floor. It was a simple country dance that allowed them to relax and converse, needing no real concentration, and meant as a warm-up for the more lively dances that would follow. 'I know my father fears it but I had hoped it would not happen.'

'Oh, I believe it must,' he said and smiled kindly at her, clearly thinking her a delicate female. 'But you must not fear, my dear Estelle, we shall protect you. I myself am raising and paying for a troop of men, and I shall personally see to it that you come to no harm.'

He gave her what was meant to be a smile of reassurance, but made her tremble inwardly. She did not want to be beholden to this man for anything. The touch of his hands made her want to recoil, and it was only her strict upbringing that stopped her giving any sign of her feelings. He held her too tightly, and his hands were hot, the palms damp and sweaty. She could see that beads of perspiration were already appearing on his brow, and he moved heavily. Some big men were light on their feet and danced well, but Frank Erskine had no notion of timing, becoming out of step with the music.

She breathed a sigh of relief when their dance ended and she was besieged with admiring young men asking for her favour. Most of them were well known to her, the sons and younger brothers of her father's friends, including André de Varennes. He secured one dance with her but, to her disappointment, did not beg for another as most of the men did. She wished that one of her friends would speak, mostly she wished that André would speak, but he seemed more interested in another young lady that evening. She was French and had come on a visit to her uncle, Monsieur Leclerc, and was attracting a great deal of attention for she was pretty and dressed more stylishly than any other lady present.

Estelle's heart sank as she saw André dance with Suzanne Leclerc three times in a row. Clearly he liked her very much. Besides, if he had wanted to speak to Estelle's father he might have done so long ago.

She danced a second time with Frank Erskine, who was perspiring freely by now and looking very hot and bothered indeed. He had also been drinking and she could smell the wine on his breath. He was less respectful towards her now than he had been earlier, and his hand slipped down from her waist to her bottom until she pulled away, giving him a look of reproach, when he mumbled an apology and replaced his hand at the arch of her waist. However, she had seen the hot, lustful gleam in his eyes and the thought of him touching her intimately made her feel physically sick.

As soon as she could after their dance, she slipped outside into the gardens, seeking some fresh air after the heat of the ballroom. The air inside had become heavy with a pungent mixture of perfumes and body odour, and she felt as if she could not breathe. Suddenly, her eyes filled with tears and they came tumbling out of her before she could stop them. It was impossible! How could she marry a man she disliked so much?

'Why do you weep, beauty of the night?'

The man's voice was like the soft purr of a cat, stroking her like a hand in a velvet glove, making her head jerk up and her eyes open as she looked for him and saw him standing in the shade of an old and gnarled magnolia tree. He had been smoking a cigar, which he now abandoned and ground into the dry earth beneath his boot. He was not dressed as most of the men that evening in formal attire, but wore a grey coat and riding breeches of pale buff, his neckcloth tied carelessly as if he had been on a pleasure jaunt with his friends rather than attending a ball. Yet even dressed casually, he had more presence than any man she had seen here, arresting and compelling as she looked at him.

'What are you doing here?' she demanded, tears forgotten as she felt a spurt of anger.

'Believe it or not, Mademoiselle Lebrun, I was invited. However, I have been away and returned too late to change into suitable clothes. Since I wish to make a donation to the cause, I came as I am and hope to appease my hostess with the generosity of my gift.'

'Who are you, sir?' Estelle asked, realising that she knew nothing about him. 'Why have you come here to New Orleans? I wish that you had not, for you have ruined my life.'

Justin was momentarily stunned by her attack. 'I am Justin St Arnaud,' he murmured. 'Here for business and to collect a debt – but pray tell me what I have done to blight your life, mademoiselle, for I swear I do not know of a single cause.'

'You have ruined my father,' Estelle blurted out. 'He must pay you a debt when he has no money and we must either sell our house – or I must marry a man I cannot like.'

'Hence the tears?' Justin raised his brow. 'I begin to understand. But your father should have made provision for the debt he owed my friend. It is not my fault if he has been foolish with his investments.'

There was truth in his statement but she was beyond reasoning as she cried, 'You are cruel to demand it of him, sir. He is ill and likely to die if he has cause to be anxious, and he worries for my sake. He fears that he will die and I shall be left alone . . .' The tears sprang to her eyes again. She tried to brush them away, but for a moment her emotion overcame her. 'And I cannot marry Mr Erskine. I cannot . . .'

'Marry that brute? I should think not,' Justin muttered. What was her father thinking of? He must be mad!

He acted instinctively, moved by her distress, closing the distance between them to draw her into his arms, meaning only to offer comfort. When she looked up at him, her eyes wide and startled, something swept over him, a desire, a need so fierce that he hardly knew what he did as he lowered his head, kissing her on the lips. Yet despite the need in his loins, it was a soft kiss, a tender kiss, sweet and generous, giving more than it took, and Estelle instinctively responded to it, her body melding with his, swaying into him, clinging helplessly.

When he let her go, she seemed bemused, unable to fight back for a moment, her defences destroyed, vulnerable. Justin never knew why he made the unforgivable offer, for it was a cruel, thoughtless act. He ought as a gentleman to have told her that he would give her father longer to find the money and escorted her back to her friends immediately, instead he did something that sealed the future in a way he could never have imagined.

'I will make a bargain with you,' he said, his eyes hot with the desire that raged inside him and would not be denied. 'I will forget your father's debt, absolve him of it – on one condition.'

Estelle's heart did an odd somersault in her breast as she saw that look in his eyes and responded to it as she felt the throbbing ache inside her. What was happening to her? She could not understand why she did not run from this man at once. He was dangerous, her instinct told her that she was headed for disaster but she could no more move than she could turn her gaze from his.

'What is your condition?' she asked breathlessly. 'What would you have of me?'

'One night,' Justin answered, and wondered what had made him say such an outrageous thing to her. She was no whore to be taken lightly and discarded. She would surely pull her skirts away from him and walk away in a fury. 'For one night in your bed, in your arms, knowing you fully as a woman, I shall give you a paper that absolves your father of debt to me. I shall repay the sum owing to my friend's son myself.'

Estelle's cheeks flamed as she understood what he was saying. For one night he would pay her all the money her father owed him, absolve him of his debt. She need no longer think of marrying Mr Erskine. They could sell their house and move to a smaller one, and she could stay at home to care for her beloved father.

But oh, what a price he demanded! She could not, must not do it! She would be ruined in the eyes of the world if it were ever known. No, no, it was outrageous, infamous. She must deny him at once.

'And if I gave you what you want . . .' Estelle could not believe she was saying it. 'What then? You will boast of it to your friends I daresay? My reputation will be ruined.'

'It shall be our secret,' he promised. Why was he going on with this foolishness? Why was he riding the wolf to destruction, for he sensed his own destruction as well as hers in this foolish act. 'You shall have the paper and your father need know nothing of it. I shall go away and he will think I have forgotten the debt.'

'I am not sure . . .' Estelle felt as if the breath were being squeezed out of her. She was near fainting at the suggestion. How could she even contemplate such a wicked thing? And yet she would prefer this infamous seduction to marriage to a man she disliked. All he asked was one night, just one night

38

of her life. Perhaps he would keep his word. Perhaps it would not be so very bad. His kiss had not shocked or distressed her, indeed she had wanted it to continue.

Oh, but she was shameless to think of such things!

'Perhaps you would prefer to marry Frank Erskine?'

'No! I cannot. . .' Estelle shuddered at the thought. 'If I must pay your price for my father's debt then . . . I shall. Come tomorrow night and I shall be waiting for you in my room. There is a balcony and the window will be unlocked.'

'You will let me come to you?' Justin was disbelieving. She intended some trap, thinking to have him arrested for attempted rape. 'Shall I find your father and his servants waiting for me?'

'I am not so base,' Estelle cried, head up and eyes bright with temper. 'If I give my word I keep it.'

Justin recalled another woman who had promised much and met his naïve eager response with mockery, and wondered. He was a fool to trust her – more, he was a fool to have suggested the bargain. What woman was worth six thousand sovereigns for one night? It was so ridiculous that he found himself laughing inside.

Damned if he would not call her bluff! No doubt she would lock her window to keep him out, but he would give her a sleepless night worrying about it.

'Very well,' he said and smiled oddly. 'It is a bargain, Estelle. Keep it and I shall pay your father's debt, but play with me and you may be sorry.' He bowed his head and walked away, leaving her staring after him in dismay.

His departure left Estelle numbed with shock. What had she done? She had accused him of ruining her life when they first met that evening, but if she allowed him into her bed she would truly be ruined in the eyes of the world.

Yet her father would be free of his debt and they could be happy again. Perhaps the loss of her personal honour was not so very much after all. Once it was over she could put it from her mind, forget that it had ever happened.

After a night spent tossing restlessly on her pillows, Estelle opened her eyes to a sunny morning and wondered if she had been mad to agree to such an infamous suggestion. What could have possessed her? How could she have been so far lost as to say that she would accept his outrageous bargain?

She would bar her window, call for her servants if he tried to break his way in through the shutters. She was hot and cold by turns as she remembered that interlude in the gardens, when she had responded to his kiss and given him her promise.

He could not keep her to it! She would deny ever having spoken to him. He could not force her to honour their bargain ... but if she did not, what would happen to her father? St Arnaud would be angry and he might take his anger out on her dearest Papa. Unless she could find some way of paying the debt before he came to her?

Estelle thought of André de Varennes. He had danced only once with her at the ball it was true, but he had always been kind and attentive to Estelle. Perhaps if he understood how desperate she was he would offer her marriage, and his father could easily pay the debt for them instead of giving her a marriage settlement.

Estelle dressed in her most becoming gown. It meant she must humble her pride, but she would do that and more to save her father. Surely André cared enough for her to help her? She put the memory of him dancing three times with Suzanne Leclerc from her mind. Gentlemen always flocked about a pretty face they had not seen before, it did not mean anything.

She glanced at herself as she set out for the de Varennes' house. She was a pretty girl herself, and there was no reason why André should not favour her as much as any other. Her heart was racing wildly and she was nervous, but it was very daring of her to propose marriage to a young man, even if she had known him since they were both small children. Besides, she had no choice. Her only other alternative was unthinkable.

She was admitted into the small parlour and asked to wait, her heart thumping as the servant went to fetch André. He had given her a rather odd look, for young ladies of her standing did not generally ask for the son of the house, nor had she ever done so before.

It was a few moments before André came. She thought she

saw a flicker of annoyance in his eyes, though in a moment it had gone and he was smiling.

'You only just caught me, Estelle. I was about to leave for an appointment.'

'Forgive me, I shall not keep you long . . .' She took a deep breath, then raised her head, meeting his eyes steadily. 'We have been friends for many years, André. It is because of this friendship that I dare speak as I do.'

'Yes, we are friends,' he replied and his frown deepened. 'There is something you wish to ask of me?'

'My father is in some trouble and I must marry a man of substance, a man who might pay a pressing debt instead of settling the money on me as is our custom,' Estelle said. 'I came here today to ask if . . . you would marry me, André. I have always admired you and I would be a good wife if you would help me in this.'

André stared at her, a look of dawning horror in his eyes. It was clear that he was shocked by her proposal, and that it did not appeal to him. Indeed, he could not wait to repudiate it.

'Forgive me, that is impossible. I am promised to another lady. My father arranged the match some years ago, and Mademoiselle Leclerc has come to New Orleans so that we may become acquainted before our marriage.'

'Oh . . .' Estelle's cheeks flamed with embarrassment. 'I see. Forgive me. I did not realise. I thought . . .' She broke off, feeling overcome with humiliation. She ought to have guessed the previous evening when he spent so much time with the newcomer, but she had not really thought it through. Her impulsive nature had brought her here on a fool's errand and now she wished that the floor might open up and let her through. 'I am sorry. I shall go . . .'

André caught her arm as she tried to pass him, a speculative expression in his eyes as he looked at her and saw her distress.

'Do not be hurt, Estelle. It is not that I do not admire you. Indeed, I had thought in the past . . . but my father had other plans for me. Unfortunately, your father has been careless with business matters and lost much of his wealth. Had it been otherwise we might have considered the match suitable.'

41

Estelle felt as if he had thrown cold water over her. Did he imagine that his words were of comfort to her? To know that he might have thought her worthy of him had her father not thrown his money away? That hurt more than all the rest, but she had brought it upon herself by coming here. She saw now how foolish she had been to imagine that André had ever cared for her. His smiles and his perfect manners meant nothing, and concealed a calculating mind.

That calculating mind was at work now as he said, 'Of course I might be able to pay a part of the debt myself for . . . certain favours. If you were to consent to be my mistress, Estelle, I would do what I could to help your father. I have no mistress for the moment and Suzanne has been strictly reared and schooled. Until our marriage she will not let me touch her . . .'

Estelle recoiled, feeling as if he had struck her. Was he implying that her upbringing had been less proper than his fiancée's? She was even more insulted by his offer than she had been by St Arnaud's the previous night. At least he had offered her a bargain, her father's debt for one night in her arms, and he had kissed her in a way that made her melt inside.

Anger and humiliation battled inside Estelle, but pride came to her rescue and she managed to lift her head and give him a haughty look. Somehow she managed to control both her anger and her tears as she said, 'I thank you for your generous offer, sir, but I must decline. I had thought you truly cared what became of me, but I see I have presumed too far on our friendship. Forgive me. I shall not bother you again.'

Somehow she walked from his house with her head high, and somehow she found her way home without collapsing in the street. Once inside her bedroom, she locked the door and fell to her knees on the floor, covering her face with her hands as the sobs of humiliation and shame shook her body.

Oh, how foolish she was! To let such a man distress her, to have believed herself in love with him! He was betrothed to a beautiful girl and yet he had offered to make Estelle his mistress, betraying both the friendship she had treasured and his future wife.

After a while her sobs subsided and she got up, going to wash her face in cool water. Her head was aching and she felt drained, unsure of what to do next. André de Varennes thought so little of her that he would only have considered marrying her had her father's fortune been intact. Was that how all men saw her then, as an object to be bargained for, bought or sold?

Why did Frank Erskine want to marry her? She knew that he lusted after her for she had seen it in his face, heard it in the rasp of his breath, felt it in his touch. But was he under the impression that her father was still rich? He was rich enough himself, perhaps he could afford to indulge his baser needs by buying himself a wife. After all, she was of gentle birth, and attractive.

It was a stark choice that awaited her, Estelle realised. She could marry Frank Erskine, a man whose very touch made her shiver with revulsion, or she could give herself to Justin St Arnaud for one night of desire.

There was no choice, Estelle realised. Besides, she recalled Justin St Arnaud's kiss with pleasure and knew that whatever he did to her that night would not displease her.

Oh but she was wicked! Shameless! Yet it seemed that men thought of her as a plaything, something to be used and discarded – so she might as well accept the highest bidder, for she doubted that Frank Erskine would be prepared to settle as much on her if they had married.

Justin mocked himself as he signed the paper he had had his lawyer draw up. It said that he was prepared to forgo the debt owed to Robert Marshall by Henri Lebrun but made no mention of the price paid for the concession.

She would refuse, of course. He smiled wryly as he tucked the paper inside his coat. He was dressed as if for a reception in the drawing rooms of high society, his linen of the finest, his hair washed, combed and lightly scented, his cheeks freshly shaved. He would do Mademoiselle Lebrun the honour of appearing to take her word, he thought, though he was sure that he would find her window tightly barred.

It was an infamous thing he had asked of her, he admitted it, knowing that it was perhaps the worst of his crimes. She would have spent the day denying that she had ever made the promise, thinking up ways of trapping him. Perhaps she hoped to secure the paper he had promised, without giving him anything. She would not succeed. He was no longer a green youth to give his trust to a pair of sparkling eyes – even if they were the most devastating eyes he had ever seen.

Yet he found himself impatient for their meeting, indeed, he could scarce wait for the appointed hour. Was he fool enough to believe she would keep her bargain? He mocked himself for the need she had aroused in him, but could not help anticipating a night of sheer pleasure. He could not remember another woman who had made him feel this way – nay, not even she who had so betrayed him as a green youth.

Estelle lay on her bed trembling as the hour drew near. She was wearing a pretty silk nightgown, her long hair brushed loosely from her face as it fell about her shoulders in soft waves. Three times she had shut her window, only to open it seconds later. Perhaps she need give him nothing. Perhaps he would relent and give her the paper if she cried a little. Papa had always given in to her if she cried . . . poor dear Papa, who had looked so tired and anxious all day.

She must keep her bargain. She must for her father's sake!

Hearing a noise outside her window, Estelle's heart caught with fright. He was coming! She curled her hands into tight balls, the nails digging into the palms to stop herself crying out. Her pulses raced as a dark shadow appeared at her window, and then he was climbing through it, standing at the foot of her bed, staring at her in the pale glow of the single candle she had left burning.

'So, you have kept your word,' he said softly.

His voice sent little shivers winging down her spine. She pushed herself up against the pile of pillows, which had been covered with fresh linen and smelled of lavender. He looked so big and powerful standing there, so very masculine, an adventurer, all conquering. She was trembling all over, but it was a kind of nervous excitement. She was not afraid of him. Her heart quickened as she realised the truth. She was not afraid of him!

Her mouth felt dry and she hardly knew how to speak as he came to the side of the bed and sat down, reaching for her hand, which she allowed him to take, her heart hammering in her breast.

44

'Did you think to find my window locked and barred against you, monsieur?'

'It would not have surprised me,' he said in that husky voice that made even her toes tingle. 'I drove a hard bargain with you, Estelle.'

She smiled up at him, a glow in her eyes that made him in his turn catch his breath. 'In that you are not alone, sir. I believe that men often make bargains of a similar nature for their lady's favours – is that not so?'

'Yes, with their mistresses, and indeed their wives,' he said, an odd smile flickering in his eyes. How brave she was, how beautiful. Surely she would draw back soon, weep and beg him to give her the paper for nothing. It was the way of women to use their tears to gain the advantage. 'What else is a marriage settlement but a payment for favours given?'

Brought to a new and painful awareness of how truly he spoke, she smiled. 'Indeed, you are right. It is a bargain blessed by God but a business transaction none the less.'

'And this is so much better is it not?' he said, daring her to continue, pushing her to the point of no return. 'For one night your father's debt is absolved and you free to live as you please . . . a sweeter bargain than marriage I think?'

'Yes, I believe you are right, sir,' Estelle said, stunning him. 'Father may sell the house and we shall be quite happy in a small cottage together. I have no wish to marry anyone.'

Had someone hurt her? He felt a spurt of anger and, more out of a wish to comfort than to tease, he bent his head to kiss her softly on the lips. His tongue brushed over their sweetness, gently invading the fresh clean moistness of her mouth, tasting her. Desire rushed up in him, hot and strong. Her arms slid up about his neck in a trusting, lovely innocence that was both his and her undoing.

She truly intended to give herself to him. He knew that a gentleman would withdraw, apologise and give her the paper she sought, but although born to follow a strict code of honour, he found himself swept away by the need to possess her. She was so sweet, so loving in her giving that he could not turn away now.

Instead he began to make love to her with a gentleness and tenderness he had shown no other woman in all these years.

He stroked and caressed, drawing her with him so that she followed along the path he trod, a path of primroses and violets. They were in a clear green glade, apart from the world, lost in Paradise as he kissed and explored every inch of her lovely body.

His tongue teased at her rose-tinted nipples, so that they became erect and firm beneath his caress. He took them into his mouth, sucking at her more gently than a babe sucks at its mother's breast, all the while stroking the length of her hip and thigh. Her skin felt so silky smooth beneath his hand, her flesh firm and sweet, lighting such a fire in him that he burned and moaned. And then his mouth travelled downward, his tongue probing the sweet mystery of her inner citadel, making her writhe and moan with pleasure. For a long time he contented himself with stroking, kissing, teasing her into such pleasure that when he slid his hard, swollen length into her moistness she hardly cried out, though for a moment she flinched and he stilled. But then she was pressing herself closer and he thrust even deeper, tearing the delicate hymen as he made her his own.

She arched her back to meet him as he began a slow rhythm, pushing inside her, withdrawing almost, such sweet torture, to plunge deep inside her once more. For a while he rested within her, whispering sweet words close to her ear, his warm breath tickling her, his hand stroking once more, and then he moved again. Slowly, almost too slowly as she felt a rising tide of impatience within her for something she only vaguely glimpsed, and moaned, pushing up to meet him, her body begging for what? Only when she felt the spasms begin inside her did she begin to understand what her body had cried out to his for, and to whimper as the exquisite pleasure washed over her. It was almost pain in its intensity, a feeling she could not describe other than as like dying to be born again as a part of the man who had so utterly possessed her.

'Oh . . .' she whispered on a sobbing breath. 'Justin . . .'

'Estelle, my lovely woman,' he murmured against her throat as he lay across her, passion satiated for the moment, replete with a satisfaction he had never quite known before. 'You were beautiful, beautiful . . .'

She buried her head into his moist shoulder, tasting the saltiness of his sweat, shy and uncertain of what to do next. If this was seduction then she wondered why women spoke of it in such hushed tones. She had never felt so wonderful, so happy in her life, and she wished this night might never end.

She wondered if he would leave her now, but when he stroked her hair and told her to sleep she obeyed, just as she had followed him in their loving, so she instinctively trusted him now. She slept peacefully but was woken by his kisses before dawn. His deep kisses and urgent caresses aroused her once more and they made love again. It was as sweet and pleasurable as the first time, and she lay in his arms afterwards, sensing that he would leave her soon and wishing that he would stay forever.

'I must leave you now,' he said at last. 'If I do not someone may see me – and you should wash yourself and remove the sheets for if not your servants will know what has happened here.'

Estelle wanted to protest that she did not care. How could she feel shamed by something so beautiful? And yet she knew that the world would not see it so – her father would be shocked and horrified. She remembered suddenly why he was here in her bed.

'The paper . . .'

'Yes, I have it here.' Justin rose from the bed and began to dress. He had been about to speak to her of something else, but her words made him pause. She had given herself to him for this paper. He did not know why but he found that disappointing, wanted it to be for another reason. 'I would not have left you without giving it to you.'

'No, of course not. I did not think it.'

Did she trust him then? Most women would have demanded to see the paper first – why had she given herself to him without appearing to think of it?

For a moment he hesitated, uncertain of what he ought to do next. Things could not be left like this, that thought was central in his mind. He did not know how he felt exactly – surely he could not be thinking of a permanent arrangement? He had absolved her father's debt for one night in her arms and that was an end to it – or was it?

'I must leave you, Estelle,' he said and bent to kiss her once more on the lips, softly, tenderly. 'I thank you for the gift of last night, and I shall see you very soon, sweet lady.'

'But why?' Her heart beat faster as she gazed up at him. Did he want more for his paper? Would he come to her again like this? With pulses racing, she knew that she longed for him to say it.

'Because . . .' Justin shook his head for he did not know why he felt it so important that they would meet again. What he had done was unforgivable. Why should she care what he felt? She ought to hate him. Suddenly he knew that the paper was not enough, he owed her more, much more. 'Your father will receive an offer for his house very soon. It means that you will be able to continue living here, and you will no longer need to worry for money's sake.'

'But . . .' Estelle did not understand. 'You have kept your bargain – why should you do more, sir?'

'Call it my conscience for lack of better,' Justin told her, and laughed softly. 'I did not think you would keep your side of the bargain – though I meant to give you this either way.'

He laid the paper down beside her.

'You would have given it to me . . .'

'Perhaps I would give you much more.'

'What do you mean?'

'Perhaps something, perhaps nothing, impatient one.' His soft laughter sent the shivers running through her as she wished he would return to the bed and never leave her, but he was leaving and she felt suddenly bereft.

Estelle watched as he climbed out of the window, hearing the soft thud as he landed in the garden below. He would have given her the paper for nothing . . . No, she did not believe that. He was merely mocking her. He could not have meant it, surely?

Suddenly the realisation of what they had done, of what she had done, the way she had welcomed his loving, swept over her and her cheeks burned. In the same moment she realised how difficult it would be to give her father the paper that absolved him of debt. He would ask her how she came by it.

She puzzled over the problem, knowing that she would have to arrange for it to be delivered without his knowing where it came from, that she could never tell her father what she had done for his sake.

And yet, was it for his sake alone? Had not Justin St Arnaud's passionate loving assuaged her feeling of humiliation, washed away the sting of rejection she had felt at André's hands?

Was it possible that when she gave herself to him she had forgotten the reason for her surrender altogether?

Four

Justin's first business of the day after leaving his lodgings was to visit his lawyer, the same man as he'd had write out the deed for Estelle. The man looked at him in a puzzled manner as he described his business, then something clicked inside his head and he beamed.

'Am I to wish you happy, sir?'

For a moment Justin paused, knowing that his thoughts had been running in the same direction, though against his will. 'Not for the moment, Saunders, but who knows? In time it may happen.'

The lawyer nodded, thinking he understood his client's generosity. Not that what St Arnaud was proposing was any great thing for a man of his wealth and prospects. He was known as a coming man and would no doubt grow much richer in the future. Henri Lebrun might not be the wealthy businessman he had once been, but he still had contacts and knowledge that might assist St Arnaud if he wished to make a name for himself here.

'I shall begin work on this immediately, sir,' he promised, and was thanked by an absent-minded Justin, who left him almost at once to proceed with his next task of the day.

Justin had decided to spend the rest of the morning finishing the work he had begun on Marietta's house, for it was in his mind that he might soon begin his preparations for a new voyage. He had already tentatively agreed to carry a small cargo to the West Indies, where he could be sure of finding an even bigger one to bring back. Unless he decided to make a longer voyage this time, he mused, perhaps to France?

Marietta was waiting for him, sitting in her chair by the fire as always, for she was never warm these days until the sun was high in the sky, and her bones ached. Her probing eyes met his as he came in to tell her he was about to finish the repairs to her roof, and for a moment he felt as if he were falling into a black pit, and his mind went reeling before he wrenched it back again.

'So it has begun,' Marietta said nodding to herself. 'You will remember my warning, Captain? Give me your word that she shall not regret knowing you and I shall give you something you need yet know not that you need it.'

'You speak in riddles again,' he replied with a frown. 'I have no need of your charms, madame, but I give you my word that she shall not suffer for what I do.' Yet how could he promise such a thing, knowing that he had stolen her innocence?

'If I did not believe that your heart is good I would make you suffer the tortures of hell,' Marietta told him, and for a moment her eyes burned with a cold fire that struck ice into his heart, for he suddenly believed that she had the power if she wished to use it. 'But despite what I see, I know that she will need you and therefore I shall use my strength to protect you and not to harm you.' She reached inside the bodice of her gown and brought out a small leather bag, holding it out to him. 'Keep this with you always, Captain St Arnaud, for there is one who ill wishes you. Her magic is not yet as strong as mine, for she is young and vengeful and she has not learned that to do evil is to weaken yourself. Wear this inside your jerkin, sir. Keep it next to your heart and it will protect you.'

Justin took the pouch dubiously, sniffing it and finding that, far from giving off an evil stench, it had a sweet, pungent scent that he quite liked.

'Very well, old woman,' he said with a wry smile. 'Since it concerns you that I might come to a bad end, I shall keep your charm with me.'

'Do it,' Marietta said and closed her eyes, then opened them again. 'And mind you mend that roof well! It will need to be watertight in the months to come, and you will regret it if you shirk your task.'

'Yes, madame!' Justin swept her a mocking bow, picked up his tools and went out, but not before tucking the charm inside his jerkin.

He was smiling as he began his work, but as his thoughts crowded in on him his grin faded. Supposing Estelle was to have his child? Their night of sinful pleasure could not then remain a secret.

He puzzled over the answer to his problem. It would not suit him to be tied to a wife at the moment; he needed to be free to expand his empire, and she was gently reared. It would mean that he must leave her here while he sailed away, and yet the idea of making Estelle his own was gaining ground with him.

Perhaps it was the old woman's charm working its magic, he thought, his lips quirking at the thought, only to be dismissed as nonsense. Yet he would remove it from his clothing when he reached his lodgings.

However, when Justin left Marietta's house some hours later and made his way home, stopping once or twice to speak with people he had become acquainted with these past days, it was to find a letter from his agent waiting for him. It seemed that there was news of Piers, but if he wanted to find him he would have to leave immediately.

There was no time to ponder the problem of Estelle, for his first duty lay to Robbie and his son. No time even to remove the charm or think of it again.

The morning brought new fears in its wake for Estelle. Supposing she were to have a child? She had not given it consideration before for she knew several ladies who had been married for many months, even years, before they managed to carry a child to its full term. Yet it could and did happen to unfortunate girls, and the thought of carrying a bastard child sent cold shivers down her spine. If such a thing were to befall her she would have to leave New Orleans, go somewhere far away, where she was not known – but that would mean she must desert her darling Papa. Unless she told him of her

51

shame, of course, which she might be forced to do should it become necessary.

But it would not, she decided, knowing she must be strong. She had not been forced, nor had she needed much seducing. Indeed, she had been shamefully eager, and that thought brought a hot flush to her cheeks.

After Justin had gone, she had managed to sponge the blood from her sheets, and to wash herself. She did not think that even her faithful Jessie would suspect anything, though as the morning wore on and she was oddly quiet, her servant looked at her intently a few times.

'Ah declares you'se like a cat with hot butter on its paws,' Jessie said. 'What got into you, honey chile?'

'I had a restless night,' Estelle told her, which was no more than the truth. 'My head aches a little. I think I shall go for a walk this afternoon. I might visit Marietta.' Was it a walk she wanted, or the hope of seeing Justin again by chance?

'Then Ah'se comin' with you'se,' her servant told her, shaking her head sorrowfully. 'Ain't gonna let you expose youse'self to them bad girls without me there to look after you.'

Estelle looked at the set of her mouth and sighed inwardly. It had been a mistake to mention the girls from the House of Pearls to Jessie, for she had made up her mind that her child was in moral danger from the girls and would watch over her visits to Marietta like a dragon from now on. Estelle wondered what she would say if she knew how she had spent the night!

She could never tell her, of course. She prayed to God that she would never need to, for she wished to keep her wickedness to herself if it was possible.

Somehow she must find a way of having the paper Justin had given her delivered to the house. She could not simply hand it to her father, for he would be immediately suspicious, though he would never think her so lost to decency that she would throw away her honour.

What she had done was a sin, and no lady of quality would deign to know her if her shame was revealed to the world. She must have been mad to agree to Justin's infamous bargain.

Why could she not hate him? Estelle looked into her heart and knew that her feelings for Justin were far removed from the proper outrage she ought to feel for a man who had seduced her.

She thought that she might have fallen in love with him, but that was foolish indeed. What had love to do with what had taken place the previous night? On his part it had been merely lust, the gratification of his senses. And yet, had a woman ever been so sweetly parted from her maidenhead?

Estelle smiled as she recalled the touch of his lips, the way her body had quivered beneath his hands, and the feel of him inside her. Her eyes widened unconsciously and her breath quickened, for she realised that if he came again that night she would welcome him into her bed.

'What you smilin' like that for?' Jessie said, giving her a suspicious look, and Estelle shook her head and looked down at the flowers she was arranging. If she were not careful she would give herself away.

'It was merely a thought,' she said. 'Nothing that need concern you, Jessie. Yes, you may accompany me to visit Marietta this afternoon, and now – I am going to see my father.'

She found Henri in his office, going over some papers. He looked up and she saw that his face was grey with anxiety. Clearly he was trying to discover a way of paying his debt to Captain St Arnaud.

'Do not worry, Papa,' she said. 'I am sure we shall find a way of solving our difficulties.'

'I can think of only one way,' her father told her. 'But I have been puzzling over these papers, for I could see the other night that you did not care for Mr Erskine and I would not have you marry against your will, child.'

'It is true that I do not care for the gentleman very much,' Estelle told him. 'But I would do it if there were no other way.'

'Do not give him your answer just yet,' her father said. 'I may find enough somewhere to pay St Arnaud a little on account. I must hope that he will be generous and allow me to spread the repayment.'

'If you ask him to be patient I am sure he will,' Estelle told him. 'I am going out this afternoon for a walk with Jessie – may I not deliver a letter for you, Papa?'

'Yes, that is a good idea,' her father told her. 'I shall write a letter to his man of business and explain my position, and you shall take it for me.'

Estelle smiled at him, for it suited her purpose admirably. She could deliver the letter and bring back the paper, once she had sealed it and written her father's name on the front. It would be an excellent way of covering her deceit.

Justin wished that he might have seen Estelle before he left, but it would mean several hours hard riding to where the ship lay off Pointe A La Hache and there was no time to be lost. His informant had told him that Piers had been seen with a sea captain, and that the captain's ship had been provisioning for the past two days, which meant that it was probably ready to leave with the next tide.

If Piers left before Justin could reach him his chance might be lost, for there were many dangers waiting at sea for a young boy. Should anything happen to him, Justin would never forgive himself. If Piers wanted a life at sea, he would prefer it if the lad began his career with him. Although he was fourteen years of age, he would find the life harder than he might imagine, unprotected and without friends.

It was night when Justin finally arrived at his destination, the dark of the night lit with a brilliant array of stars. He breathed a sigh of relief as he saw that the ship still lay at anchor and that men were camped on the shores, clearly intending a feast on this their last night ashore for some months to come.

Justin sought the captain himself first, and discovered that they had met some years earlier, though the acquaintance was slight. They shook hands for each remembered the other as a decent man.

'I am glad to see you, St Arnaud,' Captain Wolf Harrod said, and gripped his hand firmly. 'And what brings you here at this hour? I can see that you have ridden hard to catch us.'

'I seek a boy – the son of Robbie Marshall,' Justin said with a quick frown. 'I was told he might be here and that you had taken him on to serve with you.'

'Aye, I offered the lad a berth,' Wolf answered with a grin. 'He's fourteen but looks older, and he has been making a nuisance of himself long enough on the waterfront. The wonder is that no one took him before, for he works well and is strong for his age.'

'You know that his father and I sailed together and that I am now the master of the *Dark Angel*?'

'Aye, I had heard a rumour,' Wolf raised his brows in question. 'You've come to take the lad?'

'I have been searching for him since I returned to New Orleans. I have news for him. His father was a rich man and Piers will have a substantial inheritance.'

'I doubt you'll change him from his purpose. He is set on a life before the masts.'

'I do not wish to dissuade him, though the choice must be his, for he might prefer to further his education first.'

'Not Piers,' Wolf said and laughed harshly. 'I've had the devil of a time taming the boy, and you may take him with my blessing if you wish. Watch out for his right foot, St Arnaud, for he has a kick like a mule.'

Justin smiled oddly, for Wolf was not the first to speak of the boy's temper. 'I shall remember your warning, my friend. And now, where may I find the lad?'

'He is with the watch on board ship,' the other said with a frown. 'But before my men row you out there, stay and share a tankard with me? I have a proposition that may catch your interest.'

'I heard that you were sailing for the West Indies, is that not so?'

'Aye, that is my first port of call,' Wolf replied. 'I carry a cargo there and shall bring another back, but not before I sail first to Cartagena. I have business there that may make us both rich.'

'Indeed?' Justin raised his brows. 'What cargo do you seek? I do not trade in slaves, Wolf. I will not carry black gold for you or any man.'

'I am one with you in that,' Wolf replied. 'But I think you would have no objection to the yellow kind – gold and silver. A treasure stolen from the Spaniards nigh on fifty years past and lost until now.'

'Lost treasure?' Justin stared at him, his disbelief manifest upon his face. 'I have heard many such stories during my time at sea, though most are but stories, legends and myths.'

'I do not doubt it,' Wolf said and grinned. 'But I have seen a part of this treasure, St Arnaud, held it in my hands, and I know its secret.' He tapped the side of his head. 'I hold it up here.'

'Then why share it with me?'

'Because you are by reputation a man of honour. Only such a man would have ridden so far and so fast to find the son of a friend, when to do so means he must pass on a fortune he might have kept.' He held up his hand as Justin would have spoken. 'Besides, I cannot do this alone. I trust most of my men but some might try to betray me for gold – few men do not when faced with such a treasure. I need someone to watch my back when we are in Cartagena, and I can trust you – if you give me your word.'

'You will need a man you can trust at your back in that hotbed of thieves and pirates,' Justin said with a nod for the city had long been a meeting place for such men, although founded in 1553 by the Spanish Conquistadors. The pirates lived and sailed in the waters of the Virgin and Leeward Islands, presently owned by the British, and many of them were English by birth. They hated the Spanish and had for more than two centuries past preyed on the ships carrying treasure from the New World. It was more than likely that a Spanish ship had sunk in those waters, though whether it would be possible to retrieve its cargo was another matter. 'But what is in it for me?'

'One half share of the treasure we recover,' Wolf said. 'To be shared by you and your crew as you direct.'

Justin was silent for a moment. Wolf was being very generous, and he suspected there must be more here than he was admitting.

'And this treasure is hidden in Cartagena itself?'

'I did not say that, only that my voyage takes me there,' Wolf said, and then, seeing the frown on Justin's forehead. 'I need to go there first to retrieve something – a paper I hid when I left in a hurry.'

'You were made unwelcome there I collect?'

'I have enemies,' Wolf admitted. 'A man who goes by the name of Hinckston – an English renegade who turned on his own for the sake of gold. We got drinking and he lost his secret to me in a card game. Afterwards, he swore that I had cheated him but it was not so. I won his part of the map in fair play and it will lead us to the treasure once we reach the island.'

'Ah, now we approach the truth,' Justin said. 'You dare not retrieve this paper yourself and would have me do it for you.'

Wolf grinned and spat out the tobacco he had been chewing. 'I might have told you the whole once we reached the West Indies,' he said with a rueful look. 'Yet I should have known you would guess it from the start. Well, will you join me?'

'Yes. My hand on it,' Justin said and offered his, finding it gripped firmly. 'For if there is no treasure to share there will be a fine cargo to carry from Cartagena to the West Indies and there I may pick up another.'

'I had heard your bent was to trade,' Wolf said. 'I hope you have not lost your taste for fighting, my friend, for we may have to fight our way out of a few places once whispers of our search get out.'

'You will not find me lacking,' Justin assured him. 'And now, if it pleases you, I shall find Piers and take him back with me. I prefer that he sails with me until he is older.'

'As I said, take him with my goodwill,' Wolf said and signalled to one of his men, telling him to prepare the long boat. 'You will need time to follow me, but we shall meet soon in Kingston.'

Justin smiled and inclined his head in agreement. He had shaken hands with Wolf on their bargain, and he trusted him as much as any man he had met during his time at sea, but he was not sure that the older man had told him the whole truth.

No matter, he had found what he sought. Now, at last, he could keep his promise to Robbie.

'You say St Arnaud's man of business gave this paper to you?'

Estelle swallowed hard for she did not like to lie to her father, but she had no choice. 'Yes, Father. It was given to me by a gentleman . . .' There, she had not quite told a lie for Justin was a gentleman, even if he had not treated her as a lady. 'Is it important?'

Her father had broken open the seal and was staring at the paper, his face pale. He sat down at his desk, his hand shaking, and for a moment she was afraid that the shock might make him ill.

'St Arnaud has absolved me of debt to him,' Henri said in a hushed whisper. He turned the paper over as if looking for something more, a puzzled expression in his eyes. 'He asks for nothing in return. I do not understand, Estelle. Why should he do something so incredibly generous? He seemed determined to be paid when he was here.'

'He must have changed his mind,' she said, her heart fluttering.

'But why?' Her father shook his head over it. 'I fear the Greek bearing gifts, child. St Arnaud is not a man to give way so easily. Is this some kind of a trap?'

'Is it properly signed and witnessed, Papa?' she asked, though she knew the answer.

'Yes, indeed, it is a legal document, drawn up by his lawyer.'

'Then it seems as if Captain St Arnaud has indeed decided to be generous, sir. Why do you not simply accept his kindness and forget the incident?'

'I can do no other for I could not have paid him had he come here to demand it of me. I must write to him once more, Estelle, to thank him for showing mercy.'

'If you wish it, Papa, I shall take it to the lawyers in the morning.'

'Perhaps I should go myself . . .'

Estelle's heart caught with fear, for if he did he might discover that the lawyers had given her nothing, but then her father was shaking his head.

'No, perhaps it is best that you deliver my letter, child,' he said. 'He must be a strange creature to change so easily, and I shall not tempt fate. He must be thanked, but let that be an end to it.'

'Yes, Papa,' Estelle said, and breathed a sigh of relief. 'We may forget it now and be happy again.'

'Yes . . .' Her father looked at her doubtfully. 'I am no longer in pressing need, Estelle, but our situation remains precarious. We must go carefully for I can scarcely afford to keep this house running.'

'I shall be very careful,' she promised and went to kiss his soft cheek. As always now when she touched him, she was aware of his frailty, and her mind told her that the time left to them was short, though her heart denied it.

'I shall not press you to marry against your will,' her father said. 'But there will be very little money for you when I've gone, Estelle, and I worry for your future, my dear.'

'Pray do not, Papa,' she told him. 'I should be content with much less than we have, and who knows, one of your investments may come right in time.'

'Perhaps. I doubt that any of the money I so foolishly lost can be recovered – but we might sell the house. If we moved into something smaller . . .' He sighed, for it was not what he had hoped for her. 'If only there was a better prospect for you, my daughter.'

'You would like to see me married,' Estelle said sadly, 'but I do not think I shall find anyone I could love as I love you, Papa.'

'Has someone broken your heart?'

'There was someone I liked but he . . . does not wish to marry me.'

She could never tell her father that she had given herself to a man without marriage, and could not therefore in honour wed another.

'I suppose you mean young de Varennes?' Her father nodded to himself for it had not gone unnoticed with him that Estelle had liked the young man. 'I had heard he was to be betrothed soon to a French girl. Besides, it was impossible, Estelle. It would not have done.'

'But why, Papa?'

For a moment he considered telling her the truth, but he knew that he would see shock and hurt in her lovely eyes and he could not bring himself to say the words.

'He would not have made you a good husband.'

Estelle sensed that her father was hiding something from her but she did not press him for the truth. Her thoughts were elsewhere as certain things that Justin had said to her came back to her mind.

He had promised to call on her soon, and that her father would receive an offer for the house, which would enable them to continue living here for the moment.

She smiled and left her father to his work for she had some of her own. She had taken it upon herself of late to do the sewing and mending. Jessie had too much work to be fiddling with such tasks, and there were few enough servants to run the house these days. As she bent her head over her work, she could not help thinking about Captain St Arnaud. Where was he – and when would she see him again? Perhaps even more pressing was the worrying thought that even now she might be carrying their child.

What would she do if the worst had happened? The fear of shame haunted her, for she could think of no way out if it should be her fate to carry a bastard child. Yet even so, she did not regret what she had done.

'Pa told me about you.' Piers looked at Justin with sulky dark eyes. 'Why should he make you my guardian? I don't need anyone. I can look out for myself. I've been doing so since Ma died, and I've found a berth with Wolf. Why should I leave him and come with you?'

'Because it is my wish to have you under my direction,' Justin said. 'There is money lodged safely in a bank for you, Piers. If you wish I can take you back to New Orleans and find a place at a good school for you, where you can finish your education.'

'I can write and count money,' Piers said. 'What more do I need to know to be a sailor?'

'If you want to be captain of your own ship one day you will need to read charts and do more than simple sums, Piers.'

For a moment he saw a flash of eagerness in the lad's eyes, but then in a moment it had gone. 'I can learn from others on board ship. I don't need to go to school.'

'You can certainly learn from me if you wish it,' Justin said. 'I doubt Wolf will have the time or inclination to bother. You'll work your watch the same as the other men on board his ship, and you'll find it harder than you imagine. With me you will work your watch, but my men will show you what to do and you'll spend time with me learning about the charts and how to read them.'

Piers was silent for a moment, studying the tall, powerful

man with the deep scar on his cheek. 'Where did you get that scar, sir? Was it when you saved my father's life?'

'So Robbie told you about that, did he?' Justin smiled and stroked the scar with his finger. Most of the time he forgot it was there. 'No, this happened before I met your father, lad, when I wasn't much older than you. I was set upon while riding on my uncle's estate, beaten senseless and then taken on board your father's ship by the murdering rogues who had been told to dispose of me. They hoped I would die but your father cared for me himself, and when I recovered he taught me all the things I would teach you. I worked as hard as any man aboard that ship, but I wasn't tortured and beaten as some lads are who choose their berths unwisely.'

'Is that why you want me with you, because my father was good to you?'

'Robbie was my friend, and the father I had never truly known,' Justin told him. 'I came to find you because he asked it of me, but I would keep you with me for your own sake. I think you honest and I am told you work well. I have need of someone to keep his eyes and ears open for it is a dangerous trip we plan.'

Piers looked at him consideringly. 'I heard we were looking for buried treasure on an island on the Spanish Main.'

'Indeed?' Justin smiled oddly. 'If the tales are circulating already then we must be doubly on our guard, Piers. Come, sail with me and we shall help each other.'

'Like you and my father?'

'Yes, just like that.'

Piers grinned at him, and in that moment he was very much his father's son. 'All right, Cap'n,' he said. 'I'll throw in my lot with you and I'll learn what you have to teach me – but no schools!'

Justin offered him his hand, finding his grip surprisingly strong for one so young. He was a tall lad, lanky and immature as yet, but with signs of the strong man he would become after a few years before the masts. It was a hard life, often dangerous, wet, cold, and sometimes terrifying in the middle of a storm at sea, but Justin would not change it for the richest palace on earth, and he felt that Piers was of the same bent.

'It is your choice, Piers,' he said. 'Deal well with me and

you will find me a fair master. I doubt I need to warn you of the alternative?'

Piers shook his head. He had seen little of his father when he was growing up, for Robbie had been too often away at sea, and yet he had learned to respect him, and he had heard tales of Justin St Arnaud, though until this moment he had never met him.

'So tell me, lad,' Justin said. 'Why did you run away after your mother died? Could you not have stayed in the house?'

'The owner wanted it back,' Piers said. 'Ma had no money to pay the rent for weeks before she died, and I could hardly earn enough to keep us in food. She needed medicines, but Marietta gave her things to ease her fever. We had no doctor . . .'

Justin frowned as he saw the grief in the lad's eyes, and his anger against Henri Lebrun intensified. The man was a scoundrel. He had let him get away with the debt for the sake of his daughter, but when Justin returned to New Orleans he would bring Lebrun to account for his treatment of Petra and her son.

Telling the boy to get some rest, for they would not reach the place where his ship lay at anchor until the next afternoon, Justin lay down on his blanket beside the fire he had built for their camp. At the back of his mind lay guilt for the way he had treated Estelle Lebrun. She had not deserved to be served so, despite her father's behaviour.

He wondered if she had thought of a way to give her father the paper without arousing his suspicion, and then, quite suddenly, he realised that there might be awkward consequences. Supposing there should be a child? He had not given it more than a passing thought until that moment, but talking to Piers had made him aware of a certain lack in his own life. At least Robbie had always known that there was someone waiting for him when he returned to port.

For years Justin had been content to sail and work with Robbie, needing no more than a place to lay his head and food to eat, though he had, during his years at sea, accumulated his share of the booty they had stolen, besides investing in several rich cargoes of his own. Besides the *Dark Angel* he owned two merchant ships, which were sailed by captains he trusted, and with whom he shared the profits of each successful voyage.

Robbie had known of his enterprise, saying nothing, understanding that the man he had had thrust upon him in a state of near death needed more than he could give him. Justin had a keen mind and boundless ambition, a fire burning inside him, fuelled by bitter memories and the desire to succeed. It was possible that their last voyage together might have been the last even had Robbie lived.

Justin had never considered marriage, never felt the need for the soft influence of a woman in his life, using their bodies for the mutual pleasure it gave during a brief interlude in their beds. He did not understand why Estelle Lebrun should haunt him, but it was so, her lovely face lingering at the back of his mind despite his efforts to dismiss it. But no more!

He had paid her generously for her services, he thought savagely. Neither she nor her father deserved more than he had already done for them! He would think of her no more.

Estelle heard a sound outside her window and trembled, her heart racing. Could it be that he had come to her again?

She got out of bed and went to look out. The sky was velvet dark but lit by bright stars that showed her the garden clearly – well enough for her to see that no one was there. Sighing, she stood for a moment, breathing in the air, which was heavy with the scent of night-flowering blooms, honeysuckle and jasmine amongst others.

Four days had passed since that night ... and there had been no word from Justin. She sometimes wondered if the paper he had given her meant anything for she had only his word that it absolved her father of debt, though it seemed genuine. Justin had told her there would be another letter, an offer for her father's house, but so far they had heard nothing.

He had promised they would meet again, but he had not kept his word. Had he simply ridden away and abandoned her? It made her heart ache to know that she might never see him again, and she felt the sting of tears, which she brushed away angrily. How foolish of her to regret that she might never spend another night in his arms. Better that it had never happened!

Better that she had never seen him, and that he had never come to New Orleans and upset her father. For then she might not be breaking her heart over a man who had used her as a whore. She had tried to tell herself that his loving had been more than mere lust, that he had cared for her, but in truth she knew that it was not so. He had paid a high price for her favours it was true, but it was no more than that ... but it must be!

It was too painful to believe that he had never cared for her, and so she clung to her hope that he would return to her one day. He made his living by the sea and perhaps he had gone back to sea, but surely he would think of her?

Estelle knew that she would think of him often, sometimes with anger, sometimes with love, for she could not deny to herself that he had stolen her heart. She had given herself to him to pay her father's debt, but it had been more than that, much more. She had known it in her heart when he kissed her, her body responding instinctively.

She sighed as she turned away, returning to her bed. Her back and stomach felt tender and there was a familiar ache that told her that her courses were about to start. So there would be no child, no shaming confession to her father, no terrible disgrace on their family name.

At least she had that to comfort her, Estelle thought as she lay with her knees brought up to her chest. It ought to be a relief to her – so why did she feel that she wanted to weep?

Five

Estelle left Marietta's house one morning some weeks later. She was deep in thought for her friend was not truly well, though Marietta hid her pain and pretended that nothing ailed her. She would be sad if something should happen to her old nurse, for she loved her as much as if she had been her own mother.

'Mademoiselle Lebrun, or may I call you Estelle?'

Estelle was startled from her thoughts as she looked up and saw the man standing in her path, her heart lurching uncomfortably as she felt his hot eyes upon her.

'Mr Erskine,' she said, catching her breath. 'Forgive me, I had not seen you.'

'You were lost in thought,' he said, and smiled at her in a way that made her blood run cold. 'Have you been visiting the old woman who lives here?'

'Yes . . .' Estelle's heart sank for if he mentioned this to her father it might distress him. 'She was once my nurse and I sometimes bring her food.'

'You have a kind heart,' he said. 'You must know that I admire you, Estelle – your manner, your breeding, and your tenderness. I think I may have offended you when we last met and if it was so then I beg your pardon.'

'Oh . . .' She blushed and shook her head. 'It was just . . . I am not used to such . . .'

'I was a clumsy fool,' he apologised 'and sincerely regret it. You are a lady, Estelle, and I forgot it for a moment in my excitement. Please believe me when I say it will never happen again. If you will look upon me kindly, I shall not forget my manners again.'

'My father's friends must always be acceptable to me, sir.'

'Then perhaps I may hope – that one day I may be more to you?'

'My father is frail, sir. I could not – will not – think of leaving him while he needs me.'

'Your tender heart does you credit,' he said again and smiled. 'But I shall take hope since you have given me fair words, and perhaps one day I shall find you pleased to look on me with favour.'

With that he doffed his hat and walked away, leaving Estelle staring after him in dismay. Had she said something to encourage him? She hoped not for despite his promises of better manners, she could never marry him. Indeed, she could never marry at all for she had fallen from grace, and no decent man would wish to wed her if he knew the truth.

For a moment she allowed herself to think of Justin, and to wonder where he was and if she would ever see him again.

* * *

The outward voyage had been without incident, apart from a storm that had damaged Wolf's ship slightly and caused some delay in Kingston. Now, repaired, and relieved of their separate cargoes, the two ships lay off Cartagena, where they had spent the night and where they could see the sprawl of the city and the fortress San Felipe de Barajas.

'The tavern lies at the end of the street directly behind the fortress, and cannot be seen from here. But you will find it easily enough, though it is but a poor place,' Wolf was saying. 'I hid the paper behind a loose board beside the fireplace. The best time to visit is early in the morning when the host is sleepy and hardly anyone is around.'

'And what if it has been found?' Justin asked, his brows arching. 'Have we come then on a fool's errand?'

'It will be there,' Wolf said and spat into the clear blue waters below. 'But if it is not . . . then we must trust to my memory. I have most of it up here.' He tapped the side of his head. 'It is just one small piece that is not quite clear.'

'And is the treasure here in Cartagena or sunk in these waters somewhere?'

'The ship was sunk in these waters more than fifty years ago, gold and silver being carried from the interior of Columbia to Spain they say, and perhaps emeralds . . .' Wolf saw the flash of impatience in his eyes. 'But the wreck drifted towards a shallow bank and was discovered there by an enterprising sea captain by the name of Red Bart. It was clearly visible below the water, and he was an excellent swimmer. He discovered the treasure by diving down himself. It took him a long time, but he and his crew brought up the chests of gold and silver, and took them to an uninhabited island where they buried them. And then, after the way of these things, the men fell out amongst themselves as to how the treasure should be split.'

'And how do you know this?'

Wolf grinned. 'That enterprising captain was my grandfather. He told me that there was a terrible fight one night and half the crew were killed by the other half, including all but two of the men who knew the exact spot where the treasure lay buried. One was my grandfather himself, the other his first mate. Under cover of darkness they stole away, marooning those of the crew they dare not trust, and returned to Jamaica, where the mate died soon after in mysterious circumstances. His portion of the map had been stolen . . .'

'And you believe it is this that you have secreted behind a loose board in the Inn of the Black Feather?'

'Aye, for my grandfather described it to me in detail. I know how to find the island for I have been there and seen where the cave lies, but there are many passages within the cave and without that piece of the map I cannot be certain. It might take years without it . . .' He frowned. 'I believe it has been passed on many times in the intervening years, because it is not complete. Only Bart had the rest of the map, showing the island itself. Yet this scrap of paper I hid is known to be the key to a great treasure, for the fool bragged of his treasure map before I won it from him in a game of dice.'

'So you *have* brought us on a fool's errand,' Justin said. 'If the paper is not there you could spend your lifetime in looking for this treasure.' His brow furrowed. 'Why did your grandfather never return to the island to retrieve his treasure? Surely he knew where it was buried without the aid of a map?'

'Aye, he knew, but he turned to drink, talking wildly sometimes of the evil of riches beyond a man's dreams, and most thought him an old fool. A corner had been torn from his map somehow and though he tried to show me, I think he could not quite recall it for his mind had become fuddled by drink. My mother used to scorn his tales as nonsense, but I sat alone with him often and I believed in the treasure – for he showed me a tiny portion of it. He had held back a small chest when the treasure was buried, and it was filled with silver bullion, which was intended for the Spanish mint. It was this that helped me gain my first ship.'

Justin's eyes assessed him, convinced that he at least was genuine in his beliefs. 'Very well,' he said at last. 'If the paper is where you say, my ship will accompany yours to this island, but if it is not, then this is where we part company, my friend. There is money to be made carrying hides, cocoa beans, molasses and sugar. If this is a fool's errand you may go to your island alone.'

'Fair enough,' Wolf said. 'But you would need many cargoes to earn what you may find on my island, St Arnaud.'

'That remains to be seen,' Justin replied. 'One more thing before I go in search of your paper – once the crew knows what we seek, there will be mutiny. Even my own men may think it worthwhile to cut a few throats to get their share. It must be clear that they will receive their portion as usual, according to their rights. Otherwise we shall have bloody mayhem as your grandfather did before us.'

'Of the gold and silver, yes,' Wolf replied. 'To that I agree – but if there are emeralds, they belong to us. We shall share them and no one else the wiser.'

Justin hesitated, then nodded. Emeralds were the most precious of jewels, valued not only for their beauty but also for the powers they were believed to hold. Some said they helped sufferers of the falling sickness, others that they warded off the evil eye, but they were much prized, and might drive men to dangerous actions to possess them.

'If I were you I should say nothing of the possibility to anyone,' Justin warned. 'If there is as much gold as you say, there should be enough to satisfy us all . . .'

Enough for a man to live like a king for the rest of his life perhaps, Justin thought, for as captain of the *Dark Angel* his share would be four times that of his next ranking mate. It was the law by which men such as his abided, men who had served under him and Robbie, men who had fought for what they got, sometimes to the death.

And what would he do if such a fortune should come his way? He was still doubtful that it could be found, if indeed it existed. Yet what did he want of life if he were no longer obliged to roam the seas in search of his living?

A wry smile touched his mouth as he realised that he lacked for nothing. He already possessed as much wealth as any reasonable man needed. Then why was he here on a mission that could prove both dangerous and fruitless? But he knew the answer. He was here because the love of adventure was in his blood, and the idea of buried treasure had caught his mind as it would any man's.

With it he could buy more ships, a fleet of trading vessels that would make him an important man in his chosen life. And yet what would that avail him if he had nothing more than wealth?

Justin had struggled long and hard to put that night in Estelle's arms from his mind. As the months passed he had found it harder to recall her face at will, but sometimes it came in the night to haunt him, keeping him wakeful, making it impossible for him to sleep.

Was she still living in her father's house? Had Lebrun accepted his offer to buy the property and remain there as his tenant for life? He had given the excuse that his reason for buying, and allowing the owner to continue living there, was that he wished the property not to be neglected when he could not be in residence, and therefore making Lebrun and his daughter superior caretakers. He had gained a certain satisfaction from that, for he guessed that Lebrun might feel it humiliating to remain under such circumstances. It was little enough punishment for a man who had refused help to Robbie's wife – but perhaps there had been reasons for that?

Justin's anger had cooled over the months at sea as he saw how the boy had blossomed, his skin bronzed by the sun and wind, his body rapidly filling out, growing, becoming that of a young man. And he was happy too, fulfilled by the life as Justin himself had been at his age.

Justin smiled as he came to his decision. He would take Piers with him that morning, he could serve as a diversion as he searched for the elusive paper.

Wolf dare not go to the inn for the last time he had walked through those sunlit cobbled streets, an attempt had been made to cut his throat and he knew his enemy would be waiting for him to return. He had fought off the attack but was in no mind to risk another such attempt, and he would trust none of his own men to accompany him lest they discover the secret map and seek to kill him on their own account.

Justin grinned as he went to tell Piers to be ready, relishing the adventure that lay ahead. The city of Cartagena lay shimmering in the sunlight, its old walled town whispering of a violent history. It had been built by Spaniards and attacked by pirates many times, including the English privateer Sir Francis Drake, for the riches found in the interior of Columbia and Venezuela were enough to tempt any man to madness.

*   *   *

69

As the months passed, Estelle had ceased to hope for a visit from Justin. His offer for their house had reached her father some two months after that fateful night, and she had begun to think he had changed his mind, but the letter that came from the lawyer said that it had lain forgotten in a drawer and apologised for the delay.

'It seems that the gentleman in question is a wealthy merchant who spends much of his time elsewhere,' Henri told his daughter after puzzling over the letter for some time. He did not even consider that it might have come from Captain St Arnaud for he had consigned that gentleman to a distant corner of his mind, only too relieved that it seemed his debt was absolved. 'He wants to buy the house but will not be needing it for a few years and asks that we continue to live here as his tenants for the time being. The rent is a nominal fee of one dollar a year.'

Estelle was taken by surprise and colour washed into her cheeks as her father read the letter aloud to her. 'Does it say who has offered for the house, Papa?'

'It says that the purchaser wishes to remain unknown for the moment, daughter. He will reveal himself to us when he returns to New Orleans, which may not be for a year or perhaps longer.'

'Then we may stay here for the moment and you will not need to worry over your debts, Papa.'

'If I accept the offer . . .' Her father sighed. 'There are two other debts I ought in all honour to settle, Estelle. Yet that will still leave a sufficient amount for us to continue here for the meantime, and perhaps there will be something for you when I die.'

'Papa, pray do not . . .'

'We must speak of it, child,' he said, but then as he saw the distress in her face, 'but perhaps not just yet.' He sighed and reached for her hand again. 'This trouble with the British bothers me, Estelle. They have attacked ships trying to reach our port, and I believe it is only a matter of months before they may try to attack us.'

'You have feared it for the past year or more, Papa.'

'The Americans are at war with the British and until something is settled we are in danger here.' He frowned. 'Besides, if our ships are attacked it will make prices higher here and there may be shortages of some commodities.'

'I have no desire to buy silks and French perfumes,' Estelle said and smiled. 'We shall not go short of food for much that we need comes down river.'

'You are a good girl,' her father said, his faded eyes caressing her with love. 'You have always been a blessing to me, as your mother was – God forgive me that I did not take better care of you.'

Estelle kissed his cheek and went away to busy herself about the house. She had asked one of the servants to dig a patch of earth in the back garden, and she had taken to growing vegetables for their food. Over the past few months she had learned to do many of the things that she would once have considered impossible, but it was a secret she and the servants concealed from her father. Henri Lebrun would not have allowed his daughter to get her hands dirty, but it was the only way they could manage to keep the house running on the meagre sums that came their way.

The verdant island lay glistening like an emerald in the blue sea, the sun dancing on the still waters of the lagoon so that it looked like a shower of silver pieces raining down from the heavens.

'A good omen, no?' Wolf asked as he grinned at Justin. 'So, we are here and now we shall find all that our hearts desire – no?'

'Perhaps,' Justin said. 'Have you spoken to your men yet – agreed terms with them? We do not want a mutiny such as your grandfather suffered fifty years ago.'

'Do you take me for a fool?'

Justin's eyes narrowed. 'Your promise has held true so far, my friend. I hope that the treasure is where the map says it is. My men are loyal but the mood might turn ugly if they were disappointed.'

'There will be no disappointment,' Wolf said. 'There are six chests of gold bullion and two of silver – besides the emeralds.'

'If they exist,' Justin said. 'I came for the adventure, my friend, and may return from Jamaica with a cargo and be satisfied, but I know there are rumours and whispers amongst the men. I have already told them that anything we find will be shared in the usual way, but I know that some may try to take us by surprise. We must be on our guard at all times.'

He did not add that it was Wolf's men he feared more than his own, for he had chosen his crew with care and all but a few would fight with him to the death. If the mutiny came it would be from Wolf's men.

'We shall take only a small crew ashore with us,' Wolf said. 'Just three of your most trusted men and three of mine.'

'I have already chosen them,' Justin said with an odd smile. 'Piers, Eric and Sam are men I would trust with my life.'

'You would take the lad?' Wolf raised his brows. 'He won't be of much use to you in a fight.'

'I prefer to have him where I can see him,' Justin replied. 'If a mutiny were planned on board my ship, they would use him to twist my arm. If he is with me he cannot hinder any plans I might make.'

'That is good thinking,' Wolf said, understanding his reasoning. 'But who will hold your ship for you while you are ashore?'

'I have others I trust. Look to your own crew,' Justin advised. 'We'll meet ashore in half an hour.'

'You have the map?'

It had been agreed that Justin should keep the map he had recovered in Cartagena so that no one person had the whole and could not betray the others. Finding the treasure, if it existed, was not the most pressing problem they would have to face.

The island was of a good size and lush with vegetation, exotic fruits growing amongst the wilderness and a good stock of wildlife. A man might make a good life for himself on an island like this one, Justin thought, as they trudged inland towards the mountain that brooded over the island like a squatting monster, housing the treasure they sought within a cave hidden somewhere in its mass.

Two men were left to guard the boats, for though they believed the island uninhabited they could not be certain. The cave was more than an hour's trudge from the beach, and

Justin, like the others, was drenched with sweat after hacking a path through the thick vegetation. Brightly coloured birds flitted though the trees, calling eerily to each other as the peace was broken by the intrusion of human voices and the slashing of heavy machetes.

'We'll take a rest here,' Wolf said suddenly as they came to a small spring that trickled down a fall of grey rock from somewhere high above. 'We are almost there.'

Justin saw the two crews glance at each other, sensing the heightened excitement. He felt it himself, the lure of wealth, of gold and silver, more than men like them might earn in a lifetime.

'Yes, we'll eat and drink here,' he added his voice to Wolf's. 'Break out the rations, Piers.'

They had brought food from the ship, not knowing whether they would find anything edible on the island, but already they had seen fruit they recognised and there were small animals and birds to be trapped, besides fish in the lagoon, though he had seen no sign of wild boar or larger mammals.

As the men found places to rest, some taking the chance to splash their heads and faces with cold water from the tiny spring, Wolf signed to Justin and he walked a little apart with him. Wolf jerked his head towards the jutting mass of rock and vegetation behind them.

'Look just above you, Justin. Can you see a rock that looks like a dog's head?'

Justin looked up. For a moment he could not see what Wolf meant, but then it suddenly came to him and he nodded.

'Yes, I see it.'

'The cave lies just above it. You cannot see it for the opening is overgrown with vegetation. I left it that way when I visited the island last time. I found the cave but there are three passages leading deep inside the mountain, and I am not sure which to follow. You have the map?'

Justin took it from his leather jerkin and handed it to him. 'If the map be true it is the passage to the right. It leads to another, larger cave and the treasure is buried there.'

Excitement leapt in Wolf's eyes. Justin laughed for despite his caution and reserve against the possible outcome, he felt exhilarated to be so close to their goal.

'We should take one man each,' Wolf said. 'To be sure we have it right. If the treasure is there we shall need more men to transport the chests back to the ships, but it is best that only a few know the secret for now.'

'I shall take Sam,' Justin said. Sam was a huge Negro he had discovered once in the market in Kingston, being sold by his master. Noticing that the man had a deep slash on his right cheek, which was still raw and weeping with puss, something had made him buy his bond. He had taken him back to the ship, cleansed his wound, asked him how he came by it, accepted the silence that greeted his question, and told him he was free.

'Why did you buy me?' Sam asked, his dark eyes fixed on Justin's face. 'Why do you set me free?'

Justin touched his own scar, which was on the opposite cheek to the one Sam bore, and smiled. 'I thought we might each be one of a pair,' he suggested. 'Two odd-looking fellows together.'

Sam had stared at him a moment longer, then his head went back and he roared with laughter, laughing until the tears ran down his coal black cheeks, and Justin had laughed with him.

'Odd fellows – that's right enough, Cap'n, two of a kind. And since we're bound together, I'm your man, free or slave,' he said, and they had shaken hands on it. Justin gave him a berth on his ship, trusting him more than he had trusted any man other than Robbie, and he knew that Sam would stand with him to the death.

'Bronte is my man,' Wolf said, bringing Justin's thoughts sharply back to the present.

His eyes narrowed. He would have thought twice before trusting Bronte. Yet it was Wolf's choice and he must have his reasons.

'As you wish.'

They returned to where the men were sitting. Justin beckoned Piers to him and explained what was happening.

'Keep your eyes and ears open, lad. Trust no one other than me, Eric or Sam, and say little.'

'Do you suspect treachery, Cap'n?'

'Something smells wrong,' Justin said. 'I'm not sure what

yet. It may be that I am over-cautious, but I want no useless bloodshed amongst our men.'

'They know that, Cap'n,' Piers said and glanced towards the others. 'It's Wolf's crew they don't trust.'

'I have warned everyone to be wary,' Justin said. 'Wolf is a fool if he trusts Bronte – and I do not think him that.'

Justin saw the others were waiting and left Piers to return to the other men that had been chosen to stay by the spring with him. It was not a hard climb to the rock shaped like a dog's head, and they would be in full view of the others until they went inside the cave.

So far everything had gone easily, too easily for Justin's liking. Wolf seemed prepared to share his treasure but could he be trusted once it was found?

Justin had never quite believed it would be found. Someone else might have discovered it; perhaps one of the original crew from Red Bart's ship had returned and claimed it long ago. Yet when the cave had been found, the greenery hacked away and the cave open to their view, Justin's blood heated with excitement.

What was it about buried treasure that went to a man's head? He knew that once it was found both crews would be on fire to claim their share of the gold and silver. A part of his mind wondered whether gold could ever be worth the risk of fierce fighting amongst the men, and yet a tiny pulse beat at his temple as they followed the passage to the right and found themselves within a larger cave with a high domed roof.

It had to be right! It was so like the map. Justin held his lantern above his copy of the map, studying it intently.

'It shows a skull . . .' he said, and holding his lantern aloft he looked about the cave and gave a start as he saw the skulls and bones lying almost in the centre of the cave. 'My God! It looks as if there are three of them. What happened here? You did not tell me of this, Wolf.'

'I did not know,' Wolf said and his face looked grey in the light of the lanterns as they approached the old bones. 'I knew Bart was haunted by something. It seems they left a warning . . .'

'It looks like treachery to me,' Justin said and felt sickened.

'Had I known of this I should not have joined you. This is blood money.'

'Is there milk in your veins, St Arnaud?' Wolf sneered. 'The Spanish crew were slaughtered for their gold – that did not turn your stomach I think?'

'Enemies fight and one must lose, that is the law of the seas,' Justin said. 'But these men were a part of the same crew – slaughtered to protect the secret of the treasure.'

In his mind he could see what must have happened here fifty years earlier. The crew had been brought to the cave to bury the treasure until it was settled how it should be disposed of, and shared. After they had finished their work Red Bart and his mate had killed them. Little wonder then that the crew had turned on each other or that a man's guilty conscience had driven him to drink.

Justin began to remove his shirt, indicating that the two sailors should do the same. 'Before you dig for the treasure you will carry these remains to the front cave, each set of bones wrapped in a shirt so that they do not become mixed together. We shall give these men a decent burial as they deserve.'

'Aye, aye, Cap'n,' Sam said and made a hasty sign of the cross over himself before bending to pick up the first of the skulls.

The other man scowled and looked at Wolf, who nodded and said, 'Mark the spot and do as St Arnaud says.'

After they had departed, carrying the remains, carefully wrapped in their shirts, Wolf grinned at him.

'A good ruse, Justin. It gives us time to find the emeralds.'

'They are not with the gold?'

'No – Bart said he buried them . . .' He glanced round the cave, and then pointed to a small pile of loose rocks in the far corner. 'There wasn't much time for he wanted to keep them secret from the others.' He ran towards the rocks, scrabbling amongst them with his bare hands and giving a cry of glee as he found the small leather pouch. Bringing it back to Justin, he opened it to tip the uncut jewels into his own hand. There were twelve in all, two large, the others of varying sizes. 'We'll divide them later.'

'Not so fast, my friend.' Justin gripped his wrist, preventing him from closing his fist. 'I'll take one large and two smaller – the rest are yours.' He selected his choice swiftly and slipped them into his jerkin, which he had put on over his bare chest after removing his shirt, where they nestled against the charm Marietta had given him months earlier.

Wolf was surprised to be given more than his fair share and anxious to hide them from the other men. Hearing the sound of voices, he thrust the pouch inside his jerkin and made no protest.

The two sailors returned, picked up their abandoned spades and began to dig where the skeletons had lain. It was hard work, for the earth had remained undisturbed for fifty years, but as they dug deeper they hit sandy soil and it became easier, the hole growing steadily. They had been working for some time when they all heard the noise of a spade hitting metal.

'The chests were bound with iron,' Wolf said, breaking into the sudden silence. Then he jumped down into the open pit and started to pull at the loose earth with his hands. In another moment they all saw it. 'My God! He was right. Bart was right!'

Wolf was almost crying in his excitement. Justin watched, feeling suddenly detached from the scene. The thrill of finding gold was diminished for him because of the earlier discovery of the old bones.

It was some minutes before the three men managed to drag the heavy chest out of the earth, but took seconds only for Bronte to slit it open with his axe. The dull gleam of gold bullion was there in the light of the lanterns, enough in just this one chest to make a man wealthy beyond desire. Six such chests were enough to make men kill their best friends.

'We shall need more men to dig for the rest,' Wolf said, his eyes narrowed. 'You and I will return to the ships and make the necessary arrangements, Justin. Bronte and Sam can remain here to guard the gold.'

'We'll leave another man outside the cave,' Justin agreed. 'I'll take Piers with me.'

Wolf opened his mouth to object and then shut it again. It meant there were two of his men against one of Justin's, fair enough for the moment, he thought.

77

Justin saw the struggle in him. From now on, every man would bear watching, including, perhaps especially Wolf.

To carry the heavy chests of bullion back the way they had come without horses or mules would be difficult, back-breaking work. It was Justin who came up with the solution. The men would work in shifts to bring up the gold, and each chest would be divided equally among them. Each man would carry his own share back to the ship. Another shift would take their place and the gold would be the responsibility of the man whose share it was.

'If one of my crew steals another man's share he will be hung, and his share goes to the dead man's family,' Justin warned. 'We live by and for each other. If we kill for greed we are all dead.'

A few dissenters murmured beneath their breath at his warning, but most of Justin's men were loyal, and those who complained were outnumbered and watched. Indeed, even the grumblers knew that they were fortunate to sail with him, for Wolf's men were uneasy with each other – especially when Bronte went missing one night.

A guard was left in the cave each night, five men from each crew, but on the third night Bronte said he was going outside to relieve himself and never returned. A search was made for him the next day, but nothing was found. It was three days before his body was found in thick vegetation. He had a knife in his back – but since it was his own knife it was impossible to point the finger of blame.

Wolf had made no threat to hang any man who stole another's share, and when Bronte's was found to be missing there was speculation and anger, but no one knew where to look for his killer.

Wolf had in any case taken the lion's share of his half of the gold, and his men were sullen as they saw that Justin's men fared much better. Wolf had dragooned four of his men into transporting his gold, and once it was safely locked in his cabin, remained on board to guard it with a loaded pistol.

Justin was left to the supervision of the men, and perhaps it was because his own respected him that Wolf's men did no more than grumble and envy their more fortunate brothers.

When only five chests of gold and two of silver were found, Justin suspected that Wolf had either exaggerated his claims or that some mischief was afoot. However, since he was the only other man to know how many chests there should have been, he kept his silence. The men had taken enough gold this voyage to make them rich if they were wise, though he knew many of them would lose no time in spending it once they reached Jamaica.

He himself had refused his share of the treasure, for he had told his men that they might divide it equally amongst themselves. This gesture won over the dissenters in his own crew, but raised the level of anger amongst Wolf's men. It came to a head at the end of a week, when most of the gold had been transported.

About twenty men remained on the island overnight, for one more chest was left to be divided, silver this time and smaller than the others. The men spent the night in feasting and drinking on the rations of rum Wolf had sent ashore to celebrate the end of their quest, and when they woke to discover that there was only one ship in the bay, their fury erupted.

Of the twenty, half were Wolf's and they cursed violently as they saw he had stolen away in the night, marooning them – unless they were taken on board the *Dark Angel*.

Justin was not on the beach when the desertion was discovered but his own crew soon alerted him to the fact that a fight was taking place on the island. He took another ten of his crew ashore, all armed heavily, and the fight was soon quelled. Three of Wolf's men had been killed and two of his own were badly wounded. He had them taken on board and the other men were buried in the sand, a few prayers said over their graves.

'This accursed treasure has cost enough lives,' Justin said. 'We leave on the next tide.'

'But what of the silver?' one of Wolf's men demanded. 'Our share of the gold has gone with that bastard.'

Several men echoed his anger at being cheated, murmuring amongst themselves.

'We have five hours to the next tide,' Justin told them. 'My men will join you and what can be brought here in the time will be shared amongst Wolf's men, to make up for what has been stolen from them.'

Justin's crew looked at one another and nodded. 'We're with you, Cap'n. It's fair they should have it.'

'And if I ever find that bastard again I'll put a knife between his shoulders!' one of the men shouted, waving his fist at the ocean where his ship should be.

'If I haven't shot him first,' Justin agreed grimly. 'So what are you waiting for? Don't fear we shall leave you here for you have my word on it. Return within the time and you sail with us.'

The men on the beach set off at a run, knowing that it was a race to bring back as much of the silver as they could before the tide caught them. Justin rowed himself back to the ship. It would be safer to stay on board until the others returned, just in case a few members of his crew thought about following Wolf's lead.

His treachery made Justin burn with anger, for nothing but sheer greed could have prompted it. Yet he had expected something, and in his own mind he laid the blame for Bronte's death at Wolf's door. The two men had somehow discovered the sixth chest and secreted it again, though how he could not say, and then Wolf had killed Bronte to keep the secret – just as his grandfather had killed those other men long ago.

Justin thought that perhaps he should have been grateful there had been no more loss of life. He hoped that no more ill luck would befall them on this island. For himself he could not wait to ship a cargo in Jamaica and return to New Orleans.

Six

Estelle sat quietly listening to the conversation at the dinner table. Her father had invited Monsieur de Varennes, his unmarried sister Rosemarie, André, his wife Suzanne, and another lady of mature years to dine, also Mr Frank Erskine. *He* had become a frequent visitor of late, and she knew that he had put some business her father's way. His manner towards Estelle was always courteous, attentive and kind, and if she had been able to forget his behaviour on a certain fatal night, she might have liked him. However, she could not forget, for that night was printed indelibly on her mind – and the consequences that followed.

'The British burned buildings in Washington and had they not been turned back at Baltimore they would have invaded in force,' Monsieur de Varennes was saying. 'But I think the Americans have the measure of them now for it was a great victory they scored at Plattsburg.'

'Yet I do not believe that that is an end to it,' Henri said. 'Mark my words, they will come at us yet.'

'Yes, I think you are right,' Frank Erskine agreed with him. 'But we have made great strides in our defensive measures of late, sir. Only yesterday a ship carrying arms arrived in port and they have been safely unloaded and positioned.'

'I am relieved to hear it,' Henri replied. 'It is thanks to our brave sea captains that we have not suffered more, for the British harry our ships and some have been lost.'

'Aye, for I lost one of my own cargoes,' Frank said ruefully. 'But we weary the ladies with our talk of such things.' He smiled at Estelle, who was sitting opposite. 'I hope that you mean to attend Madame de Varennes' ball next week, Estelle?'

Estelle took a sip of wine from a beautiful crystal glass. The wine had come from France and was some of the last in her father's store. When it had gone there would be no money to replace it. Perhaps even the glasses would need to be sold one day.

She felt her cheeks heat as she saw the message in Frank Erskine's eyes. 'Yes, of course. I am looking forward to it.' She glanced at Suzanne, who was looking particularly lovely that evening. The ball was to celebrate the marriage of Suzanne and André, who had been married just six months.

'Of course she is coming,' Suzanne said and her smile was warm and generous, for she had insisted on getting to know Estelle better these past months. 'I should be most distressed if she did not.'

'This man – Captain St Arnaud,' Monsieur de Varennes went

on as if there had been no interruption. 'The man is quite a hero I hear. This is not the first dangerous cargo he has carried in these waters.'

Frank Erskine nodded and scowled. 'He is little better than a privateer, sir. I daresay we are fortunate that he has thrown in his lot with us, and there is talk of Lafitte having done the same thing – but they are two of a kind, and go hand in hand they say. Pirates when all is said and done.'

Estelle saw her father turn pale when mention was made of Captain St Arnaud, for though he had put the memory of his meeting with the man out of his mind these past months, it had haunted him. Just as her own memories had haunted her. She had gradually come to accept that she might never see Justin again, but now that she knew he was here in New Orleans, she felt her heart race.

Her eyes lit with a silver fire and there was an incandescence about her at that moment that made Frank decide he would have her soon, whether she willed it or no. Unaware of his hot gaze Estelle was thinking of Justin. She hoped that she would not have to meet him, for try as she might, she could not forget the way he had made love to her, or the despair and emptiness she had felt after he had left her. It was clear that the night he had spent in her arms had meant nothing to him or he would have come to see her when he was in New Orleans. And she knew that he had brought more than one cargo to port, for he had spared time to visit Marietta. It would be painful if they should meet in company, and she dare not see him alone.

'Perhaps it is time we left the gentlemen to their port,' Tante Rosemarie said, giving Estelle a hint.

'Yes, of course.' She blushed, for her thoughts had been far away. 'Yes, we shall leave you, Papa.'

She got up and the ladies followed her into the drawing room, leaving the gentlemen to their wine and their talk of war. Erle and Jessie brought in trays of coffee and tea for the ladies, and they began to talk of fashions and domestic issues. But Estelle let the conversation drift over her head, for she could think of nothing but a certain gentleman.

'Men!' Suzanne exclaimed as she sat next to Estelle on the sofa. 'Do they ever think of anything but war or business? I declare it bores me to tears, do you not agree?'

'It worries me for Papa's sake,' Estelle said, and sighed. She must put away her thoughts of Justin St Arnaud, for if he had wanted to see her he would have come long before this. 'But you are right, we have better things to talk of. Your dress is very pretty, Suzanne – did it come from Paris?'

'It was one of my trousseau gowns,' Suzanne said. 'I thought I should wear it for I may not be able to do so before long ...' A delicate colour stained her cheeks. 'I have told no one but André and he has spoken to his Papa and Tante Rosemarie, but you are my friend, Estelle, and I would like you to be the first outside the family to know that I am *enceinte*.'

'Oh, how lovely for you,' Estelle exclaimed. 'I am so pleased, Suzanne.' She saw something in the other girl's eyes. 'You are pleased, aren't you?'

'Oh, I suppose so,' Suzanne said, and laughed. 'But it will be so uncomfortable, and I do not like to be uncomfortable. Already I have been sick and it is most unpleasant.'

'But that will soon pass,' Estelle said. 'At least, I have heard that it does ...'

Suzanne pulled a wry face. 'Tante Rosemarie knows no more than I about such things, and would not tell me if she did. But I suppose I shall just have to put up with whatever comes. Men are so fortunate, are they not – all the pleasure and none of the fuss!'

Estelle laughed. Despite her embarrassment at meeting Suzanne with André at first, she had come to like the young woman very much, and now counted her as one of her best friends.

'Well, you will just have to make your husband suffer a little,' she teased and noticed the gleam in Suzanne's eyes.

'I intend to,' she said, and laughed merrily as they saw that the gentlemen were about to join them. 'Do not worry, Estelle, I intend to do just that! If I suffer so shall he.'

Estelle smiled for she did not take her words seriously, and it was only some months later that she would recall the significance of their conversation.

'You look very fine this evening, Monsieur,' Piers said. He made his guardian a laughing bow as Justin came down dressed in the correct attire for dancing, in a dress frock coat of pale grey, with narrow-fitting pantaloons, a silk striped waistcoat and a froth of pristine white lace at his neck. 'Pleased to make your acquaintance, milord.'

Justin aimed a playful blow at his ear. 'Watch your tongue, brat, or I'll put you on crow watch the whole of our next voyage.'

Piers pulled a face at him. 'I'm going to visit Marietta while you are out,' he said. 'She was kind to my mother and I have a gift for her – just some sweets she is partial to now and then.'

'Give the old witch my love,' Justin said with a grin. 'Tell her I shall visit her soon and mend whatever she has lined up for me this time.'

Piers laughed and they left the house together, walking in companionable silence until they parted company, Justin to the grand ball to which he had been invited, and the youth to visit his mother's friend.

Justin was thoughtful as he walked to the reception rooms where the function was being held that night. He recalled the last time he had visited them, and his meeting with Estelle Lebrun, as vividly as if the intervening months had never been.

After leaving the treasure island, he and his crew had returned to Jamaica, where most of the men had gone ashore to drink solidly for nearly two weeks, until Justin had negotiated a cargo and rounded them up, some at pistol point. There had been some sore heads and sullen looks for a few days, but then the atmosphere returned to normal, and they began to bless their lucky stars that thanks to their captain they still had some part of their fortunes left to take back to their families.

After his first return to New Orleans, some of Justin's men had taken their gold and decided it was time to give up the sea. He had paid a visit to Barataria on Grand Terre to give his usual tribute to Jean Lafitte. There he had learned of the offer made to the pirate king by the British if he would help them attack New Orleans.

'English pigs!' Lafitte spat on the ground. 'I take what I want of their cargoes and ask no permission. Never have I attacked an American ship, and I have made a bargain with the Americans – when the time comes I shall fight on their side. For the moment what they need is guns and munitions. And I have a cargo waiting in the West Indies to be shipped to New Orleans under the noses of the British – are you the man for it?'

'Aye, for I am with you in this. I have no love for the English – though my father was one of them.'

Lafitte had heard stories, but knew no more of Justin's history than most others, nor did he pry. A man's past was his own, and the less said the better. The bargain sealed between them, Justin returned to New Orleans, where he had business.

Estelle had seldom been far from Justin's thoughts. He had brought in a cargo of guns and cannon, running the gauntlet of three British frigates in the Gulf, and it had brought him a handsome profit. He had been asked to bring in more vital supplies by some prominent citizens, and it was in his mind to negotiate terms that evening. Indeed, it was the main reason for his attendance – and yet at the back of his mind lay the hope that he might see Estelle.

He was not sure why he had not been to see her father as yet, though his desire to bring Lebrun to account had lost its edge over the months. Piers lacked for nothing, was growing rapidly towards manhood, happy and sure, his education leaping far ahead of what he would need to sail a ship. He was an intelligent young man and it could not be long before he was ready to command his own ship, young though he was. Petra was dead and nothing could bring her back, and there was Estelle to consider . . .

What did he want to do about Estelle? Sometimes he thought he knew, and at others he was uncertain. The life he led was not for the daughter of a gentleman. Much of his time was spent at sea, and the company he kept was not what she had been accustomed to. His men were rough tongued and rough mannered, inclined to fight, quarrel and spit. The routine on board ship was not for a delicate lady. He would be a fool to think of Estelle in those terms, and yet . . .

He shook his head. She had accepted his bargain and no doubt she had forgotten him, put the memory far from her mind. Too many months had passed since that night. She might even be married by now.

Indeed, if she had fallen for a child, she might have had no choice but to marry the first who asked to cover her shame. Yet it would be he who must bear the shame if she had been forced to such desperate measures. It would be on his conscience for a long, long time.

'You look beautiful this evening,' André said as he greeted Estelle at his wife's ball. 'Will you give me the honour of a dance?'

She felt her cheeks heat slightly, for she could never forget the day she had humiliated herself by begging him to marry her – or the offer he had made her after he refused.

'Yes, if you wish it, sir,' she told him. She gave him her dance card, which had only a few spaces taken for she had arrived with her father just a short time earlier. 'You may choose where you will.'

'Then I shall reserve two dances, Estelle.'

The look he gave her was so particular, so warm, that it made her look away. What could he mean by paying her such attention?

'If you wish.'

'Excuse me, I believe Suzanne needs me,' André said, and frowned. 'She is not in the best of moods of late.'

Estelle had little time to ponder his remarks, for the other guests had begun to realise she was there and a succession of gentlemen came to greet her and ask her for a dance. She was smiling as they passed her card from one to the other, refusing to give it back, and then, suddenly, her heart caught as a man took the card and returned it to her.

He was taller than the others, stronger, harder, his presence casting a shadow over them so that they melted away leaving him the field. His dark eyes moved over her, sending little shivers up and down her spine and she swallowed hard.

'Captain St Arnaud. I had heard that you had returned to New Orleans, and that you have done us some considerable service.' Her head was high, her manner almost regal as she met his searching gaze.

'Do not believe all you may hear, Mademoiselle Lebrun,' he replied, a faint quirk to his left eyebrow. 'I trade as I see fit and make a profit from my efforts. I give nothing for senti- ment or patriotism.'

'Yet you are much admired,' she said. 'I have heard your name on many lips these past days, for they say you fear no one.'

'Then they are but fools after all, for every man fears something. I fear that you may hate me, Estelle.'

'Have I cause to hate you, sir?' she asked with a toss of her head. She looked proud, cool, remote, as if nothing had passed between them, and Justin frowned. This was not the innocent girl who had given herself to him so sweetly. 'I have no memory of anything that should make me feel something for you – hatred or otherwise.'

'Then I have nothing to fear,' Justin said and bowed his head to her. 'Excuse me, I see someone I must speak to . . .'

He had not even asked her for a dance! Tears stung at the back of Estelle's eyes, but she blinked them away. She had been so cool to him, but inside she was a mass of seething emotion. He was right to fear her hatred, for his behaviour had aroused it! He cared nothing for her nor ever had. And she was hurting so badly that she did not know how she could continue to smile at her friends. He had taken what he wanted, discarding her like the whore he thought her – the whore she was! He had offered payment and she had accepted it; there was no escaping what she had done, and it stung bitterly.

Her pride was in shreds, her heart aching as she watched him greet the gentleman he had gone to meet, and she was not at first aware of Frank Erskine as he came up to her.

'Are you in some distress, Estelle?' he asked in a gentle voice that almost overset her. 'Did that rogue St Arnaud say something that upset you? If he did he shall answer to me for it, hero of the hour or no!'

'Oh no,' she said faintly. 'No, of course he did not, sir. We merely spoke in passing. It is just that – just that I have a little headache.'

'You look pale,' Frank said. 'Would you like to go into the garden for a breath of air?'

'Perhaps . . .' Estelle looked at him gratefully. She did feel very warm and her throat ached for want of relief – but she must not weep. 'It might help if I could walk a little in the air.'

'Allow me to take you,' he said and offered her his arm. 'You know that my first concern is always your comfort and your happiness, Estelle. I would do anything within my power to please you.'

Why had she disliked him so at their first meeting? Estelle

could not remember. For months now he had behaved in a most gentlemanly manner, and she had come to accept his company as being pleasant. He no longer repulsed her and he was clearly kind for he had been good to her father.

'You are very kind,' she said as she took his arm. 'I do not know why I should be so affected by the heat for it is not particularly hot in here, but a few minutes in the air will no doubt revive me.'

Outside, the air smelled sweet and fresh, and after a moment or two walking on the terraces, she began to feel much better. It was foolish of her to let Captain St Arnaud distress her, for nothing had changed. She had known for a long time that she meant nothing to him. It was just seeing him again, being close to him. Now she was over it, her mind restored and clear once more.

'I think we may go back now, sir,' she said. 'I am quite recovered.'

'You are sure?'

'Yes, quite sure.'

'Then may I speak?' Frank looked at her earnestly. 'I believe that you know I care deeply for you, Estelle?' She nodded but said nothing for her heart was racing. 'It has long been my wish that you will consent to be my wife – but I have not spoken for I wanted to give you time to know me. I understand that you do not wish to leave your father, but there would be no need. He could live with us.'

Estelle caught her breath. How could she marry him? It would not be fair or honourable to marry any man without revealing her sin – and she dare not, could not tell him the truth. He would be disgusted, angry – and he would tell her father.

'You are very generous,' she said, feeling faint. She did not know how to answer him! 'I hardly know what . . .' It was on the tip of her tongue to deny him when she saw Justin come out onto the terrace. He stood looking at them, feet apart, smoking a cigar, his expression brooding, resentful. She felt his anger, his disapproval, and her head went up proudly. 'I shall give your offer further consideration, sir. Indeed, I thank you for it and consider it an honour . . .'

'Estelle!' Frank's ruddy face lit up with pleasure. He had

meant to have her one way or the other, but it seemed there would be no need for coercion. To take her without her consent would give him fleeting pleasure, but to own her body and soul, that was a prize beyond measure. 'If you give me such kind words I know that you will come to accept me as your husband very soon. You have made me the happiest of men, my dear. Come, let us go and tell your father the good news.'

She had not given him her promise, had she? Indeed, her heart was thumping, her mind in such confusion that she did not know what she had said. She felt a tiny surge of panic for even though she no longer felt repulsed by him, she had no desire to marry him.

Yet he seemed to think she had accepted him, and there was an air of possession about him as he took her inside, nodding curtly to Justin as they passed him. His dark eyes followed them and he was frowning when Estelle risked a brief glance back at him.

However, she was given no chance to do or say anything. Her escort went straight over to where her father was standing with some other gentlemen and announced that Estelle had promised to marry him.

'Oh but . . .' she said faintly. She was not sure what she had promised, and she felt confused, slightly distant, as though this was happening to someone else. 'I have said I will consider . . .'

'Estelle wants to wait until you are feeling better, sir,' Frank said, his loud voice seeming to boom in her ears. 'But I have assured her that she will not need to be parted from you for I shall be honoured to have you live with us.'

'It is my dearest wish to see my child settled,' Henri said, looking so relieved and pleased that Estelle was silenced. She could not protest that she had never meant to accept Frank Erskine's proposal. It would distress her father and make a fool of the man who was even now being congratulated by all his friends. 'You have made me very happy, Estelle. Do not think you must wait for my sake. The sooner it is done the better.'

Estelle felt a sense of panic rising inside her, but she was trapped – trapped by her father's relief and happiness, and Frank Erskine's obvious delight. How foolish she had been not to choose her words more carefully, but her mind had been distracted by . . . *he* had come into the room once more and their eyes met across the room, his faintly disbelieving, challenging her, disapproving. She felt that he was mocking her and she raised her head, then turned her back on him deliberately.

He meant nothing to her! She had been foolish to accept his shameful bargain, to let him use her as a whore. The man to whom she was now promised as a wife was a far better man than that . . . pirate! She would think of him no more. That part of her life was over and she would forget it.

Yet when a gentleman to whom she had promised the next dance claimed her, she smiled at him a little fixedly as he wished her happiness and then whirled her round the room. Passing under the disapproving gaze of Justin's dark eyes, her mouth trembled and she hardly knew how to keep from weeping. Oh, how she hated him. She hated him, she did! Yet in her heart she knew that she was lying, and that she would never, ever be able to forget him.

Justin watched Estelle dancing. He had heard the little buzz of excitement, which flew about the ballroom, and knew that she and Erskine had announced their engagement. And how had that happened? She had changed her mind mightily from the last time if she was going to marry the man!

A deep burning anger had started in his guts. She belonged to him in the sight of God and man. He had made her his that night, and she had no right . . . pulling himself up, he took a long clear look at himself and realised what a fool he had been. He should have fixed his interest with her before he left New Orleans that first time, and could blame no one but himself. Yet, as he watched her, he sensed that she was unhappy.

She was not in love with Erskine and she did not want to marry him. Had her scheming father forced her to it? Justin had absolved him of his most pressing debts, but perhaps that was not enough for Lebrun. Perhaps he had sold the girl to the highest bidder.

Erskine would not have her! He was a scoundrel, an abusive brute who treated his girls abominably, and the thought of him marrying Estelle, lying with her, made Justin's blood run cold. No, she should not be made to suffer that, he vowed silently.

He would not allow it. If he had to abduct the girl to stop it, he would do it.

But things had not gone too far as yet, he thought, and he would keep a cool head. The first thing to do would be to visit Lebrun in the morning and discuss matters of business. It was what he ought to have done when he first returned to New Orleans, and he could not for the life of him imagine why he had delayed.

Estelle lay in her bed unable to sleep as she turned first to one side and then the other, seeking some way out of her dilemma. She was trapped, for it would cause too much distress to everyone if she drew back now, and she had seen how happy her father was at the news. He had been so frail of late and she knew that he was failing. He could not live much longer. The doctor had told her she must prepare for the worst – and perhaps it would not be so very bad to marry Frank Erskine.

Yet the very thought of lying with him – the way she had lain with Justin – had the shivers running through her. How had she been so foolish as to allow herself to fall into this muddle? She had been trying to extricate herself without hurting Frank's feelings, and somehow she had allowed him to believe that she would marry him. It was her father, however, who was pressing for an early marriage, and she knew that that was because he was afraid he might die very soon.

Her throat was tight and she felt like weeping, but that would avail her nothing. She had fallen into a trap of her own making and she could see no way out of it.

Oh, it was all Justin St Arnaud's fault, she thought angrily. If he had not upset her so badly she would never have gone outside with Frank Erskine and it would not have happened.

By the time that Jessie came to rouse her, she felt wretched, her eyes gritty with tiredness, and far too restless to remain in the house.

'I am going to visit Marietta,' she told Jessie when she went down to the kitchen later. 'And no, I do not need you to come with me. You cannot be running after me all the time. There is too much to be done here.'

'What got into you'se this mornin'?' Jessie asked, for she could see that Estelle was out of sorts. 'Seems to me a girl in your shoes should be happy seein' as you'se just got engaged.'

'Well, I am not,' Estelle said crossly. 'Do not fuss over me, Jessie, for I am not in the mood for it.'

Ignoring the hurt look in her dear friend's face, she fetched her cloak and a basket, filling it with bits and pieces from the larder. Marietta had a sweet tooth and Jessie had been baking blueberry tarts that morning. She was guiltily aware that Jessie had done nothing to deserve such sharpness from her, and she would have to apologise when she returned, but for the moment she was too much on edge to find the right words.

It was a cool morning, the breeze carrying a bite that was seldom found in the balmy climate of New Orleans, and she felt that a storm was gathering. She hurried towards Marietta's house, suddenly anxious to visit her friend and return home.

When she went in, she found the old woman dozing by the fire. Marietta roused sufficiently to greet her with a smile, but Estelle realised that her friend was looking frail and ill, and her heart caught with distress.

She heated some soup over the fire for her, holding the spoon to her lips when she saw that Marietta was barely strong enough to hold it for herself.

'How long have you been like this?' she asked in a gently scolding tone. 'Why did you not send word to me?'

'She would not trouble you,' a girl's voice said from behind her and Estelle turned. She knew that the girl was called Genieve and worked at the House of Pearls. 'Besides, one of us comes to see her every morning and every night.'

'Oh, that is so good of you,' Estelle said and smiled at her. 'It makes me easier in my mind to know that she is cared for – but should she not have the doctor?'

'No need for doctors,' Marietta said, and now her eyes were open and her voice was stronger. 'It's my time, child. The Good Lord is coming for me soon and I shall rest with Him, unless the other one claims me for my sins.' A harsh laugh escaped her. 'Weep not for me, Estelle. I've lived my fill and shall be ready to meet my Maker when He calls.'

Estelle felt the sting of tears. 'Oh, Marietta . . .'

'I'll see you on your way,' Genieve said when Estelle

retrieved her basket a little later, and walked outside with her. 'I will send word if she needs you – but it cannot be long now. We have been expecting it for days.'

'I have not been for a week,' Estelle said feeling guilty. 'My poor Marietta . . .'

Genieve looked at her steadily for a moment, an odd expression in her blue eyes. 'They say you are to marry Frank Erskine?'

'Yes . . . perhaps,' Estelle said. 'I have heard he owns the House of Pearls – is that true?'

'Yes, for our sins,' the girl said with a grimace. 'If you will listen to me you will break your promise to him before it is too late. Run away, hide, do what you must – but do not marry him.'

'Why do you say that?'

Estelle watched as the girl turned away from her, then pushed down the shoulder of her gown to reveal a large purple bruise that extended over her shoulder and down her back.

'He did that to me a few days ago. It is not the first time – nor am I the only one. You think that he uses whores but will be kinder to his wife perhaps?' She gave a harsh laugh. 'Within a year you will wish that you had never met him.'

Estelle shivered. 'I was not sure. I had heard rumours but . . .'

'They are true, every one of them. I tell you only because you have loved Marietta, as we love her.'

'Thank you.' Estelle swallowed hard. 'Thank you for telling me.'

'Do not let him know it was I who told you, for he would kill me.'

'No, of course not,' Estelle said. 'I shall think of some excuse to break my promise to him.'

'If you do not you will regret it.'

Estelle felt cold as she walked home. The storm was gathering fast now, and the sky was dark. She felt some large spots of rain as she ran inside her house. Tension seemed to hang in the air as she removed her cloak and went into the kitchen. Immediately, as Jessie looked at her, she knew that something had happened.

'What is it – what has happened? Is it Papa?'

'Your father, he have a visitor just after you left, chile,' Jessie said and tears started to roll down her cheeks. 'Erle, he heard them arguing and then the visitor left and in a temper some. Erle, he go in there to see what goin' on, and he find your father slumped out on the floor. We got him to bed and the doctor's with him now . . .'

Jessie spoke to air as Estelle turned and ran out into the hall and on up the stairs. Her heart was racing wildly and her chest felt tight. If her father was really bad this time, it could be the last . . .

Outside his door, she paused, gathering her composure. She must not let him see how distressed she was for it would only hurt him. She forced herself to smile as she tapped at the door and went in. The doctor was bending over her father, speaking to him as she stood quietly behind him. When he turned towards her, she knew at once that it was hopeless. The expression in his eyes was like a dagger thrust at her heart, for she understood that he was telling her that her father was dying.

'Ah, you are back,' he said kindly. 'That is good for your father was fretting for you. Come, sit with him, Estelle, for he wishes to be alone with you. I believe he has something he wishes to tell you. I shall be outside and you may call me if you need me.'

Estelle approached the bed, her heart aching as she saw how fragile her father was. It was clear to her that he did not have long to live, and she forced a gentle smile as she sat on the edge of the bed and took his hand.

'I am here, dearest,' she said. 'I am sorry I was not here when you needed me.'

'You could not know . . .' he hushed her with a finger to his lips as she would have spoken. 'I know that you visit Marietta. I had forbidden it but you could not abandon her because you loved her.'

'She was like a mother to me, Papa.' Estelle could hardly keep the sob from her voice. 'And I fear that she is . . .'

'I must talk to you, my dearest child,' Henri went on. His hand reached for hers but he had no strength and she took it in her own, holding it carefully. 'I have been a bad father to you, Estelle. I have been foolish with my money, wasting your inheritance . . .'

'Hush, Papa. I have no need of riches.'

'But because of it you will marry a man I respect but cannot entirely like or trust,' her father told her. 'Had things been different I should not have admitted Erskine to my house. He is not one of us. However, it is done and perhaps it is for the best. He is wealthy and I believe he cares for you.'

'Yes, I am sure he does,' Estelle said, caring only that her father should be at peace. There would be time enough later to face the problem of Mr Erskine. 'Do not fret for my sake, Papa.'

'But there is more I must say . . .' His eyes closed for a moment and she could see that he was in great distress. 'I must confess my sin to you, child. You must know the truth for it may keep you safe when I am no longer here . . .'

'Your secret, Papa?' she looked at him in bewilderment. 'What terrible secret can you have, dearest?'

'Ah, do not smile so,' he said in a choking voice, 'for you look so like her that it breaks my heart – my beloved Leah.'

'Leah . . .' Estelle questioned, for surely her mother's name was Elizabeth?

'Yes, Estelle. Leah was the only woman I loved, but she was not my wife. Elizabeth Lebrun died giving birth to a still-born child. On that same day, your mother also gave birth to you – and though she died, you lived. I brought you here to this house and gave you into the care of Marietta. Her own child was almost weaned and unfortunately died some months later of a fever. It was Marietta's milk that nursed you, her tender care that saved you from suffering the same fate as your mother and my other daughter.'

'Father . . .' Estelle was so shocked that for a moment she could only stare at him. 'Then I am . . . illegitimate . . . bastard born?'

'Do not look so,' he begged, and his hand tightened about hers, using the last of his strength. 'You have been my only, my beloved daughter and I have loved you as I loved your mother. Elizabeth meant nothing to me. I married her for the sake of an heir, because I could not marry your mother.'

'You could not marry my mother . . . Leah?' Estelle furrowed her brow as she tried to make sense of all that he was telling her. 'Were you already married – or was she married to someone else, Papa? How was it that you could not marry her?'

'When I first met your mother she was the loveliest girl I had ever seen. I fell instantly in love with her and our love

95

lasted until the day she died, and I have mourned her in my heart ever since. But it was impossible. I had to marry someone else – to get my heir . . .'

'But why could you not marry the woman you loved?'

'We met at a Quadroon Ball, child,' he said, and a tear slipped from the corner of his eye as he saw the bewilderment in her face change to shock as she began to understand. 'Leah's skin was as white as yours, Estelle, but her grandmother was a Negress. In law that meant that we could never marry. Even you . . .' he stopped and could not go on as he saw the look of dismay in her eyes.

'But that means I have coloured blood,' she said in a choked voice for it was so strange to her, so unbelievable. She had been reared as the daughter of a proud French Creole father and now to learn that she was both bastard born and a person of colour was stunning, making her feel that all she had known and loved was falling away from her. She was marooned on an island surrounded by treacherous waters and there was no way of escape. 'If you could not marry my mother then I . . . it would be unlawful for me to marry a white man, is that not true, Father?'

'If it was known,' he admitted. 'But I guarded my secret well, Estelle. No one knows but Marietta. That is why I sent her away for I feared she might tell you, but she kept faith. I thought it would never be necessary to tell you, but now I am afraid – for what might happen if the secret were to come out.'

Estelle nodded. Leah, her mother, had had white skin according to her father, and hers was a deep creamy colour, but there was a possibility that a future child of hers might show some sign of her Negro ancestry. Now she began to understand why her father had hesitated to arrange a marriage for her with his friends, and it shamed her.

She was not shamed to carry her mother's blood, for some of the people who were dearest to her had coloured blood and she loved them none the less for it. She was shamed that her father had seen fit to hide the truth from her all these years, and that he clearly felt it to be a stigma that might ruin her future.

'Oh, Papa,' she whispered brokenly. 'Why did you not tell me before this? Why did you let me believe that your wife was my mother?' She saw the way his hands shook and the look in his eyes and could not say the words that trembled on her lips. 'Papa . . .'

How could she blame him for what he had done? He had taken her into his home and his heart, giving her love and happiness all these years. With a few words he had destroyed her world, and yet she could not accuse him of betraying her. She loved him and it was breaking her heart to see the life draining out of him, and to show anger, to rain bitter accusations on him now, would be cruel.

'Forgive me, child,' he said, tears trickling unheeded down his withered cheeks. 'It is my sin and it has tortured me for the past few years for I know that you may suffer for it. In my grief and my selfishness I thought only of my need and my love for you – but it was wrong and you have to live now with the knowledge of what I have done to you.'

'No, no, Papa,' she said, and took a scented kerchief to wipe away his tears. 'You have done nothing so very terrible. It makes no difference. I have been loved and you have given me all that I could desire. It was right that you should tell me the truth.'

But oh, she wished that she had always known, that she had grown up with the knowledge, accepting it as right and proper. She was losing her father, losing her dearest friend Marietta – and now she had lost all right to her own identity.

She was not Mademoiselle Estelle Lebrun, she was the daughter of her father's mistress, a free person of colour and a bastard. Her world had come tumbling down about her, and she did not know what to do for the best.

Seven

Estelle sat by her father's side throughout the night as a terrible storm raged outside, the howling wind and the rain lashing against the house as though the very demons of hell were trying to enter. For some time she sat holding his hand, and then when he lapsed into a state of semi-consciousness, she dozed for brief moments in the armchair, listening to the sound of his breathing becoming more and more shallow as the night wore on. It was just before dawn that he breathed his last.

The doctor had left much earlier for he had an urgent call. 'Your father suffers no pain, my dear,' he told her before he departed. 'It is just a question of time.'

It was Jessie who came and took Estelle away at the end, forcing her to lie down on her bed.

'He's gone now, sweet chile,' she said, tears rolling down her cheeks. 'Your Papa with the Good Lord in Heaven. He ain't sufferin' no more.'

'I loved him so,' Estelle said, but she was beyond tears. 'I shall miss him so very much.' She felt so alone and there was an empty aching void inside her. Everything she had ever known and believed in had been taken from her, leaving her feeling numb.

'Ah knows you'se gonna miss him, chile,' Jessie crooned. 'Your Papa, he a good man in his way. We all gonna miss him.'

'Yes.' Estelle realised how true this was, for there had been little enough money these past months. Now there would be none at all. 'You said there was a visitor, Jessie. Someone who upset my father. Do you know who it was?'

Jessie looked at her oddly. 'It was that Captain St Arnaud,' she said. 'Erle told me he was a hero, but your Papa didn't like what he had to say. Erle heard them arguing, and your Papa, he was angry and shouting.'

'Captain St Arnaud . . .' Estelle's face became paler than before. 'How could he? Oh, how could he?'

Surely he had not come to demand payment of a debt after all this time? He had given her that paper as a sign of his good faith, and she believed it was legal. Then, if it was not the debt, what could he have said to make her father angry? Had he demanded that they leave his house?

Justin must have said something to upset her father to the point that he had collapsed immediately after he left. She felt a surge of anger and bitterness as she undressed and lay down

98

on her bed. Had he no thought for her at all? He could not care for her in the least or he would not have killed her father.

She hardened her mind against him. He had murdered her dearest Papa as surely as if he had taken a knife and stabbed him to the heart.

Lying on her bed, Estelle tried to put all thought of Captain St Arnaud from her mind. She had other truths to face, changes that must be made, decisions to be taken about her future. Yet for the moment she was worn down with grief and shock and she did not know where to turn.

Unaware of the grief and chaos he had left behind him, Justin was grim-faced as he walked across town while the storm gathered pace in the skies above him. Lebrun was a stubborn fool and he had informed him of it in no uncertain terms. If he allowed his daughter to marry that monster after Justin had told him the facts, he was worse than a fool.

He had spared Lebrun a lecture over his treatment of Petra, for the past could not be changed, and the man had looked ill. However, he had made his own position clear. He would not allow the marriage to take place.

'You will not allow?' Lebrun's voice had risen, sharp with anger. 'How dare you come to my house and say such a thing to me! Pray what is my daughter's future to you?'

'More than it is to you seemingly,' Justin answered. Pride forbade him the luxury of truth. 'I know Erskine to be depraved as well as dishonest, and I say again that I shall not allow Estelle to be forced into this marriage.'

'She has not been forced,' Henri said, though he was uneasy as he recalled his daughter's manner the previous evening. He had known something was not quite right but he had clutched at the idea eagerly in his desperation to see her settled. 'As her father, I should know what is best for her.'

'You should,' Justin agreed, a tiny pulse flicking in his throat. 'But it is clear that you do not. If you will not act to prevent this travesty, I shall.'

'By God, sir! If I were ten years younger I would kill you for this impertinence. I say again – what is Estelle to you?'

'I intend that she shall never marry that monster. For the rest . . .' Justin smiled oddly. 'We must leave that to the lady

99

herself to decide. And now I bid you good day, sir. I shall expect to hear that the marriage is cancelled, otherwise I shall do whatever is necessary. I shall call again in a few days to see Estelle herself.'

He left Lebrun's office without looking back, aware that the man's silence was controlled anger. The interview had gone badly for he had not meant to quarrel with Estelle's father. Something in the man's manner had irked him, reminding him of the interview with his mother's husband on the never to be forgotten day of her death.

'You are not my son,' St Arnaud had said, looking at Justin as if he were filth from the gutter. 'I tolerated you for my wife's sake, but she betrayed me, robbed me of the son I should have had. You are a bastard. Leave my house today for it is home to you no more.'

Lebrun had looked at him as if he were scum from the waterfront, and it had touched a raw nerve. Had it been otherwise, Justin might have told him that he intended something better for Estelle than she could expect from Erskine. Regrettably he had lost his cool reserve, said things that were better left unsaid.

He doubted that Estelle would be pleased to see him when he returned, but he would face that when the time came. He had earlier that day been approached by a man called Hinckston, who had told him that he had heard that Wolf's ship had been seen further down the coast. Knowing that Hinckston had a score to settle with Wolf himself, he did not doubt that the information was correct, and Justin had a mind to go after the rogue captain. If his guess was right, he would find Wolf at Barataria. He must see what could be done to bring the renegade to justice according to the laws of the brotherhood.

Estelle went through the next few days feeling dazed, her grief too deep to be eased with tears. André de Varennes was one of the first to call. His father, as Henri's closest friend, had asked that he might be allowed to arrange the burial. Henri's coffin would be interred in the family vault and the blessing would be in the Catholic church they all attended.

'My father wishes to do this as a mark of respect for an

100

old friend, Estelle,' André said, holding her hand a moment longer than necessary. 'Tante Rosemarie will come to be with you and to arrange the reception for your father's friends afterwards. You will of course stay here to greet them.'

'But I wish to accompany my father to his last resting place.'

'It would not be fitting,' André told her. 'Ladies are best at home until these things are over.'

'I shall go with Papa,' Estelle insisted, her face pale but determined.

'You are very brave. We wanted to spare you pain – but if you insist I shall escort you myself.' André pressed her fingers to comfort her. 'You must know that I have come to admire you a great deal, Estelle.'

Estelle drew her hand from his, feeling as if she wanted to scream. Why must he look at her that way? Why say these things now? She had humbled her pride to ask him for help and he had refused her. Now he spoke of warm feelings towards her, giving her the kind of passionate looks he ought to have reserved for his wife. Once they would have meant everything to her. Now they meant nothing.

'Please thank your father for his kindness, sir. I shall accept for I believe it is what my father would have wanted. Your family understands our ways and it will all be as Papa would expect.'

Soon after André's departure, Frank Erskine arrived. He was full of apologies for not coming sooner, the delay having been on account of business.

'You may leave all the arrangements to me, Estelle.'

'Monsieur de Varennes has agreed to see Papa properly looked after,' Estelle told him and saw his quick frown of annoyance. 'But there will be other things – matters of business on which I shall be grateful for your advice. My father's lawyers will know what must be done.'

'Ah yes, that must be my first concern. Your father's affairs must be settled, though you know that your future is secured as my wife, Estelle.'

'We cannot marry until I am out of mourning for my father,' Estelle said quickly. She saw his eyes narrow and held back the rest of what she wanted to say. Time enough to tell him that she would not marry him when her grief had begun to heal. 'It would not be proper, sir. As a gentleman you could not expect it.'

She saw the denial in his face. He would try to persuade her to break with convention, but even he dare not speak too openly this soon.

'We shall discuss this another time, Estelle.'

'Yes, of course. It was kind of you to call, sir, but I am expecting Tante Rosemarie at any moment. She is to stay with me for my period of strict mourning.'

She saw at once that he was displeased by what he believed to be interference from the de Varennes family, but Estelle was grateful for the strict protocol of her people. She would not be alone, at least for a few weeks, until she had made up her mind what her future should be.

'But you will of course be welcome to call on us, sir.'

'I should hope that you will turn to me in future, Estelle. These people are your friends I make no doubt, but I am your future husband.'

'Unfortunately, the contract was not signed nor even drawn up,' Estelle said. 'As you know, these things are done according to a strict code amongst my people. Until I have spoken with Papa's lawyers and my friends, I cannot claim to be betrothed. I beg you to be patient, sir. I am not able to speak further of this now.'

She turned gratefully as Tante Rosemarie entered the room, giving Mr Erskine a surprised, slightly haughty glance, for she did not approve of a young woman receiving a gentleman alone, even if they were promised to each other. Estelle greeted her with a feeling of relief. The lady might be a gossip and a little tedious, but she had never been more pleased to see her.

Justin met with disappointment at Barataria. Wolf's ship had certainly been seen anchored just off the coast during the night of the storm, but by morning it had sailed.

'You are not the only one to be disappointed,' Jean Lafitte told him with a cold smile. 'Some of the men he deserted have joined us here, and the feeling runs high against him. We live by and for each other, and if one betrays another it must be dealt with according to our laws. If Wolf comes here, he will be held until those who wish to speak against him appear here at our court to do so – and then punishment will be decided by his peers.'

Justin nodded, agreeing with Lafitte's verdict. 'If he should come you will send word – if I am in New Orleans?'

'You are thinking of leaving again?'

'Shortly, I think,' Justin said. 'Though it will be a swift run this time. I believe the British will attack soon and I intend to be there to help defend New Orleans.'

'As I shall,' Jean said and nodded grimly. 'There is no need for you to delay here on a fool's errand, my friend. You have my word on it.'

Justin left almost at once, for he had unfinished business in New Orleans, but not before he had a brief meeting with Sinita. She was waiting for him on the beach, near the boat that was to take him out to his ship.

'The time is coming,' she told him, her eyes dark with hatred. 'She who has protected you is no more. Her magic dies with her, St Arnaud – and soon my time will come. You will suffer as never before. I promise you.'

'I thank you for your warning,' Justin said, and then his hand shot out and gripped her wrist, his fingers biting into her flesh. 'I need no magic to kill you, Sinita, and if you push me too far I will do it with my bare hands.'

He saw a flash of fear in her eyes, but she broke away from him, and the fear had gone to be replaced by anger.

'Your will may be strong enough to fight me, but there is one who is not, and you will suffer for her sake.'

'You speak in riddles and I shall not heed you,' Justin said as he climbed into the boat. 'Practice your arts on those who believe in them. You waste your time on me.'

He saw the hatred in her eyes as she stood watching the boat, and felt chilled. She was an evil woman and it had been foolish to make an enemy of her, but he'd had no choice for he would not bed with her, and she felt herself scorned. Well, so be it. He did not fear her, though he knew that she practised the black arts.

It was as his ship sailed back up the coast to the port of New Orleans that he recalled something she had said and wondered. Marietta had been able to see things by looking into a person's eyes, and if Sinita had similar powers . . . but no, that was nonsense.

When he returned to his lodgings in New Orleans to be met by Piers with the news that Marietta had died the previous night, it brought a sense of sadness. But the news that Henri Lebrun had also died, and that his funeral had already taken place was the greater shock.

Had he in some way contributed to the man's death? If so he had harmed Estelle in a way he could never assuage.

Estelle sat in the parlour with Tante Rosemarie, her head bent over her work, which was a pile of mending. Her companion had pulled a wry face when she saw what she was about, hinting that embroidery would be a better occupation for a young lady.

'It is a matter of necessity,' Estelle replied. 'Jessie has too much to do and we cannot afford new sheets for the beds. I must do it myself or they will not get done.'

'Surely your father's affairs have not come to this?' Tante Rosemarie pursed her lips in an expression of disapproval. 'I know my brother spoke of his having had some trouble but this . . .' She shook her head over it and tutted as she worked at her fine embroidery.

Estelle made no further comment. If Tante Rosemarie disapproved of her doing this work, she would no doubt be horrified when she discovered that Estelle also worked in the kitchen garden. Estelle had neglected her tasks until after her father's funeral, but she knew she would have to resume them soon or there would be no food on the table.

As yet, she had heard nothing from her father's lawyers. She was hopeful that there might be something to be salvaged from the ruin of her father's fortunes, but it would not be very much. Perhaps enough to allow her to live here for a few months, though she could not be sure what Captain St Arnaud intended to do with his house. It might be that he would wish to claim it now that her father was dead.

Her eyes stung with tears, for it was hard to accept that her beloved father was gone. She would never see him again, never hear the sound of his voice or feel the touch of his hand on hers. As the parlour door opened to admit Jessie, she looked up.

'Begging you'se pardon, Miss Estelle,' she said formally, minding her speech. Tante Rosemarie had imposed a new regime on the household since her arrival, and Jessie was careful not to antagonise her for her darling's sake. 'But there is someone wishful to see you.'

'Is it my father's lawyer?'

'No, miss,' Jessie made a face at her behind Tante Rosemarie's back. 'It's a lady.'

'Then I shall come at once.' Estelle stood up, laying her sewing down. 'There is no need for you to disturb yourself, ma'am. I shall speak to this lady and return in a few minutes.'

Had it been a gentleman caller, Tante Rosemarie would have insisted that he be shown into the front parlour, for it would be most improper for Estelle to meet him alone. However, a lady visitor did not require her presence, and she was working on an intricate design. Silks had a habit of tangling if they were put down at the wrong moment, and she allowed Estelle to go without demur.

Estelle looked at Jessie once they were outside in the hall. 'A lady, Jessie? Did she give her name?'

Jessie sniffed disapprovingly. 'She said as she was a friend, and that she had brought you some news. Ah guess she talkin' 'bout Marietta. Ain't no lady, but Ah cain't tell Miss Rosemarie that else she don't let you see her.'

Estelle nodded, for already she had guessed who her visitor might be. She went into the small back parlour where the girl was waiting.

'Genieve?' she said, for the girl was staring out at the garden. 'You have come to tell me about Marietta. Is she worse?'

'She died last night,' Genieve said and turned to face her. 'She was peaceful at the last and I was with her. She spoke of her love for you and bid me bring you this. It is a letter she wanted you to have, I believe.'

'Thank you,' Estelle said and took the letter from her, slipping it into the pocket of her gown. 'When is she to be buried? Is there sufficient money to see that it is done properly?'

'All that is taken care of,' Genieve said, and smiled. 'She had a friend – Captain St Arnaud. He came to see her whenever he was in port and he made her house watertight for her.

105

When he learned of her death he came at once and has promised that everything will be done properly, as she would have wished.'

'Oh . . .' Estelle turned away, tears stinging her eyes. 'When – when will it be?'

'Tomorrow at noon,' Genieve said. 'I believe she wanted the service to be simple and quiet. She is to lie beside her husband in the tomb she had erected for him and their child.'

'Marietta was married? I knew she had a child but she never spoke of her husband . . .'

'He died before their child was born. He was a sea captain I believe,' Genieve said. 'It was he who bought her the house and the furniture was his too.'

Estelle's eyes stung with tears, her voice breaking as she whispered, 'She never told me. I wonder why she never spoke of him.'

'She told no one – it was Captain St Arnaud who told me,' Genieve said. 'He discovered it for himself, though I do not know how. I think he made it his business to find out all he could.'

'Yes, I see, thank you.' Estelle forced herself to smile. 'It was kind of you to come, Genieve.'

'I was curious to see where you lived,' the girl admitted. 'And she asked me to give you her letter. I shall go now. Your servants did not want to admit me, until I told them why I was here.'

'No, I do not suppose they did,' Estelle agreed. 'Please forgive them. They think . . .'

'I know what they think,' Genieve said and smiled wryly. 'It does not matter. Most think as they do, that I am gutter-trash and should not be allowed near decent folk.'

'But I do not think as they do,' Estelle said, moving towards her with her hands outstretched. 'I know you to be a good, kind person and I thank you with all my heart for what you did for my dearest Marietta.'

Genieve nodded, blinking hard as if Estelle's declaration affected her. 'Marietta loved you, and for her sake I would be your friend if ever you should need one.'

'Thank you – and I shall take your advice concerning Mr Erskine. I shall not marry him, though I daresay he will not be pleased over it.'

'He will be angry,' Genieve said. 'Be careful of him, Estelle, for you do not know his temper yet.'

Estelle promised her she would be careful, walked with her to the front door, and thanked her again for coming. After the girl had gone, she ran swiftly upstairs to her own room for she wished to read Marietta's letter alone.

The package Genieve had given her felt quite thick, and when Estelle opened it she found that it contained the deed to the house that had been home to Marietta for some years. The letter was brief and simple. It spoke of Marietta's love for Estelle, and said that the house now belonged to the girl she had always thought of her as her own child. She made no mention of the secret Estelle's father had told her as he lay dying, and it made the girl's eyes prick with tears to know that her friend had kept faith until the end.

Yet she had thought that Estelle might have need of a place to live one day, for that was clear in her letter. She had left the house to Estelle in order to give her a home. Marietta had seen so much, Estelle thought. She could not have known that Henri Lebrun was in financial trouble or that he would die before she did, and yet she had known.

Estelle's tears fell thick and fast, the loneliness welling up inside her as she came to terms with her double loss. Her Papa and her dearest Marietta were gone from her, and she believed that when her lawyer finally came to see her she would discover that there was nothing left of her father's fortune.

In that she was proved right, for the gentleman visited her that afternoon. She asked Tante Rosemarie to sit with her in her father's office, where the interview was to take place, and listened in silence as he explained gravely that there was nothing for her.

'But that is impossible,' Tante Rosemarie exclaimed. 'Surely there is the house at least?'

'I believe not,' the lawyer said. 'Monsieur Lebrun sold it and leased it back under a private agreement some time ago. I have not heard from the owner, but the agreement may hold. I cannot say for certain until he makes his wishes known to me.'

'My father had no money at all?' Estelle felt numbed, for

even though she had sensed it, she had hoped there would be something.

'The contents of the house are yours, of course, Miss Estelle,' the lawyer said kindly. 'I suppose they might fetch a thousand dollars or so if we are lucky, but there are two small debts, which would swallow up most of that money if it was raised.'

'I see . . .' Estelle swallowed hard as she heard a little gasp from Tante Rosemarie. 'Tell me, are the gifts my father gave me mine or should I give them up to pay his debts?'

'Anything your father gave you is yours to keep,' the lawyer said. 'I should not even think of asking you to make such a sacrifice, my dear.'

'Then . . . would it be possible for you to sell one or two items for me?' Estelle asked, her hands trembling though she clasped them tightly in her lap. 'I do not know how I am to feed us all if I have no money.'

'You could bring your wedding forward . . .' the lawyer suggested tentatively, but Tante Rosemarie protested at once.

'That would not be proper. Estelle will do no such thing. I daresay I might ask my brother for a small contribution in the meantime.'

'No, I thank you for your kindness, but it will not be necessary,' Estelle said quickly. 'Papa told me it is a matter of honour not to borrow from your friends, ma'am. I shall sell some of the things Papa gave to me, and we shall manage somehow.'

'You will need time to think this through,' the lawyer told her. 'I shall make inquiries about the house and whether you are required to leave or not, Miss Estelle. We shall then decide what needs to be done next. If you bring the items you wish me to sell to my office, I shall do the necessary for you.'

'You are very kind, sir,' Estelle said. She was close to tears as she stood up. 'And now, if you will both excuse me, I should like to be alone for a while.'

'My poor child,' Tante Rosemarie said, and her eyes filled with tears. 'Had I money of my own I would buy a house for us and take you to live with me, but I live on my brother's charity and have nothing to call my own.'

'Thank you . . .' Estelle whispered in a choked voice and fled the room before the emotions spilled over.

Alone in her room, she sat on the edge of the bed and let the tears trickle down her cheeks. It would break her heart to part with anything her father had given her, but she must do it to live. Whatever Captain St Arnaud decided, she could not go on living here for long. It was too expensive for her to keep a houseful of servants, for the food alone would cost too much, and there were other things she must supply for them.

Her father had refused to have slaves in his house, and all his servants were free persons of colour, working for what Estelle knew was a mere pittance and a roof over their heads. Her father had fed and clothed them, giving them a small wage each month, now she could not even afford to feed them. It would mean parting with all but Jessie, and perhaps Erle – though Erle might be able to find work elsewhere. The others must make their lives as they chose.

They were all like family to her, for she had known them since she was a small child, and they had given her their love as well as their unquestioning service. To turn them off would be like betraying her friends, and it hurt to know that she had no choice. It would break their hearts as well as her own.

But she would give them all something, a small pension that might keep them from starving until they found a new place. And if it must be done, then the sooner the better, Estelle decided. It was foolish to sit here behaving like a lady, mourning her father in the proper way, when it was all a lie. Her grief was true and real, but the rest was a sham. She could take her grief with her, but she needed very little else from this house.

Tomorrow she would attend the service for Marietta, and afterwards she would tell Tante Rosemarie of her decision. Jessie could pack her clothes and any small items she treasured, and she would give all of her jewellery to the lawyer, save for one small gold locket that had been a gift from her father when she was a child. It was of little value, except to her. The more expensive gifts would provide a pension for her servants and food for herself and Jessie over the next few months.

When it had gone she would have to find some kind of

work. Perhaps she might take in sewing. She would ask Tante Rosemarie if perhaps some of her friends might give her work.

Getting to her feet, Estelle wiped away her tears and went to wash her face. Weeping would avail her nothing. She must look to the future for she had no one but herself to provide for her.

'Is this true?' Frank Erskine looked both angry and disappointed as he listened to what Estelle had to say later that evening. He had called to see her, and Estelle had begged Tante Rosemarie to stay with her. 'Everything has gone other than the furniture?'

'It is what the lawyer tells me, and I have no reason to suppose he would lie,' Estelle said. 'But I am sure you already know this, sir, for you have spoken to him yourself, have you not?'

His skin turned a dark red colour. 'I came to see you at once, Estelle. This alters things as you must understand. I had thought . . .' he stopped, clearly feeling himself cheated.

'You believed I would be an heiress I suppose,' Estelle said evenly. 'I am sorry that you are disappointed, sir, but I absolve you of your promise to me. It is clear that we cannot marry now. It would not be fair to you, nor would I expect it. Tante Rosemarie will bear witness that I released you, and that it was not you who jilted me.'

'But . . .' His eyes narrowed as he looked at her. She was beautiful and there was something about her that haunted him, but he had believed Lebrun to be a rich man. He would not marry her now, and he could say nothing more while that dragon guarded her, but the time would come. He inclined his head. 'Your decision must be my guide, Estelle. I shall say no more to you now, for it is clear that you are in distress – but I remain your friend and we shall speak of this again.'

With a nod of his head to Tante Rosemarie he left the room, and Estelle breathed a sigh of relief. At least her father's ruin had made it easier for her to extricate herself from the promise Mr Erskine had had of her – though she had never intended to give it in the first place.

'Well, I am glad that is over,' she said and smiled at Tante Rosemarie. 'And that you were with me, ma'am.'

'Yes, I think it was good that I was here,' the older woman said, her eyes narrowing. 'Do not be too trusting of that man in future, Estelle. I believe he may try to mislead you, my dear. I have not heard good things of him, and it distressed me when I learned that you were promised to him.'

'Yes, I have heard things that I could not speak of to you, ma'am,' Estelle said with a little flush in her cheeks. 'But it does not matter now for I shall not see him again.'

'Be careful,' Tante Rosemarie said again. 'I am glad that you will not marry him, Estelle – but what will you do, my dear?'

'I shall manage somehow,' Estelle replied. 'We may be able to stay here a little longer, but after that I must close this house and find somewhere smaller to live.'

'Yes, perhaps that would be better,' Tante Rosemarie agreed. 'But do nothing precipitously, Estelle. I shall speak to my brother in a day or so. It might be that he would offer you a home. Not with him, but in a little house somewhere.'

'You are so kind to suggest it,' Estelle said, her throat caught with tears. 'But you must see that it cannot be. I cannot accept your brother's charity.'

'I have been forced to do so, for my father made no other provision for me,' the older woman said. 'It was thought that I would marry, and there was a small dowry, which at least pays for my clothes, but is insufficient to buy me independence. I would willingly offer you a home if it was within my power, Estelle.'

'Yes, you said as much when the lawyer was here.' Estelle blinked hard. 'I am grateful for your kind thought, ma'am, but I must fend for myself. There is a house that belongs to me. It is not grand or beautiful like this, but the roof is watertight and I may live there cheaply with Jessie and perhaps Erle, if he will consent to stay for the pittance I can pay him.'

'Oh, you poor child,' Tante Rosemarie cried, and her eyes were damp once more. 'It is wrong that we should be treated in this way. Women have so few rights, my dear. My father died a wealthy man but left the care of his only daughter to his son. I should have shared in his fortune. Your father left you nothing but debts, yet to find work you must beg for favours from your friends. It is a cruel fate to be born a woman, Estelle.'

'Do not distress yourself on my account,' Estelle begged her, though she sensed that some of Tante Rosemarie's anger was for her own plight. 'I daresay I shall manage.'

She was determined that she would not beg for favours from the de Varennes family. Somehow she would provide for herself and her servants, no matter what she had to do.

Estelle followed the other mourners into the church, choosing a pew right at the back. She was wearing the deep mourning she had donned for her father, her face covered by a thick lace veil. It hid the tears that poured down her cheeks when she saw that Marietta's only mourners were a handful of girls from the House of Pearls, and Captain St Arnaud.

It was because she did not wish him to see her that she sat right at the back, remaining where she was as the casket was taken away to be interred in the tomb Marietta had had built for her husband and son. She waited until the church was empty, and then said a prayer for her friend before leaving.

However, as she was walking away, she heard a man's voice call her name, and she stopped, turning reluctantly to face Justin as he came up to her.

'Did you think to run away from me?'

'There was no reason for me to stay . . .' she caught back a sob. 'Besides, I should not have come here alone today. It would not be thought proper.'

'Be damned to those who think ill of you!' Justin said, his eyes glittering angrily as he tried to see her expression and could not for the thick veil she wore to hide it. 'I was coming to your house later, Estelle. I wanted to tell you how sorry I am that your father . . .'

She held up her hand to stop him. 'Pray do not, sir. I do not wish to hear false sympathy.'

'Why do you say that? What have I done to harm you?'

'You visited my father on the day he died. I do not know what you said to him, but I know you quarrelled. When his servant went in after you left he found Father lying on the floor. He died that night – and I blame you for his death, sir.

Had you not been so harsh to him, he might have lived a few more months.'

'That is monstrously unfair,' Justin said. 'You must know that your father had been ill for some time.'

'And that being the case you should not have quarrelled with him!'

'It was your father who quarrelled with me,' Justin said. 'I told him something he ought to have been grateful to know, but he lost his temper with me. We both said things that ought not to have been said, but it was not my intention to cause him distress. Nor did I know at that time how ill he was.'

'Then I absolve you of the intent,' Estelle said coldly. 'But in deed you were my father's murderer.'

'No! That is not true,' Justin protested. 'Your father could have died at any time. You know that to be true, Estelle.'

She did know it but she could not admit it, because his behaviour at the ball had hurt her too much. 'Pray let me pass, sir. I do not think we have anything further to say to each other.'

'I have a great deal to say to you,' Justin said, catching hold of her arm as she would have passed him. 'I came to warn your father that Erskine is a monster. You must on no account marry him, Estelle. I cannot allow it.'

'You cannot allow it?' Her eyes flashed beneath the veil, though he could not see them. 'I think you forget yourself, sir. My marriage has nothing to do with you.'

'Yet you will not marry him for I shall prevent it.' His fingers tightened about her gloved wrist, making her wince with pain. 'Forgive me, but Erskine will hurt you more if you give him the right to do so. You do not know what kind of a man he is.'

Estelle's temper snapped. 'If you must know, and I do not think it your business, he has decided that he does not wish to marry me since my father left me nothing but debts.'

'Nothing but debts? Was his situation so bad then?'

Estelle had not meant to blurt the truth out and she avoided his eyes as she said, 'Not enough for Mr Erskine at least. So there will be no marriage – does that content you?'

'For the moment,' Justin replied with a satisfied nod of the head. 'But this matter of your father's situation – are you in trouble, Estelle? Do you need money?'

'I need nothing from you,' Estelle said. 'I have been paid for past services. I ask nothing more – and your house will be yours again very soon.'

'Do not be foolish! You will remain there for the time being – and your lawyer may apply to me for any monies you need.'

'I do not wish to live on your charity or anyone else's,' Estelle said. 'Please let me go on my way, sir.'

'You are the most stubborn creature I have ever known,' Justin said his temper rising once more. 'Did that night mean nothing to you but the bargain we made?'

'Nothing at all,' Estelle lied, her head up. She was glad that he could not see her face for she knew that her cheeks were burning. 'No more than it did to you I daresay.'

'Ah, then perhaps it meant something,' Justin said and smiled oddly. Her pride was driving her. He would need time and patience to overcome it. 'You will remain in your father's house until I call on you, do you hear me, Estelle? I have some business that cannot be neglected even for your sake. I must leave New Orleans this evening with the tide but I shall return within a few weeks. When I do I shall expect you to be at your home, and I shall not expect to see an engagement ring on your finger. You belong to me, Estelle, and when I return I shall claim what is mine.'

'How dare you!' Her hand snaked out but he caught it, pulling her closer, trying to see her eyes beneath the veil. Cursing, he lifted it and gazed down at her for a moment before pressing his lips to hers. To Estelle it felt like a kiss of possession. 'You insult me, sir,' she said when she had breath enough. 'I am not your possession and I shall not do your bidding. You paid for one night of my life, not the right to order it as you choose.' In her pain and grief she struck out blindly, wanting to inflict pain, because she was hurting inside.

'Damn you for that,' Justin said, his mouth thinned with anger. 'Will you not let me forget that infamous bargain? You *are* mine, Estelle, whether you know it yet or not. I shall come for you when I return and I shall have you, whether you will it or not.'

Estelle gasped, for the menace in his voice was terrifying. She struggled against him, and after a moment he let her go.

'I shall never be yours, Captain St Arnaud,' she said coldly.

'You ruined any chance I might have stood of a good marriage when you seduced me, but I shall not become your plaything, to be used and discarded when you tire of me. I hate you and nothing will change that. I hope that I never have to see you again. Is that plain enough?'

She was breathing hard, and she looked magnificent. He applauded her even though he burned to chastise her for her foolish obstinacy. Why could she not understand that this bond between them could not be broken?

'Plain indeed. Very well,' Justin inclined his head. 'Do as you please, Mademoiselle Lebrun. I was a fool to waste one thought on you. I wash my hands of you. In future, you may go to the devil with my blessing.'

Leaving Estelle staring after him in dismay, he turned and walked away from her.

Eight

'But you cannot go and live in a place like that with just your maid for company,' Tante Rosemarie said, and she was close to tears. 'I know you must see me as an old fusspot, Estelle, but I am not thinking of what is held to be proper now. I am concerned for you, my dear.'

'You have been very kind to me since Papa died,' Estelle said and smiled, for she understood the lady now in a way she never had before. Tante Rosemarie had been forced to become old before her time, to live the life of a maiden, destined to be aunt to her brother's children and never know the happiness of having her own life. 'But it is time for you to return to your brother's home, ma'am. I must close this house for it does not belong to me, and I cannot afford to live here.'

'What will you do if the British invade us? Besides, there are all those American soldiers in the town.' A British fleet had sailed into the Gulf that autumn, its presence threatening the security of the port and its people, and prompting General Andréw Jackson to garrison the town early in December. 'It is not safe for a young lady like you to live alone in these troubled times.'

'I have no choice. I cannot stay here any longer.'

'But surely . . .' Tante Rosemarie's protest died as she saw Estelle's stubborn look. 'It grieves me to think of you alone, for you will be at the mercy of rogues. You are young and beautiful, and there are men who will try to take advantage of that, my dear. Not just the soldiers – but others who you may think trustworthy.'

'I am not so naïve that I shall let them,' Estelle replied, for she knew more of such men than poor Tante Rosemarie would ever know. 'I shall be quite safe for I am acquainted with many of the people who live nearby and they are good, kind folk. I shall be safe enough with Jessie and Erle to look after me.'

'Erle is to come with you then?'

'Yes, it seems so. He cried when I told him he should look elsewhere, and said that he had served my father all his life. He asks only for food and a place to sleep, and there is a wooden shed at the bottom of the garden where he may put his bed. We shall take some of the plain furniture with us, most of the rest must be sold to pay the last of Papa's debts.'

'That money should rightfully be yours.' Tante Rosemarie's mouth twisted in a moue of disapproval.

'But I am in honour bound to pay what Papa owes,' Estelle said, 'and I have things of my own I can sell.' She did not tell the older woman what she intended to do with most of the money she raised that way for she knew she would be horrified. But Erle had not been the only one of her father's servants to weep when she told them that the house would be closed and they must look elsewhere for work.

'And you wish me to return to my brother's house tomorrow?' Tante Rosemarie sighed for she had been happy here and did not particularly wish to return to her home, where she was treated as a poor relation, with respect but very little kindness. 'Had your house been a little larger I would have come with you. I have a small amount of money and we might have managed together, Estelle.'

116

'Had my house been fit for you I should have been glad of your company, ma'am,' Estelle said and was surprised to discover that she meant it. Tante Rosemarie's fussing was not so bad when you understood it. She was at heart a kind, loving woman who had been denied her own home.

'Very well, I shall send a note to my brother, warning him to expect me in the morning.'

As she turned away, Estelle went up to her own room to see how Jessie was getting on with her packing. Many of the gowns she had worn for parties in the past would not be suitable for her new life. They too could be sold to raise money. She saw that Jessie had lain them to one side, as if undecided what to do with them.

'Do you think they could be sold?' Estelle asked, running her fingers over the silk of the gown she had worn on the night she'd made her infamous bargain with Justin St Arnaud. 'All except this one. I shall keep this.'

Oh, how foolish she was to cling to her dreams! She recalled her last stormy meeting with Justin, when he had ordered her to remain in his house. Her pride would not allow her to do so when she could no longer afford to pay the bills, and she would not take more money from him. Yet she could not prevent her heart from aching nor her thoughts from wondering where he was and what he was doing.

Justin was staring out to sea as his ship left the Gulf of Mexico, having slipped away in the night, under the noses of the British fleet. He had given his word that he would bring in the cargo needed so desperately in the face of what many people thought to be an imminent attack from the British. Yet his thoughts were with Estelle, and her tear-laden eyes as she accused him of killing her father.

He admitted in his own mind that it was probable that the quarrel between Henri Lebrun and he had precipitated her father's last illness, but it could have happened at any time and she was unfair to lay the whole blame on his shoulders. Yet in truth he had only himself to blame. His foolish pride had kept him from telling the irate father that he loved her, and that he intended to marry her himself.

He ought to have secured Estelle's promise and her father's

consent after that night he had spent in her bed, for he had known then that she had touched something in him that no other woman ever had. He had fought against offering her marriage, his pride making him hold back the words that ought to have been said long ago.

His anger was abating now as he felt the wind on his face; it whipped the hair he wore long into a tangle and he could taste the salt of the sea on his lips. Why was it that she could drive him to fury with a look from those magnificent eyes? She had said that she hated him and he had told her that she might go to the Devil with his blessing, but he knew that the memory of her would haunt him, as it had all these months. When he returned to New Orleans next time he would make an end to this nonsense between them; he would make her see that her future lay with him even if he had to shake some sense into her.

He began to smile as his thoughts led him down a pleasurable path and he knew that what he must do was to take her in his arms and kiss her until neither of them had the breath left to argue.

It was a very strange time. New Orleans seemed full of General Jackson's men, and there was an air of siege, though some ships were managing to avoid the British and bring in necessary supplies. Estelle had done her best to make the house cheerful, and with her own things about her, it was comfortable enough. Someone had done all the repairs necessary this past year, and the roof kept out the heavy rainstorm that had occurred the first night they moved in. Since then, Estelle had managed to rescue the vegetable garden that Marietta had tended until she became too ill, and had found various herbs and roots that had helped to flavour the stews Jessie made for them.

Estelle had given her father's lawyer one of her last items of jewellery to sell and with that she intended to purchase roasting pork and chicken for their Christmas dinner so that they could at least try to celebrate the festive season. But for now they were forced to manage with whatever Jessie could buy cheaply in the market.

'Better that Ah does the marketing,' Jessie told her when

118

Estelle mentioned that they had very little money to spare. 'Them ole boys would likely cheat you, chile. You'se looks as if you was born rich, and you ain't gonna know what they ought to charge you.'

'But you must let me come with you so that I can learn,' Estelle said. 'I must begin to stand on my own feet. You can no longer keep me wrapped in cotton buds, Jessie. I am not Papa's spoiled daughter any longer. Indeed, I was never quite what I seemed.' Her eyes clouded with sadness as she recalled her father's confession on his deathbed.

'Ah knows what you is, chile,' Jessie said and sniffed. 'You'se no different now than you ever was, and that's the chile Ah loves like my own. Ain't gonna let nuthin' happen to you'se – and that Erle, he think the same.'

Estelle hugged her, tears in her eyes. 'I'm so lucky to have you both,' she said. 'I don't know what I would do without you, dearest Jessie.'

'Ain't gonna have to whiles Ah got breath in ma body, chile.'

Jessie had accepted that Estelle must learn how to market, and they usually did it together, but this morning Jessie had gone alone for Estelle was busy working on a piece of sewing. Tante Rosemarie had brought the work to her.

'It is merely mending, Estelle,' she said apologetically. 'But Suzanne pays someone to do it for her and I thought you might as well have the money as anyone else.'

'It was very kind of you to take this trouble,' Estelle said. 'Does Suzanne know where I live?'

'She asked me to tell her, but I pretended not to know. She is a good girl, but she would ask you to live with us, and then she would expect you to do as she tells you all the time. I fear she has become bad tempered and spiteful of late. I know she carries the child badly, but she is driving André away from her.'

'That is sad,' Estelle said. 'But it is just an irritation of nerves and she will be better once the baby is born.'

'Perhaps – but I fear it may be too late. If André looks elsewhere . . .' She sighed and shook her head for she knew her nephew all too well. 'But that is not my affair.'

Tante Rosemarie had promised to return another day with

more work for Estelle, and so when someone knocked at her front door a day or so later, she went to open it expecting to see her friend. However, she experienced a slight shock as she saw André standing there.

'May I come in, Estelle?' he asked. 'I brought some fruit from our garden, and I thought you might like these preserved peaches. They were a late crop and we had more than enough.' He handed her a large basket, which contained much more than the peaches, and Estelle blushed.

'You should not have done this,' she told him. 'Please come into the parlour. I was working but I can offer you one of Jessie's cordials or some coffee.'

'Nothing for me, thank you,' he said, following her into the parlour and then into the kitchen as she set his basket on the table. 'You have made this house very comfortable, Estelle. I like it.'

'Please do not try to humour me,' she said, her head raised proudly. 'How can you like it? I know it must seem a poor place to you, but it is my home now and I am content.'

As content as she could ever be with the empty aching place inside her where her heart should be.

'Anywhere would seem like home to me with you in it,' André said and the look in his eyes made her drop her own. There was such burning passion in his look, such desire! 'I wish I had acted differently when you came to me that day. I was such a fool to refuse you, Estelle. My father had arranged a good marriage for me – but it was always you I admired. Indeed, I have realised since then that I love you. You are the woman I should have married, not Suzanne.'

'You must not say such things to me now,' Estelle said. She looked at him then, a hint of condemnation in her eyes. 'Suzanne is your wife and she is carrying your child.'

'Suzanne is a sour-tongued harpy,' he said, a note of bitterness in his voice. 'Nothing is ever right for her. She complains all the time, never gives me any peace – and she is cold in bed. Even when we were first married she did not like me to touch her. You would not have been like that, Estelle. I would swear there is fire in you, and loving warmth. You would make a man want to rush home to you, not drive him out of his own home.'

'But you chose her not me,' Estelle replied, lifting her eyes to meet his. 'It would have meant everything to me if you had married me then, André – but it is too late.'

'Surely it need not be too late,' he said, moving closer to her. 'I know we cannot marry, but we could be lovers, and that is a much sweeter arrangement. I do sincerely care for you, Estelle, and I would see that you never lacked for anything. Believe me, I can be faithful to the woman I respect and love. Such arrangements last for years. I believe your father had such an arrangement in his youth.'

Estelle turned away from the eager light in his eyes. She knew what he was offering her, and it was the most she could expect of any man now. Perhaps she ought to consider well before refusing for life was sure to be hard for them in the future, and the little bit of sewing Tante Rosemarie brought her would hardly bring enough to feed them all.

She felt the touch of his hands on her shoulders and a shiver ran through her. All at once she knew that she must refuse him, now, immediately. She could not bear to think of him touching her intimately any more than she had been able to bear the thought of Frank Erskine touching her. She turned to face him, her manner proud and cold.

'I thank you for your offer, sir, but I shall be no man's mistress. Poor as I am, I have pride. I shall manage as best I can.'

'I did not mean to insult you,' André said at once. 'I do truly admire and love you, Estelle. If I were free I would offer you marriage, but my faith will not allow me to divorce Suzanne.'

'Then you must honour and cherish your wife,' Estelle replied coolly. 'Again, I thank you for your gift, but believe me when I say that I shall accept no more of them. It would be best if you did not come here again, André.'

'Perhaps I came too soon,' he said, and there was a faint flicker of annoyance in his eyes. 'When you have lived here for a while you may discover that what I have to offer is worthwhile.' Now there was a faint threat in his voice and she felt this was the real André; spoiled and rich, he did not care to be thwarted.

Estelle did not answer him, and after a moment he turned

and left her. She felt the sting of tears but would not let them fall, anger and pride coming to her rescue. Was this her fate now? Would other men think they could make her their mistress now that her father's ruin was known?

Justin returned to New Orleans in the middle of December. There was a new feeling and a bustle about the port and he saw that American soldiers were much in evidence on the waterfront, their smart uniforms making them stand out from the men who travelled the river. Clearly the expected attack was imminent.

After dealing with the business that had taken him away from New Orleans, Justin paid a visit to Estelle's house and discovered that it was closed and shuttered, only one old man remaining as caretaker.

'I wish to see Mademoiselle Lebrun,' Justin told him. 'Can you tell me where she is living please?'

'Ah don't know,' the old man said. 'If'n you'se the new owner, does you want me to stay here?'

'Yes, and I must provide you with others to help you,' Justin said with a quick frown. 'I want this house opened up again and ready to receive Mademoiselle Lebrun when she returns.'

'Miss Estelle, she comin' back?' The old man's eyes lit up. 'Ah thought she gone for good.'

'She had no need to leave, the foolish girl,' Justin said, the line of his mouth grim with frustration. 'Do you know if any of her old servants are still in need of work?'

'Ah reckons I can find out, sir.'

'Do it and I shall arrange for you all to be paid,' Justin told him. His eyes narrowed speculatively. 'I dare say Mademoiselle Lebrun was sorry to turn you off?'

'She done cry and we all cry with her,' the old man said, his own eyes bleary. 'She like our own chile, sir, and we don't like to see her so unhappy. But Miss Estelle, she gives us all money so we don't starve and she ain't got nuthin' left for herself.'

Justin swore beneath his breath as he left. The foolish, stubborn wench! He had left instructions that she should be given money if she asked for it, but of course her pride would not

122

let her. A reluctant smile touched his mouth as he reflected that he would have done the same in her place. The truth was that there was little to choose between them. It was small wonder that they struck sparks off each other.

Where would she go? His brow furrowed as he thought it over. Marietta had owned her house, therefore it was likely that she had left it to Estelle. With any luck he would find her there.

Estelle was working in her garden. She had been picking herbs and a basket of edible roots lay on the ground beside her. In a moment she would take them in to add to the soup Jessie was making. They had been lucky enough to buy a small piece of stewing meat in the market that morning, and it would make a good broth to eat with the bread Jessie had baked earlier. She straightened up as a shadow fell across her, turning to see who had come up on her unawares. Her heart took a sudden dive as she saw it was Frank Erskine.

'You startled me, sir,' she said. 'I did not hear you coming.'

'I saw you working and could not resist the impulse to surprise you,' he said, his eyes going over her hungrily. He had thought of her for weeks, almost regretting that he had allowed her to slip away so easily. The money was not so very important, it was more a matter of pride, and from what he had heard there was more to her history than he had guessed. Watching her at work in the garden his blood had heated and he was aware of a fierce desire to bed her. But there was no need to marry her after all, especially if the rumours he had heard were true. Talk had been rife since she left her father's house and came to live here, people remembering Lebrun's long liaison with his mistress Leah. 'Forgive me if I frightened you, Estelle. That was not my intention. I came to see you and ask if there was anything I could do for you.'

'That is very kind of you,' Estelle said. Something in the way he looked at her made her uneasy, but she lifted her head proudly, meeting his hot gaze. 'But I have all I need. We manage well enough.'

'It is not fitting that you should labour in the garden,' he said. 'You will ruin those lovely hands of yours . . .' He reached out and took her hand, turning it over to trace the red marks on the palm with his finger. 'See how your lovely white hands suffer . . . and they are perfectly white, Estelle. It is strange how deceiving these things can be, is it not?'

Estelle snatched her hand from his. She shuddered at his touch, and the look in his eyes frightened her. She was sure that he was hinting at her secret – but how could he know? Her father had told no one and nor had she.

'I do not understand you, sir.'

'Do you not?' His brows rose slightly. 'Well, it is no matter to me whether the tales be true or not, Estelle. I have come to make you an offer either way.'

'I do not know what you mean, and I have no wish to receive an offer of marriage from you.'

'It was not marriage I had in mind. I thought to make you my wife once, but that is no longer the case – I am offering you my protection, Estelle. You will be my mistress and I shall give you presents and keep you safe from the scum that frequent this part of town.'

'How dare you!' Estelle was incensed by the manner of his offer, which was insulting. He thought to buy her as he would any commodity. At least André had spoken of loving her! 'I have no intention of accepting any kind of offer from you and I wish you to leave at once, sir.'

'And supposing I do not wish to leave?' Frank Erskine said with a sneer. He took a step towards her, his manner menacing. 'Supposing I decide to take what I want here and now. Who is to stop me? Not you, Estelle, or your servants.'

'Perhaps not,' a cold, crisp voice said from behind him and Estelle gasped. She had seen him coming towards them, though Erskine had not been aware of him. 'But I shall. Lay one finger on her, Erskine, and you will answer for it to me.'

The older man spun round, staring at Justin as if he were a two-headed monster sprung from the ground. 'What the hell are you doing here?' he demanded.

'I am here on business,' Justin said. 'And I heard what you said to Estelle. You are a foul-mouthed braggart, Erskine, and it would please me to put a ball through your head. Indeed, it would be a service to the community.'

'Murdering devil,' Erskine muttered, clenching his fists as if he wished to strike, but apparently thinking better of it. 'You are a pirate and should be hung for your crimes.'

Justin's smile mocked him. 'I'll willingly swing for you, Erskine. If you bother Estelle again you won't live to watch me die.'

Erskine turned a deep purple, veins standing out at his temple as his hands curled into fists at his sides, but Justin was armed, and he was not. Nor was he brave enough to demand satisfaction for the insults thrown at him.

'You will regret this,' he muttered. 'Both of you . . .' He gave Estelle an evil glance before striding off.

'Be careful of him in future,' Justin said as Estelle stared at him in silence. 'He will be your enemy now.'

'He was already my enemy,' she said, 'though he offered to be my protector.'

'Damn his impudence!' Justin said. 'Did he think you no longer good enough to be his wife because your father left you penniless?'

'Something of the sort,' Estelle said, though she suspected there was more to it. Somehow Erskine had heard rumours concerning the truth of her birth, and considered her fair game. 'I thank you for your timely arrival, Captain St Arnaud – but why have you come? Please do not ask me to be your mistress, sir. I have already turned down two offers and they will doubtless not be the last.'

'If you persist in laying yourself open to insult by living here alone you cannot expect otherwise,' he told her severely. His tone was so like that of her father or Tante Rosemarie when scolding her that she almost laughed. He saw her eyes brighten and scowled. 'If you think it funny, I assure you the reality will prove far from that, Estelle.'

His warning sobered her and she would not explain why his severe manner had amused her. 'No, indeed you speak truly. I am aware that I have made myself more vulnerable, sir. However, I had no choice.'

'Ridiculous wench!' Justin cried, on the verge of losing his temper but reining it in as he realised that it would do no good. 'I told you to remain at your own house, and that I would see you had money for your needs.'

'You told me to go to the devil, sir.' Estelle raised her head proudly.

'Because you drove me to it,' he said and ground his teeth in frustration. 'You deserve that I should put you across my knee and spank you.'

'My Papa ceased to do that when I grew up, sir.'

'Yet you behave like a sulky child,' Justin said and moved closer to her. His pulses raced and he knew an urgent desire to take her in his arms and kiss her until she quietened, but to do that after he had threatened to murder Erskine for taking advantage would put him on the same footing as that brute. 'Why will you not believe me when I tell you I want to look after you?'

'Why should you?' Estelle's heart was fluttering like a bird against the bars of a cage. 'If you wish me to be your mistress . . .' She broke off as she saw the fire leap in his eyes. What would she do if he said that he did wish her to be his mistress? No other man could make her feel as he did; her bones were melting as she gazed up at him, and she longed for him to kiss her. If he kissed her now she would not be able to resist him.

'I know well what you would say to me,' Justin said, breaking the spell between them. 'But you gave yourself to me, Estelle, and in doing so you made me responsible for you. I would be your friend, stand in place of the family you do not have, and perhaps . . .'

'Please do not,' she begged, for the look he gave her had brought her close to tears. 'I cannot take your charity, sir. I have this house and my faithful Jessie and Erle. We can manage.'

'Yet that is not what I want for you, Estelle.'

'What you want . . .'

'You know that we are bound together, don't you? Struggle all you will against it, for God knows I have fought it, but it remains stronger than us both.' He moved closer to her, his eyes burning down into hers with an intensity that made her shiver. 'Tell me that you will move back to your home, Estelle.'

'I cannot,' she said, her cheeks heating. 'I do not belong there. This house is my home now. Pray leave me alone, sir. I need no one's help.'

126

'We get nowhere like this,' Justin said in frustration. 'You are too proud for your own good, Estelle. Very well, stay here for the moment if you insist, but a change is coming. Do not imagine I have given in so easily. I shall not abandon you to life in this hovel, though perhaps you deserve that I should.'

Estelle glanced towards the house. Jessie was at the door looking at them. 'I must take these vegetables in, sir. Jessie needs them for our meal.'

'I shall give you a little time to come to your senses, for I am like to be occupied elsewhere,' Justin said. 'After that, I shall take matters into my own hands. Whether you will like the consequences remains to be seen.'

Estelle did not answer him. Indeed, she hardly knew why she had defied him when her heart and body cried out for him. Would it be so very bad to be his mistress? After all, she could not expect more of him or any man.

She watched him walk away and a part of her wanted to cry out to him to stay, and yet that wretched pride would not let her. She had given herself to him once and he had abandoned her. She would not be used like that again.

Yet she wished that he had kissed her for then she would have had no choice but to surrender.

Christmas had come and gone, and apart from a greeting from Tante Rosemarie, life went on in the little house as usual. Estelle's time was divided between her sewing and working in the garden, and though they ate a little less frugally that day, nothing else marked the festive occasion. It was very different from the Christmases she had been used to in her father's house, and the grief of her loss had been almost too much to bear. On Christmas Eve Estelle had taken flowers to her father's tomb, standing there alone for some minutes before returning home.

She had thought that Justin might visit her, and she was torn between fearing it and wanting to see him. However, she had seen nothing of him. She believed that he must have important business, which kept him occupied. There had been rumours for days of a great battle that was to come, and that day it had finally happened.

The guns had ceased firing for some time now but a haze of smoke hung in the sky. It was not the first time that skirmishes had occurred between the British and American forces these past weeks, but it seemed to Estelle that the fighting had been much fiercer that day in January 1815. She shaded her eyes against the evening sun, looking towards the place where the attack seemed to have taken place, turning as Erle came hurrying up to where she was standing in her garden.

'I done hear as it was a victory for General Jackson,' he told her. 'They say his men held out against the odds and more than seven hundred British were killed.'

'It must have been a terrible battle,' Estelle said. 'Were many killed on our side?'

'Less than eighty so I heard tell,' Erle told her. 'They do say as that pirate Lafitte, and some of his men, helped to win the day.' He looked at her anxiously. 'I hopes it all over now, Miss Estelle.'

'I hope so too, Erle,' Estelle said. Her chest felt tight with fear as she looked at him. 'Were any of Lafitte's ships sunk?'

'I don't know that,' Erle said and shook his head. 'You don't want to worry none over that Cap'n St Arnaud, he can take care of hisself I reckons.'

'What do you know of Captain St Arnaud, Erle?' Estelle was curious, for there had been a distinct note of approval in her faithful servant's voice.

'He ain't a bad man, Miss Estelle. I heard he a man of his word. If'n he say he look after you, he do it right.'

'Thank you, Erle,' Estelle said and sighed inwardly. She had not seen Justin for almost three weeks and despite his promise not to abandon her, it seemed that he had forgotten her. 'It seems we are safe from invasion for today at least.'

'They sayin' the British are done now, Miss Estelle. After what done happen today, they ain't gonna attack us no more.'

'I do hope you are right. Papa was always afraid they would invade us and take us over. I fear he did not like them.'

'No, Miss Estelle, your Papa, he set in the ole ways. French people and the English, they at war for a long time, and old feelin's run high I reckons. Your Papa, he got no cause to hate them people, but it in his blood.'

'Yes, perhaps you are right.' Her father had been a monarchist at heart, and did not truly approve of Napoleon Bonaparte, who had been the main enemy of the British these last years. Yet even though England had provided a refuge for French émigrés, he could not put aside his prejudices. It seemed that Erle had understood his master well, perhaps had loved him in his way. She smiled at him as he went off to find Jessie, bending to pull a particularly stubborn weed from the ground.

Had Justin been fighting with Lafitte's men? She knew that the two men were said to have a close relationship, so it was likely that he had thrown in his lot with the pirate rather than the Americans, though of course they were all fighting on the same side.

A cold fear gripped her heart as she wondered if he had been hurt. How would she ever know if he had been injured or killed? Who would tell her? Her eyes stung with tears, which she blinked away angrily. What did it matter to her? And yet she knew that it did. She straightened up, turning to go inside the house, and then stopped as she saw André coming towards her. Immediately, she saw that he was excited, his face flushed with triumph.

'We beat them,' he cried as he saw her, and she was reminded of him as a small boy when they had played games together in her father's garden. 'It was a fine thing, Estelle. They meant it for real this time and they came at us with all guns blazing, but with our ships in the Gulf and Jackson's men on shore, we thrashed them. They've had a taste of defeat now and they will go home with their tails between their legs. They say that Pakenham was killed in the fighting.'

'The British general, Sir Edward Pakenham?' Estelle looked at him in surprise. 'Is he not their commander?'

'That is why they will go,' André said, and laughed excitedly. As he moved towards her she caught the smell of strong drink on his breath and guessed that he had been celebrating with his friends. 'Oh, Estelle, you look so beautiful. I think about you all the time. I can't sleep for wanting you. . .'

Estelle moved back as he made a grab for her; his eyes were bright with the excitement of the day and the strong drink that he had consumed.

129

'No, André!' she said holding up her hands to ward him off. 'I told you I would not be your mistress, and I meant it.'

'But I love you . . .' he muttered and lunged at her, grabbing her about the waist and forcing his wet mouth over hers, kissing her until she managed to struggle free and push him away. 'I would be good to you and I can't live without you.'

'That is foolish talk,' she said and was relieved to see that Erle had left the house and was coming to her rescue, Jessie close behind him. 'Go home and sober up, André. You have been drinking too much.'

'You do what Miss Estelle tells you, sir,' Erle said, his manner respectful but firm. 'You gonna be sorry in the mornin' if'n you does somethin' you ain't got no right to do, sir.'

'Who gave you the right to interfere?' André demanded angrily.

'We Miss Estelle's guardians,' Jessie said, coming to stand beside Erle. 'Now you just do as she tells you and go home, sir.'

André looked at them, then back at Estelle, muttered something insulting beneath his breath and turned away. Estelle stood where she was, staring after him as he walked away.

'He will come back,' Jessie said. 'We ain't seen the last of him yet, Miss Estelle.'

'Why won't they leave me alone?' Estelle asked, feeling close to tears. 'Oh, why won't they leave me alone?'

She ran into the house and up the stairs to her bedroom, locking the door after her. It seemed that Justin was right. She had laid herself open to insult by living here without protection – but what else could she have done?

It seemed that she would have no peace unless she became some man's mistress. And if she had to choose, there was only one man she would want to be with. Yet if she gave herself into his keeping, how long would it be before he deserted her? And what would she do then?

'Oh Papa, Papa,' she whispered. 'Why did you bring me up to be a lady? Why did you not tell me the truth?'

Justin saw the young man drinking in the corner of the tavern. He sat alone, muttering into his cups, his mood sullen and angry. Something about him was familiar, but it was a moment or two before he recalled why the man's face set the alarm bells ringing. And then he remembered. He had seen Estelle walking with him some months ago, and thought there was something between them, but then André de Varennes had married another lady.

'Are you celebrating our victory?' Justin asked, pulling out a chair at his table. 'Will you join me in a glass of wine, sir?'

'A great victory,' André said raising his empty glass. 'More wine! Damn that waiter! Why doesn't he bring more wine?'

Justin signalled and the waiter approached and took Justin's order. 'It is a fine day for New Orleans,' he said. 'But why are you not celebrating with friends, sir? A man like you should not be alone on this night.'

'Damn them all,' André muttered. 'I wanted her but my father said it wasn't suitable. She wasn't good enough for our family. Married the one he told me to and now look what happened . . . nag, nag, nag, all day and night. *She* is beautiful and warm . . . what does it matter if her mother was Lebrun's mistress and not his wife? Estelle has skin like a camellia, damned if I care whether her mother was . . .' He moaned and slumped forward onto the table, his eyes closing. 'If I don't have her Erskine will. Heard him plotting to . . .' A trickle of saliva ran from the side of his mouth and his eyes closed.

'What is Erskine plotting?' Justin asked, lifting André's head off the table. 'Damn you, man! Tell me . . .'

André opened his bleary eyes for a moment. 'House of Pearls . . . take her there . . .' he muttered, and closed his eyes once more.

Justin took the jug of wine the waiter brought and poured it over André's head, but it failed to bring him round. Clearly he was too far gone and would sleep it off until morning, when he would have a very bad headache indeed.

But he had said enough to alert Justin to the danger. If Erskine was planning to kidnap Estelle and imprison her in the House of Pearls he could not afford to wait any longer. Her stubbornness must not be allowed to continue. He must act now for her own good and take the consequences for his actions later.

Nine

Estelle saw Tante Rosemarie as she left her lawyer's office, where she had deposited the last item of value she had to be sold. Tante Rosemarie waved a gloved hand and came immediately to meet her, a smile of welcome on her lips.

'How fortunate that we should meet like this. I was going to visit you tomorrow, my dear,' she said. 'My brother is giving a party to celebrate the victory, and I wanted to ask if you will come as my guest.'

'How kind you are,' Estelle said. 'But I do not think I ought to visit your brother's house.'

'But why?' Tante Rosemarie looked hurt. 'Just because your father left you with no inheritance to speak of, it does not mean that you must give up all your pleasures.'

'It would not be right. I thank you for inviting me, but I must refuse your offer.'

'Is it because of André?' The older woman's expression was a mixture of concern and anger. 'I know he regrets his marriage, and I have seen the way he looks at you.'

'André is a part of it,' Estelle agreed. 'You were right to fear that Suzanne was driving him away from her. He asked me to be his mistress and I refused. If I came to the house he might think that I would change my mind, and I could not do that. Suzanne is my friend and to steal her husband would be a betrayal of that friendship.' She would not tell Tante Rosemarie that Monsieur de Varennes might refuse to admit her if he knew the secret her father had revealed as he lay dying, for it would merely distress the kind woman.

'Yes, I do see that, and I honour you for your decision. Others in your situation might have acted differently.' Tante Rosemarie sighed. 'Well, I must not press you if you have made up your mind. I shall call to see you another day, my dear.'

Estelle thanked her and they parted company. Estelle walked swiftly, leaving the pleasant streets and quadrangles of the French Quarter behind her as the light began to fade. Dusk was falling when she found herself near the House of Pearls. She could see bright lights in all the windows and hear music and laughter coming from inside, and then a man's voice was raised in anger and a woman's scream issued from an upstairs window.

A tiny shudder ran through Estelle as she hurried on, anxious to be home. Her money was almost gone and then she would have nothing other than what she could earn from her sewing. She might find herself having to work in a place like that one day. Pray God it did not come to that!

She was lost in thought and did not hear the soft tread of a man's footsteps behind her. When rough hands reached out for her she screamed and fought her assailants.

'Come quietly, you bitch,' one of the men muttered. 'Or you'll be sorry you were ever born.'

She heard the words but they only made her fight harder, kicking and scratching as she struggled violently, and then something hit her on the back of the head. She was unconscious when another group of men arrived hot on the heels of the first, so she did not witness the fierce fight that ensued, nor did she hear the sound of a pistol being fired. Happily, she was unaware that when she was carried off, two men lay dead in the street.

It was some hours before Estelle regained consciousness. She lay for a time wondering where she was, for it was dark and she could feel a strange rocking motion. Perhaps she was still dizzy . . . A flash of memory brought pictures of a violent struggle and made her give a cry of alarm. She sat up hastily, only to fall back against the pillows as the pain struck. Her head hurt and she felt very unwell. She whimpered and reached up to touch the place where the pain was centred, discovering a large lump. As she did so something moved in the shadows across the room, and then there was light in the darkness as someone brought a horn lantern to her bedside.

'Are you in pain? You were sleeping when I last looked at you so I left you to rest.'

133

'Justin?' she whispered, her mind spinning in confusion. Yet there was also relief for she had begun to feel frightened and his voice calmed her. 'Where am I? What happened to me?'

'You are on board my ship, the *Dark Angel*. You are safe now, Estelle. I give you my word that no harm will come to you.'

'On board your ship? But why? I do not understand. I was walking home and someone . . . was that you? I remember screaming and calling out for help. Did you abduct me?'

'Two men were trying to abduct you. You were to be taken to the House of Pearls on Erskine's orders. You may imagine for yourself to what purpose and what might have been your fate when he tired of you.'

'Taken to . . .' Estelle was shocked, confused. 'But how came I here? Why am I on board your ship?'

His face looked strangely pale in the lantern light. 'Try not to worry about it,' he said and laid a hand on her brow, smoothing back her hair. It felt so good that she was comforted. 'I am taking you away from New Orleans. It is not safe for you there for the time being.'

'But Jessie . . .'

'She knows you are with me. Do not fret, Estelle. Your servants are being taken care of and will want for nothing. Sleep now. We shall talk again when you are rested.'

It was all so strange and muddled in her head, and she could not think properly. Justin poured some liquid into a cup and held it to her lips. She swallowed a little of the sweet drink. It was pleasant and seemed to calm her and she felt herself drifting off to sleep.

The light was pouring into the cabin when Estelle awoke once more. She looked about her and saw that she was in a large cabin, and that from its furnishings it must belong to the ship's captain. She was on board Justin's ship! Now it was all flooding into her mind.

Someone had tried to abduct her. Justin had told her so. She was to have been taken to the House of Pearls, but she had only *his* word for that. Could she believe him or had he planned her abduction himself?

Estelle got out of bed carefully. Her head was swimming

and she had to clutch at the bedpost to steady herself. After a few moments the faintness began to clear but her head felt sore, and it was very tender in the spot where she had been struck. Someone must have hit her hard. She felt a surge of anger against whoever had treated her so ill.

The ship was moving. She could feel the motion of the waves and went to look out of the portholes. There were three of them, and this was the stern of the ship. There was nothing to be seen but sea and sky as far as the eye could focus, the foaming waves leaving a trail behind them as they surged through the water. Where was he taking her? She felt a surge of anger. He had no right to carry her off like this! She turned as the door opened, ready to accuse him of abducting her, but saw that a young sailor had entered carrying a tray of food.

'Cap'n sent me with some food for you,' Piers said. 'Shall I set it on the table, miss?'

'Yes, thank you,' Estelle said and looked at him more closely, liking what she saw. He was tall and strong with dark hair and an open honest face. 'Pray tell me, what is your name?'

'It's Piers, miss. I'm Cap'n St Arnaud's cabin boy, but I'm learning to be a ship's master.'

'Are you? That must mean a lot of studying.' Estelle walked over to the table, where several maps and papers were spread. Piers was clearing the papers away, rolling them and stacking the rolls on a shelf with a grille to hold them in place when the ship lurched, as it did every so often. Instruments of navigation were also stored on the shelf, some of them in wooden boxes with brass bands, locks and escutcheons to keep them safely locked away. 'Where are we going, do you know?'

'Cap'n didn't say. Might be the West Indies – or Cartagena this time. We're not carrying a cargo outward, but we'll bring one back. We've been running guns and supplies beneath the noses of the British for the last month or more. We'll be back to normal now though I expect. The war is over – bar the shouting. Cap'n says we'll not be needing to run guns anymore, so it's further afield we'll be going this time.'

'And what is normal?' Estelle asked, breaking a piece of soft white roll between her fingers. It seemed fine food for ship's fare but she did not guess that it had been baked especially for her. 'What do you usually carry aboard this ship?'

'Now there's a question,' Piers said and grinned at her. 'Might be pirates' gold or a cargo of hides and cocoa beans. All the same to Cap'n St Arnaud.'

'Pirates' gold?' Estelle's attention was caught. 'Tell me more, Piers. It sounds as if . . .'

'It sounds as if Piers has been talking too much,' Justin said from the doorway. 'Off with you, lad. I need to speak to Mademoiselle Lebrun alone.'

Estelle stood up as he came into the cabin, moving away from the table towards the portholes. She glared at him from a safe distance. 'Where are you taking me? Who gave you the right to bring me on board your ship?'

'I see you are feeling better this morning, Estelle.'

'Do not avoid the question, sir. Why did you bring me here?'

Her eyes were bright and it was clear that she was angry, her head held proudly as she looked at him. He smiled inwardly. Did she have any idea of what that look did to him? He felt a burning need to take her in his arms, and only the knowledge that he would be being unfair to her when she was vulnerable held him back.

'Would you have preferred it if I had left you to Erskine's tender mercies? Had my men and I not been following you when you were attacked, you would even now be incarcerated in a special secure room at the House of Pearls, a room they use to bring reluctant girls to heel. Have you any idea of what would have happened to you there?'

Remembering the bruises she had seen on Genieve's back, Estelle shuddered, but she was not ready to give him best just yet.

'Why were you following me?' Her eyes narrowed as she pounced like a cat on its prey. She saw the little nerve flicking at his temple and knew that he was fighting his temper. 'You meant to kidnap me yourself. Don't lie to me, Justin. It is the only possible explanation.'

'I intended to bring you here for your own safety.' Justin's mouth thinned grimly as he admitted it. 'André de Varennes told me that Erskine meant to imprison you in his brothel. Good grief, Estelle, you can't want that?'

136

'No, of course not, but you could have taken me home.'

'To that hovel?' Justin's fists balled at his sides. 'What good would that have done? I killed two of Erskine's rogues but he would have sent others, and I might not have been there to help you. You are no longer safe in New Orleans, Estelle.'

'You killed . . .' Her face paled and she felt cold all over. 'But you could be accused of murder . . . hung!'

He shrugged his shoulders, face expressionless. 'The men Erskine employed were scum from the waterfront. Fights and violent deaths happen often enough where they come from. Erskine might try to make trouble for me if he knew I had you, but I have friends – powerful friends. I do not fear him. Besides, I have the whole world to trade in. I do not need to return to New Orleans. We do not need to return there, Estelle.'

'I have friends there, and they will worry about me. It is my home. I have no other.' She was defensive, afraid to trust him. 'I want to go home. I beg you, turn your ship about, sir. Take me back.'

'I cannot do that,' Justin said. 'My men expect to earn good profit from this voyage. Nor would I if I could. To do so would be to abandon you to Erskine's tender mercies, of which he has none. You must accept that your future lies with me, Estelle. There is nothing for you now in New Orleans.'

'Yet I would return there.' Her magnificent eyes flashed defiance at him.

'Damn your pride, woman! You will do as I bid you.'

'I shall not. You cannot compel me.'

'Can I not?' He crossed the space between them, glowering down at her for a moment before reaching out to take her into his arms. Estelle caught her breath as she saw the determination in his eyes and then he bent his head to hers. His kiss was hungry, demanding and yet sweet. When at last he lifted his head to gaze down at her she was silenced, her eyes wide and dark, melting with desire, silver shimmering in their depths. 'Know that you are mine, Estelle. It is your destiny – my destiny. Neither of us can escape our fate for it was sealed that night. If you wished to run from me you should have locked your window. You did not and there is no going back.'

'It seems I have no choice,' Estelle whispered. She was reluctant to give in, and yet something in his eyes called to her, making her want to be back in his arms, to belong to him in truth.

'I shall not force you to accept me in your bed,' Justin told her softly. 'But I believe it will happen, because you want me as I want you. This thing is in our blood. We must take what it offers and glory in it while it lasts.'

'You will tire of me one day.'

'Nothing lasts forever,' Justin said. 'But if that day should come, you will not suffer for it. I give you my word as a gentleman. I shall never abandon you, Estelle.'

Estelle knew that she would feel the pain of their parting when it happened, as it surely must, but she could not fight him any longer.

'You are too strong for me. If you will have it thus, then so be it.'

He smiled and touched her cheek softly. 'But I will have you come to me willingly, gladly. For now I offer you friendship, and my protection. For the future – who knows?'

She gave him a tremulous smile, her heart racing. 'Where are we going?'

'To Cartagena first, then to Jamaica to sell our goods. After that the world is open to us. We may go where we please.' He touched her cheek softly with his fingertips. 'Where would you like to go – Paris or London? I have business that might take me to England one day.'

Estelle shook her head wordlessly. What did it matter to her where they went? All she truly wanted was to be with him, and for the moment it seemed that she was to have her heart's desire.

Estelle saw the men looking at her curiously as she went on deck. She knew that some of the crew were made uneasy by her presence, for they thought it unlucky to have a woman on board, but others were friendly enough and tried to mind their manners when she was near. She was undoubtedly a lady and they were not sure how to treat her at first, but as time passed, they grew used to seeing her on deck.

Piers could not do enough for her; he was her devoted slave and spent much of his free time talking to her. Discovering that he had a quick keen mind, she offered to help him with his studies, and they took mutual pleasure in the books they discussed together. They had also found a mutual bond in their memories of Marietta, and the youth often talked of his childhood and his mother. Sometimes, he talked of Justin, and of the way he had tried to run away to sea with Captain Wolf Harrod.

'I do not like to think what might have happened to me if the Cap'n had not come that night,' he said. 'For we were to have sailed on the tide, and I might have been left on the island as some of Wolf's men were when he crept away under cover of darkness. I might have been one of those killed or marooned.'

Estelle's curiosity was aroused as she encouraged Piers to tell his story. 'And you say that Captain St Arnaud took nothing of the treasure for himself?'

'He gave his share to the crew to be split amongst us all,' Piers said. 'He was interested only in the cargo we shipped in Jamaica and carried back to New Orleans.'

'Do you know why?'

'I heard that there were dead men in the cave where the gold was buried, and that he called it blood money,' Piers said. 'But the men respected him all the more – especially when Wolf sailed away and took the gold belonging to ten of his own crew for himself. Men died because of him and others might have if it had not been for Captain St Arnaud.'

'It sounds as if Wolf is an evil man,' Estelle said with a little shudder. 'I am glad that we do not sail with him this trip.'

'Cap'n St Arnaud has sworn to bring him to justice,' Piers told her. 'If he is taken to Barataria he will be tried by the brotherhood and . . .' He drew his hand across his throat and grinned at her. 'That's if one of the men he marooned doesn't get to him first.'

'You bloodthirsty little monster,' Justin said, coming up to them. 'Off with you or I'll put you on crow watch.'

Piers grinned even more and ran off, leaving Justin and Estelle together. She smiled up at him, thinking how well it suited him to be at sea. His skin had a deep golden colour, and his eyes glowed with vitality.

'Piers thinks you are a kind of demigod,' she said. 'I believe you have bewitched him.'

'I leave enchantment to others,' Justin said with a wry twist of his lips. 'Marietta was a great one for spells – did you know that? She gave me a charm to keep me safe against the magic of one who ill wished me. I do not know if it worked, but I keep it still.'

Estelle's smile dimmed. 'I believe that Marietta knew many things that other people might think were evil or born of the black arts. She saw things that would happen in the future, and I know she tried to keep me safe from harm.'

Justin saw the sadness in her eyes. 'You miss her I think?'

'I loved her. My mother died when I was born and she nursed me, loved me, and gave me her milk and her kindness. She was the mother I never had.'

'Yes, I see that,' Justin said. 'I know she cared deeply for you. She was prepared to tolerate me because she thought I would look after you.'

'I am not sure she would approve of what you did when you carried me off with you.'

'Perhaps not – but Marietta saw more than most.' He shook his head as she looked at him questioningly. 'We shall soon reach the island I told you about. I have decided to visit there before we take our cargo on board at Cartagena.'

'Is it the island where you found the treasure?'

'No, for that one is known to a man I no longer trust. Wolf may return there and it would be too risky. No, my island is slightly larger and has running water as well as fruit and wildlife. It is a pretty paradise, one day's sailing west from Wolf's island. The entrance to the lagoon is not easy to negotiate, for it is guarded by treacherous rocks and currents that could drive a ship to its doom. There are many such in these waters. I thought you might like to stay there for a few days, Estelle.'

'But will not your crew grow restless?'

'I am master of the *Dark Angel* and the men will do as they are told,' Justin said, a hard glitter in his eyes. 'We shall take on water and fruit, but in truth we have had some chancy runs of late and I think they will enjoy the chance to relax for a while.'

Estelle gazed up at him. 'I know so little of you – where you come from, who you truly are. I have heard that you were once a pirate, and that you are on good terms with Jean Lafitte, who some call privateer, though others are less kind.'

'They owe the saving of New Orleans in part to Lafitte,' Justin said with a frown. 'You know that he rules Barataria almost as a king, and that he controls much of the sea in those waters. We must all pay a tribute to him if we wish to trade safely in his kingdom. I have forsworn piracy, though I am not above attacking a British ship if it seems necessary. I do not attack either French or American ships – in this I am at one with Jean.'

'But what of the man within?' she asked, wanting to know more of him. 'I believe you are of French birth but I know no more.'

'My mother was French, my father an English Marquis,' Justin said, a little nerve flicking at his temple as if the memory pricked some nerve within. 'I was the result of my mother's betrayal of her marriage vows, and my coming robbed her husband of the chance of a legitimate heir. When she died he told me the truth and threw me out. I went to England to seek my father and . . .' He shook his head. 'It matters not for I met the man who was to be as a true father to me. Robbie Marshall was my friend, my mentor and my benefactor. Had I not been fortunate enough to meet him I might have ended very differently.'

There was something in his past that he did not wish to tell her. Yet it was a beginning, an opening in the barrier that she felt he held in place against the world.

'Come and sail the ship with me,' Justin invited, holding out his hand to her. 'We are three days sailing from our island and I want to teach you much that you do not know about life on board a ship.'

Estelle gave him her hand. As yet he had not sought her bed, but she knew that it would not be long now.

'Oh, but this is beautiful, truly a little paradise,' Estelle said, taking Justin's arm as he halted at the foot of a fall of cascading water that tumbled from the rocks above. 'Is the water good to drink?'

'We filled our casks with it when we called here after leaving Wolf's island,' he told her with a smile as she dropped to her knees on the soft earth and cupped her hand beneath the water, sipping from its coolness. 'I believe this island has everything a man might need to find his own paradise – if he gathered those about him that he cared for.'

'It is certainly lovely,' Estelle said, looking up and giving a cry of wonder as a brightly coloured bird fluttered from the treetops to their right. 'Oh, Justin, how beautiful that bird is . . .'

He gave her his hand to help her stand. 'You are beautiful,' he said, gazing down at her with such tenderness, such desire, that she melted inside and swayed towards him. 'Estelle, my love, are you ready to trust me now?'

'Yes . . .' she whispered hoarsely, for she could hardly speak. Her heart was racing madly and she found it difficult to breathe. Over the past weeks she had learned to look for him, to anticipate the time they spent together eagerly, to know that all she wanted was to be truly his. 'Yes, Justin. I do trust you. I – I think I love you.'

She could say no more for he gathered her up in his arms, carrying her to a shady place where they were hidden from the eyes of any that might have strayed this far away from the beach. Though she knew that his crew had orders to remain there and prepare the feast for that evening.

She lay gazing up at him as he bent over her, touching his lips to hers lightly at first and then with increasing passion. His tongue explored her mouth, tasting her sweetness, teasing, and flicking at her delicately as she opened to him. And then he was helping her to remove bits of her clothing, kissing each piece of her glorious body that was revealed to him, caressing her, bringing her to a quivering anticipation.

He loved her more sweetly in that shaded place than the first time, playing upon her body so that it sung with pleasure, responding to his lightest touch, moving with his. Slowly at first, and then with increasing urgency, they let the sensation mount until it spilled over in a tumult of raging desire. And even then, when passion was slated, they lay thigh to thigh, flesh cooled by the drench of perspiration that had slicked their skin at the height of their passion, still drinking in the sweet fulfilment that their loving had brought.

Above them the sun stole through a canopy of leaves, birds flitting overhead and calling to each other, and somewhere nearby was the rustling of a small animal in the bushes. It was a moment of pure tranquillity, of peace and oneness that is seldom found other than between true lovers.

'You are so lovely, so warm and loving,' Justin murmured close to her ear. His hand was stroking the arch of her satiny smooth back, down her thigh, holding her pressed close against him as though he would never let her go. She pushed herself even closer, wanting this moment to go on forever, and she felt him harden against her as his desire was rekindled.

'Justin, I love you,' she whispered, her tears mingling with the sweat of his skin as she buried her head against his chest. 'I love you.'

'Do not weep, my darling,' he murmured as he stroked her hair, kissing it softly, inhaling the fresh clean scent of her and the intoxicating musk of her sex as he sensed her own arousal. 'I want you more than you will ever guess . . .'

He moaned softly as he moved across her, beginning once again the slow, sensual dance of love, sliding into her warm depths, withdrawing . . . almost . . . only to plunge deep inside her again. She was whimpering, writhing beneath him as her mind and body dissolved into one and she became a quivering mass of sensation and pleasure, her breathing coming faster and faster as she was carried with him to that far place where she glimpsed paradise itself.

Afterwards they lay together, and then Justin suddenly laughed and pulled her to her feet, sweeping her up into his arms and carrying her beneath the waterfall so that the cold water cascaded over them. She shrieked at him, but they were laughing like children, glorying in their happiness and joy in each other.

Truly this must be as Eden had been before the serpent tempted Eve she thought, as she laughed up at her lover. All her doubts had flown, though she knew that they might return to plague her one day, but for now she had all that any woman could ever ask of life.

It was not until dusk, when the light of the crew's bonfire turned the sky red, that they wandered back to the beach, hand in hand, as close now as a man and woman might be, bonded by that special feeling that comes from finding true happiness in loving.

They stayed for four days on the island, and Estelle wished that they need never leave. For those days she had lived in a world of their own, despite being aware of the crew. At night they joined the others by the fire on the beach, partaking of the feast cooked over a slowly turning spit, listening to the laughter and the music, applauding those who sang and played for them on penny whistles and a fiddle.

Some of the men carved toys from wood or bone, spending hours whittling away until the shape gradually became clear, the model of a ship, or a bird or some animal. She knew that they were meant for children left behind in a port somewhere. At times the men drank too much rum and grew boisterous, and then there were quarrels and fights amongst them, though most were settled swiftly. When that happened, Justin took her away, back to the ship, where they lay together in his bed, content in the warmth of each other's arms, loving, talking, and laughing as they made their plans for the future.

Justin had decided to make one more run to New Orleans after he had unloaded his cargo at Kingston, and then they would go to England.

'I have business there that will be best put behind us,' he said. 'After that we shall go wherever you wish, Estelle. We might spend some time in Paris. We could buy you pretty gowns and trinkets. I want to spoil you, my love.'

'Oh, Justin,' she whispered against his shoulder. 'What a fool I was to run away from you. You told me to stay in my father's house where I would be safe, but I would not listen to you.'

'That was my fault,' he said, and stroked her hair. 'I used you ill, my love. I went away after that night without speaking. I went so swiftly because I had heard that Piers was about to go to sea and I was afraid that if I missed him it might be too late. Many young lads die on their first voyage, for the life can be hard. I had to keep my promise to Robbie, and in doing so I abandoned you. Had you been with child . . .' A little shudder ran through him. 'God forgive me. I cannot bear to think what might have happened to you.'

'It did not happen,' Estelle said. 'But your going broke my heart. I thought that I meant nothing to you – and so when you returned I was cold to you. I was so distressed that night at the ball that I did not know what I said when Mr Erskine asked me to marry him, though I do not believe that I said yes to him.'

'He thought you an heiress then,' Justin said with a frown. 'The man is a braggart and a bully, Estelle. When I learned that you were to marry him I lost my temper. I told your father that I would not allow it and we quarrelled. If I contributed to his dying I am sorry for it.'

'It may have precipitated the hour,' she admitted, 'but it could not have been long delayed. The doctor had prepared me for it weeks before that day. In truth it was not your fault, Justin, though in my grief I blamed you.'

'Nevertheless, I do beg your pardon for it,' he said. 'I should have made myself plain to him that day.'

Estelle was silent, for she did not think that her father would have been better pleased to know that Justin intended to make her his mistress, but she did not wish to spoil this perfect time by raising such objections. She would take the happiness he was offering her and face the future when it came.

After leaving the island, Justin steered the ship to Cartagena, where they took a valuable cargo on board, and then set sail for the British-owned island of Jamaica. Estelle wondered at his choosing to sell his goods there, but he explained that it made the voyage more profitable for they could sell one cargo and load another to be sold in New Orleans.

'Often I can find a ship there still laden with goods from France or the east,' Justin told her. 'They will sell to me rather than make the run to New Orleans. It may not be so easy to pick up a lucrative cargo in the future, for now that the war with the British is over ships may find it worthwhile to continue on to New Orleans. Yet some will always take a quick profit and save themselves the trouble of paying Lafitte a tribute. Not all captains could be sure of being allowed the freedom of those waters.'

Estelle looked at him curiously. 'Are you a very rich man, Justin? Piers told me you did not take your share of the pirates' gold. Were you not tempted by it?'

'Blood money,' he said soberly. 'Red Bart killed his own crew to protect the secret of where the gold was buried. I did not want tainted gold – and yet I took something from the cave that day.' He kissed the top of her head, then left their bed to fetch something from his sea chest. Bringing it back to her, he placed the small leather pouch in her hand. 'I chose these for you, Estelle, and had them cut and set for you in New Orleans. I have waited for the right moment to give them to you.'

'For me?' She looked at him in wonder, opening the pouch and tipping the contents into her hand. A beautiful emerald pendant in the shape of a pear hung from a fine gold chain, and two smaller emeralds were set with gold wires to hang from her ears. 'But these cannot be for me, Justin – they are flawless and must be worth a fortune.'

'That is why I chose them,' he said, and smiled. 'Wolf had the largest share of the stones, but I think I had the best of it though he knew it not. I always meant them for you, and they do not carry the stain of the crew's blood.'

He did not mention the Spanish crew who had been sent to a watery grave, for to Justin the law of the sea meant such incidents were inevitable. A treasure taken in fair fight was one thing, comrades killed for greed was another.

'Are you sure they are for me?'

'Of course. Put them on, let me see if they are fit for my lady.'

'Your lady?' Estelle laughed as she got out of bed, standing there unashamed in the light of their lantern, the soft light showing her creamy skin to perfection as she fastened the necklace about her throat, and fastened the earrings to her lobes. She turned to face him. 'Do I do them justice, my lord?'

'Ask whether they do you justice, Estelle,' he said huskily and pulled her down to him, crushing her beneath him in the rumpled sheets of their bed. 'And the answer must always be that no jewel however flawless could do you justice.'

'Justin . . .' she teased him, laughing up at him, her dark eyes lit with a silver flame. 'You almost convince me that you truly love me.'

'Only almost?' he asked, and bent to kiss her with little pecking kisses that made her giggle and squirm against him. 'Then it seems that I must find a way to convince my lady . . .'

Estelle sighed and arched her body to meet the onslaught of his passionate loving. Sometimes it seemed to her that they had reached the peak of sensation, that nothing could be more perfect than the content she had known in his arms. But then he showed her that the horizon was far away and that it would take forever to reach it, each new discovery perhaps better than the last.

She gave herself up to his loving, wanting nothing but the moment, the feeling of being a part of this man she loved. Let tomorrow go, it did not matter for she had today.

Had any woman ever known such happiness? Estelle could not believe that it was possible. Her man, her lover, her pirate loved her so thoroughly that she had no thought for anything but him.

When they reached Jamaica and Justin told her they had had one of the best runs the ship had ever made, he swore that it was because she was on board the *Dark Angel*.

'You have brought us luck, Estelle,' he told her. 'Some of the men murmured against it when I brought you on board, but now they think you are an angel.' He touched her hair. 'The dark angel my ship was named for perhaps.'

'You spoil me,' she said when he took her on shore and bought her a pretty skirt and blouse that dipped low over her shoulders and set off the golden glow of her skin. 'When we are in New Orleans, will you let me visit my friends?'

'Of course. I shall see that you are protected at all times, but you are free to see whoever you wish.'

'Thank you. It is just that I would like to say goodbye to Jessie and Erle, and to Tante Rosemarie. She was kind to me and I am sure she will have been anxious for me.'

'As you wish,' he shrugged, his eyes intent on her face. 'You have made up your mind that you do not wish to stay there?'

'Why should we?' Estelle asked. 'You said that we could go anywhere in the world – why should we not explore it together?'

'I see no reason at all,' he said, and kissed her. 'My cargo is almost loaded. I was lucky again, Estelle, for I have bought silks and perfumes, laces and all manner of luxuries – all the things the ladies of New Orleans have been starved of for months. They should bring in a fortune.'

'And when do we leave?'

'On the first tide,' Justin told her. 'The voyage has gone so well that I shall be glad to sell my cargo and leave New Orleans behind. We have only the future to think of now, Estelle.'

A chill ran down Estelle's spine as he spoke. Why did she suddenly feel so on edge? Was it because everything had been too easy, that their luck had been too good?

She did not know why, but she was aware of fear, the fear that the happiness she had known these past weeks was somehow at risk, and that she might lose everything.

Ten

Justin had gone ashore to make some last minute arrangements before they left Jamaica. He had told Estelle he would be no more than an hour, but it was more than two before he returned, and she saw a look of unease pass between the crew, for if he were much longer they would miss the tide. Something must be wrong! It was unlike the Cap'n not to keep strictly to his word. When he came at last, he was grim-faced and gave the order to weigh anchor immediately.

'Has anything happened?' Estelle asked looking at him in concern. 'I was beginning to think you had met with an accident.'

'Go below and stay there,' Justin told her. 'Do not come on deck unless I send for you. No matter what happens, you must not try to come up. You will hamper the crew and make things more difficult for us.'

'But what . . .'

'Do as I tell you, Estelle,' he said harshly, and the look on his face made her obey.

What could be wrong? Why was he angry with her – and what had happened to keep him so long in Kingston?

It was more than an hour later that she heard the sound of a cannon booming and then a splintering crack above her head. The ship was being attacked. Her first impulse was to go up on deck but she recalled the stern look in Justin's eyes when he told her not to come up unless he sent for her. He had known they would be attacked!

Yes, of course. He had discovered something while he was on shore. He was not angry with her, but concerned for her – for his ship. She felt better now that she understood, so when the cabin door opened a few minutes later and Piers came in, she turned to him anxiously.

'What is happening? Are we being attacked – is it the British?'

'No, not the British,' Piers told her, and his expression was a mixture of frustration, pride and fear. 'It is Wolf's ship. It was anchored down the coast in a sheltered cove that hid it from us. Cap'n St Arnaud heard about it, and about Wolf. Seems he has been bragging that there's a reckoning due between him and the Cap'n, and that he was going to destroy us when we left port. Cap'n hoped to outrun him, for he did not wish to risk a fight with you on board – but he was waiting for us.'

'Wolf is attacking us,' Estelle looked at him, feeling a flutter of apprehension. 'What will Justin do now?'

Her answer came in the form of a cannon's roar from above her head. The *Dark Angel* was firing back, and battle was fairly joined. She rushed to the porthole, trying to see what was going on, but there was for the moment only sea.

'Where is the other ship?'

'It was close behind us, but Cap'n brought us about,' Piers said, and there was a note of regret in his voice. 'It was a fine thing to watch him manoeuvre for we are faster and lighter than the *Sea Serpent* and we had the advantage, but he sent me below. Cap'n says it's my job to stay with you, to make sure you do not try to go on deck – and to protect you if the ship is lost.' An odd, half-guilty look had come into his eyes and he touched the pistol at his waist.

'The ship will not be lost,' Estelle said, but her voice was a thin whisper. 'It cannot be . . . surely it cannot be . . .'

149

'Don't be frightened,' Piers said and took his pistol from the belt about his waist. 'Wolf's men won't get you. I've had my orders.'

Seeing the look in his eyes, Estelle shivered, for she had guessed what Justin's instructions must have been. 'If the ship is lost you must do your duty, Piers,' she said softly. 'I would rather die than fall into that murderer's hands.'

'Aye, I know it,' Piers said. 'But the Cap'n was only taking precautions. He won't lose the ship. He's foxed the British time and again, and he'll show Wolf a trick or two believe me.'

Estelle nodded, then gave a little cry of fear as the ship shuddered. Wolf's cannons had clearly found their target once more, and they could hear crashing sounds and cries of pain from on deck. She glanced at Piers anxiously, only his presence kept her from disobeying Justin's orders not to go on deck.

'We have been hit!'

'It's nothing,' Piers told her, though she could see that he looked pale. He swallowed hard, conquering his own fear. 'Cap'n will bring us through, you'll see.'

'Yes, I am sure he will,' she said, though her nails curled into the palms of her hands, and her stomach was churning. 'But it will do no harm to pray a little.'

'Maybe not.' Piers laughed at that. 'Though Cap'n says the devil looks after his own, miss.'

'Perhaps,' Estelle said and smiled, but she was offering up a prayer just the same.

The battle raged above them for what seemed an eternity to Estelle, but she did not feel another shudder run through the ship such as the first, though it was tossed this way and that as Justin's crew followed his orders. It was clear that the *Dark Angel* was lighter than the other ship, more able to come about and change tack, to move faster, so that Wolf's cannon shot fell short of their target, and it was this strategy that Justin was using to outwit his enemy.

Watching from the porthole, Piers told her that they were gradually gaining the advantage, and when they heard a rousing cheer from above, he gave a cry of jubilation.

'We've brought his main mast down,' he crowed, looking out of the porthole. 'And he has sustained a great hole amidships. The *Sea Serpent* is listing badly, severely damaged. We could board him now or sink him, and there's no way he could prevent us.'

'What will Justin do?' Estelle asked, her stomach churning at the thought of bloody hand to hand fighting. 'Will he try to board Wolf's ship?'

'No, we're leaving them to save themselves,' Piers said. 'The Cap'n didn't want to fight this time. He was forced to it, but he's wounded them badly; they may sink if they do not take care. At best they can only limp back to Kingston.'

'So it is over,' Estelle closed her eyes for a moment, whispering a prayer of thanks. Yet in a moment her eyes were opened as she heard a shuffling noise outside the door and the sound of heavy breathing. 'Who is it . . .' She gasped as the cabin door was flung open and three men entered, two of them supporting the third, who had clearly been injured and was barely conscious. 'Oh no . . .' The man being supported was Justin and he had a crude bandage round his head, also a wound to his shoulder, which was bleeding profusely. 'Bring him to the bed. Is he badly hurt?'

'Just a flesh wound,' Justin's eyes flickered open at the sound of her voice, but then he gave a little moan and sagged at the knees.

Estelle had drawn the covers back, and the men laid him down on the bed, staring at him anxiously, seemingly lost without someone to give them orders.'

'What happened? she asked. 'How bad are his wounds?'

'The head wound was slight,' a voice said from the doorway and she turned to see Sam standing there. The sight of his large frame filling the opening was somehow comforting. 'A splinter of wood grazed his temple when our foremast was hit, and he took no account of it, but the wound to his shoulder is worse. We went in too close that last time. It won us the battle but someone fired at him from the *Sea Serpent*, and he took a ball in the shoulder. An inch or so lower and it would have finished him.'

'We must wash the wound and bind it,' Estelle said, bending anxiously over Justin. His face was pale, his eyes closed, and his breathing had a ragged edge to it. 'I have no experience of these things. Do you have a surgeon on board?'

'He was killed in the first attack,' Sam told her grimly. 'I can take the ball out and bind him, mademoiselle, as I shall for others of our crew, but I have no knowledge of healing. It will be your task to nurse him.'

'Do as you must,' Estelle said. 'I shall take care of him once you have finished your work.'

'Where shall we head for?' The two crew members were looking to Sam for guidance. 'Do we go to New Orleans or Grand Terre?'

'Grand Terre,' Sam told them gruffly. 'We're sure of a welcome there and Wolf will not dare to come after us – if he survives.'

Estelle brought a bowl of water to the bed. She cut away the blood-soaked remnants of Justin's shirt, revealing the ugly, jagged hole where the ball had entered, and then began to wash away the mess and dirt so that Sam could examine the wound. As he lifted Justin to look at him, they both saw that the ball had entered his flesh at an acute angle between shoulder and arm and passed straight through, somehow missing the bone altogether.

Sam grunted with satisfaction as he saw the deep gash. 'It is well that the ball did not lodge deeply,' he said to Estelle. 'The best thing we can do for now is to wash this with some of the Cap'ns brandy. That should help to prevent infection, but if it doesn't heal it may need to be cauterised. I would do it, but if we wait until we reach Barataria there should be someone with more knowledge of these things than I.'

'Marietta once told me that she tended a man who had been shot on the waterfront. She said that it was necessary to cauterise such wounds at once for if infection sets in the limb could be lost.'

'It will be painful,' Sam warned.

'Yet you could do it?'

'Aye. I've done it before for a mate – though it didn't save the limb nor yet his life.'

'Was it done immediately?' Sam shook his head. 'All the more reason to do this now.'

'You're the Cap'ns lady. It must be for you to decide.'

152

'Then do it,' Estelle said. Her stomach was churning and she felt as though a drum was beating in her head, but she believed they had no choice. If only Marietta was here to tell her what to do! She had only her instinct, and the memory of Marietta's words. She took a deep breath as she looked down at Justin's white face. The blood was oozing from his wound again, and she knew it must be stanched or he would likely die. 'Do it, Sam. It is his only chance.'

'I'll be back,' Sam said and nodded to her.

She bent over Justin as Sam went out, tending the wound to his head, which she saw at once was slight. She washed away the blood and dirt, then washed the wound again with brandy. Justin flinched but did not wake, though his eyelids flickered.

She became aware of Piers standing beside her and, turning, saw that tears were running down the youth's cheeks.

'Will he die?'

'Not if we can prevent it,' Estelle said. 'We must do whatever is necessary, Piers. I shall need your help until we get to Barataria. Once there we may find someone who will help us.'

'You have only to ask.'

'Yes, I know.' Estelle smiled at him. She had just cleared away the water and linen she had used to bind Justin's head when the door opened once more to admit Sam and three members of the crew. Sam was carrying a bar of iron, the tip of which had been heated until it glowed.

'It will be necessary to hold him,' Sam told her grimly and she nodded. 'I should leave him to us for the moment, mademoiselle.'

Estelle shook her head. 'If he must bear it then so must I,' she said, her face pale. Yet as she watched from a distance, saw the red hot iron applied to his open wound, heard the scream of pain that issued from his lips as he came to sudden consciousness and struggled violently against those who held him, she felt that she would die of her sorrow. How could he bear it – how could she?

In another moment Justin had slumped back against the pillows, his eyes shut. The stench of burned flesh made her stomach heave. She moved closer to the bed once more and

153

saw that there was blood and froth on Justin's lips, his face damp with sweat. The other men had turned green, and Sam was looking decidedly sick himself as he moved away to let her near.

'Is it finished?' she asked, and Sam nodded. 'Then you have done your work and you have my thanks. Piers and I will tend him now.'

'You have only to ask for whatever you need,' Sam said. 'The Cap'n is a good man. We shall all serve his lady as we served him.'

'Say a prayer for him, Sam,' Estelle replied, her eyes bright with tears. 'And for me.'

As the door closed behind them, she fetched fresh water and bathed Justin's face, and then she remembered some pots of salves that she had seen in his sea chest when looking for linen to bind him, and asked Piers to bring them to her.

'Do you think this will soothe him?' Piers asked. Justin's face was prickled with sweat again, tiny beads gathering on his forehead. It was clear that the pain troubled him.

'We can only try,' Estelle said and held the pot to her nose. 'It smells pleasant . . . like something Marietta showed me once. Perhaps she gave it to him to thank him for repairing her house. She made many salves and creams to help the girls at the House of Pearls. We shall apply a little to the bandage and hope that it may ease the sting.'

Piers took the cloth from the bowl she had used and bathed Justin's face again as Estelle prepared the bandages. Then he lifted Justin's unconscious form from the pillows while she bound him with a soft pad of muslin and more linen strips, all of which she had found in his personal stores.

'We must take turns to watch over him,' Piers said as she bathed Justin's forehead once more. 'For I think he will be in much pain when he wakes, and perhaps there will be fever.'

'Yes, he will have terrible pain,' Estelle said and her eyes stung with tears. 'We have nothing to give him to help it, save some brandy. I hope we have saved him from the fever – for I do not know how to cure it.'

Justin lay unconscious all that night and the next day, and then he began to toss and turn and cry out. His body heated and he sweated profusely. Estelle and Piers took it in turns to watch over him, and to bathe his skin, which was almost always damp with sweat. Sometimes when he roused a little they gave him brandy mixed with water to ease the pain, spooning a few drops into his mouth. He muttered and swallowed but did not wake from his fever.

Sam came several times to inquire after him in the following days, as did other members of the crew. Estelle could not doubt that he was respected and liked, indeed, it might not have been too strong a word to say that his men loved him.

She wished that she had some knowledge of healing, for then she might have brewed potions that would ease his fever, but she had nothing. She could give him only water and brandy and try to keep him comfortable. Then after three days had passed, one of the crew brought a powder he had found amongst the surgeon's belongings, and told her that he had been given it to help cure a fever when he was taken ill on their last trip.

'Surgeon mixed it with water,' he said, 'but I put wine in it to make it taste better. Look . . .' He lifted the flask he had prepared for her to his lips and took a swig. 'Ain't no harm in it.'

'No, I see that,' Estelle said and took the flask gratefully. 'I shall give the Captain a little mixed with water and we'll hope for the best.'

Piers sniffed at the flask after the sailor had gone and pulled a face. 'I don't know about this stuff,' he said. 'Smells awful to me.'

'Yet Jackson swears by it,' Estelle said. 'If we had someone to tell us what to do we might be able to help him more, but as it is . . . I suppose this cannot harm him.'

She mixed a spoonful of the powder with water as the sailor had instructed and tasted it. Finding it foul, she blended a little wine into it, which helped to disguise the bitter taste.

'We shall try it for a while and see if it helps,' she said. 'At least we know it is not poisonous.'

Piers held Justin up from the pillows while Estelle spooned a small amount of the mixture into his mouth. He coughed and choked, but then swallowed, his eyelids flickering.

For a while he seemed calmer, still hot and sweating but not so restless, and Estelle was encouraged. Perhaps Jackson's mixture would help him, but during the night he became worse again, and giving him the mixture made no difference. He was burning hot and she sponged his body with cool water, and then he was cold and shivering and she lay down beside him, gathering his body to her in an effort to still the convulsive shudders.

'Oh, Marietta,' she whispered in the darkness of the cabin, which was lit by only one small candle. 'If only you were here. If only you could tell me what to do.'

'Do as you are doing,' came the answer to her mind. "Tis love will save him, keep true to your heart and all will be well.'

'Marietta?' Estelle looked about the cabin, for in that moment she felt as if her dear friend was close by and was comforted. 'I do not want to lose him now . . .'

'Love will overcome,' Marietta's voice was close to her ear, or was it only in her mind? Estelle did not know, yet she felt reassured, as though her friend was watching over them.

Estelle sighed. If Marietta were here in truth she would brew potions and cures to make Justin better, but even she could do nothing from beyond the grave. She bent over Justin once more, stroking his hair back from his forehead. Was it her imagination or was it cooler again? Cool but dry, free from the drenching sweat that had plagued him for days.

'I love you, my darling,' she whispered close to his ear. 'Do not leave me, my love. I beg you, be strong for me. I cannot bear to live without you.'

'Estelle . . .' the word was merely a sigh on his breath, barely audible, but it made her eyes prick with tears. He knew she was there, he knew she was caring for him.

Wiping away her tears, Estelle prepared a little of the mixture Jackson had given her, making it stronger than usual. She spooned a good measure of it into his mouth, and heard him make a sound of rejection, as though it tasted foul. A smothered oath issued from his lips, and then his eyes flicked open.

'Trying to poison me?' he asked, jerked up and immediately fell back with a curse. 'Bloody pain . . . what the hell have you done to me?'

'Justin?' Estelle bent over him again as he muttered something more. 'Justin, my dearest . . . can you hear me?'

But he had lapsed back into his state of semi-consciousness. She blinked away her tears. It was the first time that she had been given a sign of hope, the first time that he had shown any sign of recovery.

'Praise God,' she murmured on a sob of relief. He would not die now. Though it was clear the pain was terrible and he was far from recovery, in her heart she knew he would not die.

Justin became fully conscious the following day. He woke when Piers was bending over him, bathing his face with cool water, his eyes staring up at him for some seconds before he spoke.

'And what the hell do you think you're doing?'

Piers jumped and almost dropped his bowl of water. 'Only what Estelle told me to do, Cap'n – that's to keep you cool. You've been mighty hot and fretful these past eight days or more.'

'Eight days?' Justin groaned and tried to sit up, failing because of weakness rather than the pain, though that was severe enough. 'I'm as helpless as a kitten. Get me some brandy, lad.'

'I'm not sure what Estelle would say . . .'

'Damn you!' Justin grunted. 'Is she the captain of this ship or am I?'

'She has been in charge of you, sir. I do as Estelle tells me . . .'

'You'll damned well do as I tell you or I'll have your hide,' Justin said. 'And it's Mademoiselle Estelle to you and the rest of them!'

'Yes, sir.' Piers grinned for it seemed that Justin was on the way to being himself again. 'Brandy coming up, Cap'n.'

He poured a small measure into a cup and brought it to the bed. Justin made a face at it, downed it in one go and demanded more. When Piers hesitated, he glared at him.

'Bring me the bottle and be quick about it.'

'Piers will do no such thing,' Estelle said from the doorway. She was carrying a tray with a bowl of steaming hot broth and a spoon. 'Very well, Piers, you may leave us now. I shall deal with this.' She set down her tray.

Piers scuttled, giving her a conspiratorial look in passing.

157

Estelle smiled inwardly but did not let it show as she approached the bed and looked at her patient. His eyes were focusing on her for the first time in days, and she knew that her assumption in the night had been correct. The fever had worn itself out, and he had survived for he was a healthy man and his will to live was strong.

'Does it hurt very much?'

'Like all the devils in Hell had been at me with hot pincers,' Justin said, glaring at her. 'What did you do to me?'

'The wound was cauterised,' Estelle told him. 'I believe it did its job for though you have had a fever the wound itself is healing well and there is no infection.'

'It was well done,' Justin admitted ruefully. 'But it hurts like hell.'

'Yes, I know it must. I wish we had not had to do it, but I was afraid it might become poisoned and I did not think you would wish to lose your arm – or your life.'

'No . . .' He eased himself up against the pillows, grimacing as he felt the lancing pain begin again. 'Have I been a terrible patient?'

'No, for you hardly knew what we did for you.' She smiled at him, a naughty light in her eyes. 'I fear you will not be so easy to manage now that you have regained your senses.'

'I should like some more brandy.'

'You should eat something first,' Estelle said. 'Cook has prepared some good broth for you. It will help you to regain your strength better than brandy.'

'The brandy is for the pain. I need it now.'

'Very well, a little,' Estelle said. 'But then you must eat some of the broth.'

'Give me the bottle,' he said, but she poured a generous measure into his cup and took the bottle away again. 'Damn you, Estelle. I know what I need.'

'Normally, I accept that you are master here,' Estelle said calmly. 'But for the moment you must allow me to judge what is best for you, Justin. When you can get out of bed and fetch the brandy yourself, you may drink your fill of it.'

'I shall not need it then!' Justin cursed but tossed back his measure of brandy. 'How long do you mean to treat me like an invalid?'

'Is it so very bad to be looked after?' she asked and smiled at him. 'It will be only for a little while, my dearest, and then you may order us all as you will.'

'You make it sound as if I were some mincing popinjay!'

'Do I? I assure you I meant no such thing – at this moment you resemble a growling bear more than anything else.' She fetched the bowl of broth and dipped her spoon into it, holding it to his mouth. 'Please try a little. It smells very nice.'

'Am I a child that I cannot feed myself?'

'You may try if you wish. I will hold the bowl for you.'

Justin took the spoon and dipped it in the broth, but his hand shook so much that it was all spilled again before he could lift it to his mouth. He snarled with frustration, and let the spoon drop. Estelle filled it and carried it to his lips once more. He opened his mouth and swallowed obediently, discovering that he was ravenously hungry. The delicious broth went down swiftly and he looked hopefully at the bowl as if wishing it full again.

'That is a good start,' Estelle said. 'You may have more later, and bread with it – and now you may have a little more brandy so that you sleep.'

Justin watched her as she walked to the table and brought him another small measure of brandy. The sway of her hips was enticing, and the food had made him sleepy. He lay back and closed his eyes contentedly.

Estelle smiled as she looked down at him, for he was sleeping peacefully. She believed that he might sleep for some hours now, and when he did wake he would no doubt demand something more substantial than broth. She left the brandy on the bachelors chest beside the bed and went out, closing the door softly behind her.

Justin was not a good patient; indeed, it would be wrong to use the word patience in relation to his manner at all, for he became irritable and difficult to manage from that day on. Most of the crew were afraid to go near the cabin, for if they so much as poked their head in the door they might have something flung at it. Piers begged to be allowed back to his normal duties, for he could not stand the Cap'ns temper, and Estelle let him go once he had shaved Justin, for it seemed the youth could do nothing right.

159

Estelle was the only one who seemed unaffected by his temper. She continued to visit him and sit with him, finding ways of amusing him in the first days when he was so frustrated that his anger boiled over at the slightest thing.

'I shall not be kept in bed like a weakling,' he raged at her on the third morning after the fever had left him. 'I have never spent so much time in bed in my life – and this is not the first time I have been wounded.'

'Yet the first time you have lain in a fever for days I think?'

Justin glared at her but said nothing, for it was true. 'I shall get up now,' he told her. 'I refuse to lie here any longer.'

'If you believe you can do so – the brandy bottle is on your table,' she invited with a sweet smile.

Justin glared at her and threw back the covers, swinging his legs over the side of the bed. He grimaced, and beads of sweat stood out on his forehead for the effort had cost him dear, but he managed it and to take a few steps, but then he stopped and could go no further.

'Damn it!' he muttered. 'I feel as if a herd of elephants had trampled over me.'

'You are still weak,' Estelle said. 'But you are much better than you were. Shall I help you to your chair? You may sit there for a while if it pleases you.'

'It would please me,' he said and put his arm about her shoulders as she offered her support. 'I am a terrible trouble to you, Estelle. Why do you bear with me?'

'Oh, I suppose I must like you a little bit,' she said, and gave him a naughty look that brought a reluctant laugh.

'I do not make a good patient.'

'No – for you have no patience, my love. But we shall be at Barataria this afternoon, and there may be someone there who will have medicines to make you strong again.'

'It would have been better to make for New Orleans,' Justin said with a little frown. 'But no matter. I shall remain on the ship until I am stronger, Estelle, and you will stay too if you please. The men may take it in turns to go ashore as always – but you must wait until I can accompany you.'

'You think it would not be safe for me there alone?'

'I have friends there but also enemies,' Justin said. 'If you would save me anxiety, humour me in this, my love.'

'Yes, if it is what you want,' she said and leaned towards him, kissing him lightly on the lips. 'I do not want you to worry for my sake. You must put all your energy into growing strong again.'

'Yes, that is true,' he admitted. 'I must look to my affairs. We have a cargo to sell – and there are other things that must be attended to. In a few days I shall be well enough to go ashore, and then we shall go together.'

They had reached the table, and he sat down with a sigh of relief. His face was pale but he looked grimly satisfied to be out of bed, and she knew he would not admit that the pain was worse for his heroic efforts.

'Do you wish for brandy?'

He shook his head. 'I told you that when I could get it for myself I should not want it,' he said and laughed softly. 'Bring me food, Estelle. Proper food not pap, I mean. I shall never regain my strength supping that stuff you've been feeding me. I need some good red meat, cheese and bread, and a tankard of ale – and then we shall see.'

'Yes, Captain,' she said and laughed as she went to the door. 'As my lord and master wishes . . .'

He growled and threw something at her, but it was only a shirt that had been left lying on the arm of his chair and it fell harmlessly to the floor. Estelle smiled to herself as she closed the door behind her. Now at last, she could truly believe that he was mending.

It was another three days before Justin could walk easily about the cabin without help. Even then his shoulder pained him, but it was growing easier to bear and in truth he made the pain worse by constant exercising. He knew that such wounds could leave a man with a dead arm if the muscles were not made to function properly immediately, and he had no intention of being left with only one arm fit to use. So he forced himself to get up, to wash, shave and dress himself, and to practise with his sword.

On the fifth day he told Estelle that they were going ashore.

'Lafitte will expect my call,' he said. 'He will know that I have been injured and he will be waiting to see if I am still a man to be reckoned with.'

161

Estelle understood that to hold his place in the violent world of the brotherhood, with whom Justin must deal to continue his trade, he needed to be strong. To show weakness would be to make himself vulnerable, and give his enemies the chance to strike.

'My father used to call Jean Lafitte a pirate,' Estelle said and wrinkled her brow. 'What kind of a man is he really, Justin?'

'He has his own values and principles,' Justin replied. 'It is not true that he is a pirate, Estelle, for a pirate cares not who he attacks. Jean is a privateer. He sails under *letters of marque* from Cartagena, and since that republic is fighting for its independence from Spain, he is licensed to attack their ships and his actions are perfectly within the law.'

'It is said that Lafitte never attacks an American ship.'

'Any of his men who did so would be punished. It is the law on Barataria, and those who break it must take the consequences. There are many laws that govern the brotherhood. Lafitte punishes thieves as we discipline men on board ship with the lash, murder will be repaid with a hanging, and a man who attacks an innocent woman will be set adrift.'

'And yet no ship can pass through these waters without being made to pay homage, which means they must give up a part of their profit to him.'

'He holds a prime position for his men occupy three islands, and together they are a fortress through which an enemy would find it hard to pass,' Justin said and smiled. 'Yet I have found friendship amongst these men, and Lafitte is my friend. I do not object to paying his tribute, for it has kept me safe in these waters for many years. I must visit him, Estelle. I can do no other.'

'You must do as you think fit,' she replied, for she knew that he was the master once more. For a while she had been able to compel him to do what was best for him, but he would not be brooked now that he felt so much better. She knew that he was still in pain, but he made light of it, hiding it from her as much as he could. She doubted that he was truly strong enough to do all that he was determined on, but there was no gainsaying him.

* * *

162

Estelle was surprised at the size and magnificence of Jean Lafitte's residence, although she had heard that he lived like a king. She was not surprised by the look of the man, however, for he was undoubtedly a gentleman, and enjoyed the good things of life. He was a handsome, strong-looking man with a thick moustache, which gave him a rakish air. His reputation and the stories told of him changed with the teller, for to some he was a ruthless pirate, to others the saviour of New Orleans, a clever man who had used opportunity to gain vast wealth.

To Estelle he was charming, taking her hand and kissing it, his eyes bright with admiration. 'So this is the lady who has finally captured the heart of a man we thought heartless. All the women on Grand Terre will be jealous of you, mademoiselle. Many have tried to capture this rogue and none have succeeded before this.'

'Indeed, I do not think they have need to envy me, for I have not enslaved him,' Estelle said, and her eyes glowed with a silver flame. 'He is his own master, sir – and woe betide any who think otherwise.'

Lafitte threw back his head, roaring with laughter. 'Oh, but I think you lie, mademoiselle. I think you are a witch, and would make any man your slave.' He slapped Justin on the shoulder, fortunately not the one that had been so recently injured, and laughed. 'You are a lucky man, my friend. When I heard the stories I thought you nearly finished, for they said she had you tied to the bed like a kitten – but I see that it was where you wanted to be. Indeed, I should not be in a hurry to get out of it if she was my nurse.'

Justin smiled wolfishly. 'I shall not wish you laid low on your bed, Jean, but if it happens I shall send Estelle to you. I daresay you will change your mind fast enough then. She can be a dragon when she chooses.'

The two men strolled off laughing, leaving Estelle to amuse herself while they discussed business. The room she was in was lovely, furnished in the latest style from France with pure Empire lines, gilded wood strung with ebony and crafted by the finest cabinet makers. One beautiful cabinet with glass and wood panels, the panels painted with swags

163

of flowers, was filled with precious items. Gold boxes with enamelling and miniature painting on the lids, delicate crystal bowls, beautiful porcelain, and *objets d'art*. Many of these fine things would have been plundered from ships that his men had taken, but no fault could be found with his taste.

The long French windows were open and led onto a veranda. Lafitte often entertained here, and palm trees shaded his hammock, where he often liked to while away the lazy hours, perhaps entertaining his mistress or playing on his mandolin and singing a ballad.

She went out for the day was fine and warm, the air as still as could be and scented with flowers and camomile. Leaving the veranda, she stopped to smell the perfume of a dark red rose, then trailed her fingers over various blooms that grew to either side of the path she followed until she came to a little stream. There were fish in the stream, their scales glinting in the sunlight as they rose to the surface, and flies skimming above the water.

'So you are the one who keeps him from me.'

Estelle turned at the sound of the woman's voice. She saw a lovely woman, a few years older than herself, her skin a pale coffee colour, hair a glossy black and eyes as dark as jet.

'Who are you?' she asked, her heart skipping a beat.

'I am called Sinita – and you are Estelle Lebrun,' the woman said. 'I have seen you in my dreams. I have conjured you up so that I should know you when I saw you, and now you are here.' She smiled. 'I knew that one day I should find the way to destroy him.'

'What do you mean?' Estelle felt chilled. 'Who are you talking about? You can't mean . . .'

'But of course I do. I shall destroy him through you.'

'No!' Estelle felt the pull of her eyes. It was as though she was being sucked into a void, dragged down and down.

'Estelle . . .' Justin's voice broke the spell and she returned to herself, as the woman turned and walked quickly away. Justin came down the steps to her. 'What are you doing out here? Who were you talking to?'

'She said her name was Sinita and she knew who I was.' Estelle looked up at him anxiously. 'She hates you, Justin. She said that she would use me to destroy you.'

'She is an evil woman who thinks she has the right to do as she pleases,' Justin said and took Estelle's arm, leading her back inside the house. 'Take no notice of her, my love. Her magic cannot touch you if you do not believe it. Just ignore her and do nothing she tells you to do. Never trust her, whatever she says to you.'

'No, I shan't,' Estelle said and shivered. She felt cold despite the warmth of the sun. 'Why does she hate you – us?'

'Because I refused her,' he said with a grimace. 'She chooses her own lovers, and few refuse her. I do not know what happens to them when she has finished with them – but I did not wish to be one of them.'

'I am glad you refused her, Justin.' She looked at him anxiously. 'I think she is evil.'

'Marietta gave me a charm to keep me safe from her magic,' he said. 'I laughed when she gave it to me, but perhaps it has worked. But you must be very careful. I fear she might try to harm you, Estelle. She knows that I care for you. When she said that she would use you to destroy me, she might have meant that she would harm you – and God knows that would destroy me.' His voice grated with emotion at the thought.

Estelle smiled up at him. 'Sometimes I almost think you love me.'

'Do you not know it?' he asked, reaching out to touch her face. 'Do you not know that you are my whole life? I adore you, Estelle, and now that we are here I can say what is in my heart. I want you to be my wife.'

'Your wife?' Estelle looked up at him, her heart hammering with a mixture of fear and excitement. 'But I am your mistress, Justin. We are happy. No, no, you must not ask me. I am yours for as long as you want me. Do not let us tempt fate by asking for more.'

'Still she does not trust me,' Justin said and smiled oddly. 'We shall be leaving for England soon, my darling, and there we shall be married. I have a score to settle with someone and once that is done I intend to marry you.'

Estelle hid her face against his shoulder as he drew her to him. She did not doubt that he cared for her, but would he still want her as his wife if he knew her secret?

Eleven

Justin was impatient to be on his way. He had sold his cargo to Jean Lafitte and there was nothing to delay their journey other than the fact that Jean had invited them to a grand dinner party that evening. Several important citizens of New Orleans had promised to attend and Justin knew he dared not offend by refusing.

'We shall go to the dinner since we must,' he told Estelle. 'But we shall return to the ship afterwards and tomorrow we sail for Jamaica. There we shall provision the ship and set our course for England.'

'What business takes you there?' Estelle asked, for his eyes held a brooding expression and she sensed that this trip held some special importance for him.

'Unfinished business begun more than eleven years ago,' Justin said and shook his head at her as she would have continued to question. 'I shall tell you when it is over. Now is not the time. Come, try on the gown I bought for you in Kingston. It should fit you but you have never worn it.'

'It was too grand for life on board the ship,' she said. 'Besides, you have been ill – or had you forgotten?'

'No, I had not forgotten,' Justin said. He flexed his shoulder. It was still stiff and painful but his strength was returning. 'Come, try the gown, Estelle. It is the same colour as the one you wore *that* night.'

'The night you made me such an infamous offer?' Estelle pulled a face at him, struggling with the hooks at her back. He beckoned her and she turned, allowing him to help her. 'This bodice took me ages to fasten this morning. You would make a good ladies' maid, Justin.'

'And you need your own maid,' Justin said. 'How would you feel about taking Jessie with you to England?'

Her eyes lit up instantly. 'Could we, Justin?'

'Perhaps. We'll see. Put this on now.'

Estelle pulled the gown on over her head. She heard someone say something and a laugh, and then, as her head emerged, she found herself looking into Jessie's smiling face.

'Jessie!' she cried and flung herself into the woman's arms. 'How came you here?'

'Captain St Arnaud sent for us – Erle, he here too, chile. We is comin' with you'se wherever you'se goes.'

'Oh, Jessie,' Estelle hugged her, eyes bright with love. She glanced at Justin, who was watching them, a look of amusement in his dark eyes. 'Thank you,' she whispered, and then to Jessie, 'I am so glad you're here.'

'You need someone to look after you, chile. Turn round and let me fasten your gown. Then you'se best let me dress your hair if'n you'se goin' to a grand dinner with the Captain.'

'Yes.' Estelle touched her hair, which was a tangle of riotous curls and clustered about her face enchantingly. 'It has become untidy of late. I cannot dress it the way you do, Jessie.'

'Ah knows that,' Jessie said, her chins wobbling as she nodded her satisfaction. 'You sit yourself down and let me look after you right, chile. Ah kin see as you'se been runnin' wild without me.'

Estelle glanced at Justin and saw that despite his grave expression he was laughing inside. She pulled a face at him but he merely inclined his head to her.

'I fear you are right, Jessie,' he said. 'Estelle is inclined to be headstrong – and to go her own way. I am glad that she will have you to look after her now.'

Estelle's eyes sparked at him but his expression did not change, as he went on, 'Naturally, I want my future wife to look her best this evening – but I know I can leave that to you, Jessie.'

'Oh yes, sir,' Jessie agreed and the look she gave him was one of total adoration. 'Ah knows how to look after my chile, Captain.'

'She is your child,' he said and allowed himself a smile. 'But she is also my lady and my love.'

'Ah knows that, sir,' Jessie said almost purring as he stroked her with his silver tongue, making Estelle grind her teeth and plot retribution for when they were alone. 'And Ah is goin' to look after you both. Don't you worry none, Captain. Jessie knows what to do for Miss Estelle.'

'Then I shall leave her in your capable hands and return later,' Justin said. He gave Estelle a look that had her wanting to batter him with her fists. 'Be good, my love. Jessie knows best.'

Estelle looked for something to throw at him, but there was nothing to hand so she took refuge in dignity.

'I shall see you later, sir.'

He smiled and went out, leaving Estelle to the care of Jessie's loving ministrations.

'It was so good of you to bring them here,' Estelle said to Justin later that evening as they were being rowed ashore. Barataria Bay looked beautiful as it basked in the evening sun, for there was a sandy beach, palm trees, huge oaks and exotic flowers. Its waters teemed with fish that were good to eat and pelicans could sometimes be seen strutting on the beach, their wings flapping. Terrible storms and hurricanes could sometimes blow across the bay, but that particular evening the air was soft and balmy. 'Jessie and Erle, they are both devoted to me and I love them dearly.'

'I am aware of that,' Justin said, giving her a look of amused affection. 'I know everything about you, Estelle. I have made arrangements for those of your old servants who wish it to follow us once we have a settled home. We shall need people we can trust about us, and my ships will carry them and your possessions to wherever we are.'

'My possessions?' She stared at him uncomprehending. 'I have none that matter. I sold everything when I moved to Marietta's house.'

'To give your people money to keep them from starving. I know. I was afraid you might do something of the kind and I arranged to buy those items you sold through your lawyer. I have managed to recover most of them I think.'

'You bought everything?' He nodded and she frowned. 'Are you very wealthy, Justin?'

'I have sufficient for all we need. My plans are not yet completely formed, Estelle. There are matters I must settle first. I shall tell you the whole one day, but for now you must be prepared to trust me.'

168

She nodded but felt a slight unease. If he was as wealthy as she had begun to suspect, what kind of a life did he plan for them? She knew that his father had been an English marquis, his mother a French woman of good birth. True, he had been born the wrong side of the blanket, but he was undoubtedly a gentleman, and could if he chose find a place in his own world. Money such as he now possessed would buy him a title if he wished, and he might mix with the aristocracy. Would he wish to return to that world, a kind of world she knew little of despite her own father's standing in New Orleans?

'You are quiet, my love.' Justin looked at her intently. 'Is something troubling you?'

'No, of course not. I am very happy. How could I be otherwise when you have done so much for me?'

'As yet I have done little, except seduce you, abduct you, and cause you endless trouble,' he said with a wry smile. 'But if these things make you happy, I am glad. I want you always to be happy, my love. If anything troubles you, you must always tell me.'

Estelle smiled but remained silent. Perhaps one day they would exchange secrets but while he kept his so would she.

The guests had enjoyed a splendid dinner, and now the ladies had retired to a grand drawing room while the gentlemen enjoyed their port and brandy. Estelle had not noticed it while the company was mixed, for the gentlemen had made much of her, but now that the ladies were alone, she could not fail to be aware of a distinct coolness towards her.

She lifted her head a little higher, refusing to let their manner disturb her. These were ladies who had been anxious to know her a few months ago. Now they looked at her as if she carried a contagious disease. She was a man's mistress, a fallen woman, no longer considered fit to move in decent circles.

Estelle got up from the little gilt-framed sofa she had been sitting on alone and wandered over to the French windows, which stood open. The room seemed stuffy and warm and the night air was cool on her heated cheeks. Justin had warned her not to wander outside the house alone, but surely it would be safe enough if she did not go far. Besides, there was something about the soft night that called to her, inviting her to venture into the moonlit gardens. It was almost as if she were being compelled to go out, as if her will was subject to the magic of the night.

She wandered outside, walking across a smooth lawn to sit on a wooden bench. The air was warm and soft on her skin. She had a clear view of the people inside the room, and felt as if she were watching a strange tableau that was apart from her. It was much nicer out here, she thought, breathing in the sweet perfume of a night-flowering blossom. Justin would soon tire of the gentlemen's gossip and then he would come to look for her.

'Come quick, chile,' a voice called to her from the darkness. 'Jessie needs your help.'

Estelle jumped to her feet, looking round. She peered in the direction from which the voice had seemed to come, but it was impossible to see or to be sure who had called to her.

'Miss Estelle. Jessie done took sick. She needs you, chile.'

'Erle.' Estelle took a step into the shadowy darkness of the bushes. 'Is that you? Where are you?' Even as she spoke the words a blanket was thrown over her head, smothering her cry of alarm. In another moment she felt herself lifted and tossed over a man's shoulder, carried hurriedly, at a run, as if her attacker was desperate to get away. She screamed but the blanket deadened the sound.

'Be quiet, wench,' a man's voice growled. 'Or it will be the worse for you.'

Estelle struggled and kicked, but the blanket hampered her movement and there was nothing she could do to escape her captor as she was carried away from the house. It seemed an eternity before she was at last set down on her feet, though she knew it was no more than a few minutes. Someone removed the blanket, and in the moonlight she saw that she was on the beach and surrounded by a small group of men.

'How dare you carry me off like that?' she demanded, her eyes bright with anger. 'When Captain St Arnaud discovers what you've done he will punish you.'

'Aye, he may try.' One of the men pushed his way through the others to face her. He was tall and heavily built, with a

170

swarthy complexion and a hard mouth. 'But we've a score to settle and this gives me the upper hand.'

'You – you're Wolf,' Estelle gasped as she looked into his harsh face. 'It was your ship that attacked us when we left Kingston.'

'Aye, it was that,' Wolf said. 'He had the advantage of me then, but he'll pay for it – and more than he bargains for. There's another wants you, Mademoiselle Lebrun. Frank Erskine would pay me to deliver you to him, but now that I've seen you I think I might get more than he is willing to pay.'

'You devil!' Estelle cried and bent swiftly, scooping up a handful of sand and throwing it into his face with all her might. He recoiled from it, spitting as the sand got into his eyes and mouth. In that instant, she turned and raced towards the trees and bushes that fringed the beach, hoping that her surprise attack would gain her enough time to hide.

Unfortunately, she had hampered Wolf but not his men. One of them, sharper than the rest, pounded after her, and with a flying leap brought her down into the sand. She screamed and fought with all her strength, but to no avail. He was so much stronger and had her fast, and in another moment had jerked her to her feet. He dragged her back to where Wolf stood, his eyes still watering from the grit that had entered them. He looked at her for a moment, then struck her hard across the face.

'Try that again, and you'll wish you'd never been born,' he said. 'Take her aboard the ship. We'll send St Arnaud a message when we're in the cove.' He leered at her, his mouth twisting evilly. 'Or maybe I'll sell you to Erskine after all. It might do you good to be humbled, bitch. Aye, and I'd take a hand in the humbling.'

Estelle shuddered but did not give any outward sign of the horror she felt. She would not give way to despair. Somehow she would find a way to escape from this brute. She was not finished yet, whatever he might think.

Justin went out into the garden in search of Estelle. He had been told she had gone outside almost an hour earlier, and he was conscious of a feeling of unease. Where was she? He had warned her not to wander the gardens alone, because he was afraid that one of his enemies might try to use her to get at him.

'Estelle . . .' he called, the tension mounting inside him. 'Where are you? I am ready to return to the ship.'

Hearing a rustling noise in the bushes behind him, he turned to see Sinita standing there, a smile of satisfaction on her lips.

'She has gone,' Sinita told him. 'I tempted her into the garden, called to her with my mind, and she heard what I wanted her to hear – and then they took her. You will not see her again, Captain St Arnaud.'

'Who has taken her?' Justin moved towards her, his fists balled at his sides. She had an evil leer on her face, laughing at him as she sensed his agony. 'You serpent! You will pay for this. If she is harmed I shall kill you.'

'No, because I shall kill you first!' Even as she spoke, Sinita launched herself at him, a flash of silver in the moonlight as she raised her hand to strike. 'One cut and you will die in agony . . .'

Before she could finish a shot rang out from behind Justin, and she screamed, jerking several times before she slumped to the ground, where she lay twitching for some seconds until she was finally still. Justin bent over her, seeing that she was dead. He looked up to see Lafitte and a man he recognised as one of Wolf's marooned crew. Todd Jones was still holding the smoking pistol in his hand. Behind him stood another man with good cause to hate Wolf Harrod – Hinckston, the man from whom he had undoubtedly stolen part of the treasure map.

'You killed her,' Justin said. 'Damned fool! Now I shall never know who has taken her.'

'It was time someone put a stop to her mischief,' Lafitte said. 'Nay, my friend, do not look so murderous. Todd knows who took your lady and why. He came to tell us and he saved your life. That blade had only to scrape your skin and you were dead.'

'You know where they have taken Estelle?' Justin asked, ignoring all the rest. 'Is this true?'

'Aye, Cap'n,' Todd said and gave him a cold smile. 'I've been waiting for this day for a long time, and now Wolf has shown his hand.'

'Wolf . . .' Justin's eyes glittered in the moonlight. 'You know it was him?'

'Aye, for I saw his men earlier lurking in the bushes, and I stayed close to them. I saw them abduct your lady, but there were too many of them and I could do nothing to help her so I followed them and watched. I heard Wolf tell her she was for sale to the highest bidder – you or Frank Erskine – and I saw her try to escape. She threw sand in his face and ran but they caught her and took her on board his ship.'

'You should have come to me at once,' Justin said. 'We might have stopped them before they left Grand Terre.'

'Then I should not have known for sure that it was Wolf who had her,' Todd said. 'Now we know – and I can take you to his ship. There is a cove just up the coast from here where he lays up in-between voyages. If we sail tonight we can surprise him before dawn, finish him once and for all.'

'I'll send two of my ships with you,' Lafitte said grimly. 'I want him taken alive, mind my words. Mademoiselle Lebrun must be returned safely to Captain St Arnaud, and Wolf . . . he will be brought back to stand his trial here.' He looked at Justin. 'You are in agreement?'

'Yes,' Justin said. 'You can have him with pleasure. All I want is Estelle's safe return . . .'

Estelle had been locked in the cabin until the ship anchored in a sheltered bay, but then one of the crew brought her a tray of food, setting it down on a small chest without speaking. Looking round, she thought this must be the first mate's cabin, for it was smaller than Justin's and sparsely furnished, but at least she had not been thrown into the hold – and it seemed they did not intend to starve her.

After she had eaten, Estelle looked out of the porthole. They were anchored quite close inshore – near enough for a strong swimmer to reach, she thought, and wondered if she dare try. Her father had taught her to swim when she was a small child, taking her on pleasant visits to his summer cottage, where she could splash at the edge of the sea and run on sandy beaches. That had ceased as she grew into a young woman, becoming too old to indulge in such freedoms, and it was some time since she had tried to swim. Yet she thought that it might be worth the risk if her situation became desperate.

The sailor had not bothered to lock the door after him, presumably because he thought there was no possibility of her escaping. The land she could see from the porthole looked to be a wild and uninhabited stretch of coastline, and it might be that she would have to walk a long way before she could find someone to help her. It was not surprising therefore that the sailor had not bothered to lock her in.

Estelle debated whether to go on deck or not. It was her only chance of escape. If she could jump into the sea while the crew was occupied, she might be able to reach the shore and then . . . her thoughts were brought to an abrupt end as she heard the sound of cannon fire. It had not come from this ship, so it must be that they were being attacked. Yet there had been no thud, nor sounds of crashing and splintering on deck. Whoever had fired had simply issued a warning.

Justin! Instinctively, she knew that he had come after her. She would not stay here to be used as a pawn, she decided and left the cabin, scrambling up the iron ladder to the deck above, and pushing back the hatch, which had been left half open. The crew was preoccupied and no one noticed her, for they were all at the rails staring at three ships out in the bay. Three ships! Was Justin's one of them? She scanned them anxiously, holding her breath – and then she saw that the central ship was the *Dark Angel*.

Justin had come to find her and the others must belong to Lafitte's fleet. She could hear shouting now. Wolf was giving orders, and her heart stood still as she heard him give the order to fetch the woman on deck. He meant to hold her in full view of Justin's ship, threatening her life unless the ships sailed away.

Without considering the dangers, Estelle swiftly slipped off her heavy skirts, ran to the side of the ship that was for the moment not being watched, climbed the rails and jumped overboard. By the time the alarm was raised, she was thrashing about in the cold water, splashing and choking as she struggled to remember how to swim. For a moment she panicked, going under the salt water and spluttering as she came up, but then she found that she was hearing her father's voice calling to her, telling her what to do.

174

She smiled as she saw him standing at the edge of a sunlit pool, encouraging her. 'That's it, Estelle, kick with your feet and move your arms at the same time.'

She was swimming after a fashion now, though it was an untidy, clumsy style that kept her afloat but did not take her forward as she tried to reach Justin's ship and failed. The current was driving her inshore. She struggled against it, but found herself being carried relentlessly towards the beach, her futile efforts leaving her exhausted. Realising that she would do better to let the current take her inshore, she gave up her struggle and let herself float as best she could until she felt something solid beneath her feet.

She had reached a sandbank, and beyond that the water looked still and calm, like the lagoon that fringed Justin's island, she thought, standing up and wading across the sandbank to where the calmer water lay sparkling in the early sunlight. A faint shout reached her as she slipped into the waters of the lagoon, splashing her way the short distance to the beach, where she lay down on the sand to catch her breath for her strength had all but gone.

When she had the will to look up, she saw frantic activity in the bay. Two things had happened while she was fighting her own battle with the current. Wolf's men had seen her – and so had Justin.

She saw that Wolf's men were trying to launch a boat, clearly intending to come and get her. But they were arguing amongst themselves, and before anything decisive could be done, a man dived into the sea and began to swim strongly to the shore. She knew that it was Justin and she stood at the water's edge, watching fearfully as he cut his way through the choppy waters of the sea to the sandbank. As Justin stood up to wade across the bank, she saw Wolf come to the rails of the *Sea Serpent*. He raised a rifle to his shoulder and took aim. He was trying to kill Justin!

Estelle screamed a warning, but it would have been too late had the shot not gone wide of its mark. It fell harmlessly into the water some distance away, and then Justin was in the lagoon, swimming the short distance to the shore. He waded through the shallows and she ran to meet him, laughing and crying at the same time as she threw herself into his arms.

'Justin, Justin my love,' she cried. 'Forgive me for putting you to so much trouble. I should have stayed in the house as you bid me.'

'Troublesome wench,' he muttered and then reached for her, holding her pressed against him as if he would crush her in the ferocity of his emotion. 'You deserve a good spanking.'

'Yes, I know,' she looked up at him, saw that he was smiling and raised her head for his kiss. 'I do not know why I went out there . . .'

'I do and it was not your fault,' he said. 'But . . .'

Whatever he had meant to say was lost, for one of Lafitte's ships had fired another warning shot at Wolf's vessel, and this time the top sail came crashing down. It was clear they did not intend to be denied. A series of flags had been run up, which Estelle knew meant they were demanding his surrender.

'He must surrender surely,' Estelle said. 'Now that he does not have me as his hostage . . .'

'You foolish wench,' Justin chided. 'Why did you jump into the sea when you cannot swim?'

'I can swim . . . a little,' she said, and laughed as he shook his head. 'I was determined that he should not use me to torment you – or to get his own way. I knew that while he held me, he had you at a disadvantage.'

'But you could have drowned. Besides which, there may be sharks in these waters.'

'I did not think of that,' Estelle said, a little shudder running through her as she realised what might have happened. 'And nor did you.' But of course he had known of the possibility and still he had come to her.

'We are both fools then,' he said, and put his arm around her. 'You are shivering. We can do nothing but wait, Estelle. But it should not be long.'

Another shot had been fired at Wolf's ship, bringing down the mizzenmast. As they watched they saw a fight break out on board, and it became clear that the crew were not prepared to sit and be slaughtered like sheep for no good reason. They had turned on their captain, and, standing on the shore, Justin and Estelle heard several shots. As they watched, they saw Wolf's body jerk as the balls entered his body, and then he slumped to the deck. Even as he fell, the flag for surrender

176

was already being run up, and a cheer went up from all the men on board.

'They must have hated him,' Estelle said, gazing up at Justin. She shivered, a feeling of horror creeping over her. 'Your men would not betray you so easily.'

'The men do not forget the way Wolf marooned their comrades on that island,' Justin said with a grim look. 'It is well done. He is dead and Sinita too. Wolf's ship will be auctioned at Grand Terre, and the profits divided between his crew.'

'Sinita is dead? Did you kill her?' Estelle's eyes were wide with shock.

'No, though I would have had not another done it for me. It was she who lured you into the garden. She called to you with her mind, making you believe you heard something I think?'

'Yes, that is true. I did feel compelled to go out into the garden,' Estelle said, wrinkling her brow as she remembered. 'It was strange but I felt that something was making me go outside – and then I heard Erle's voice calling to me. He told me that Jessie was ill and needed me. She isn't ill – is she?'

'No, she is well and waiting anxiously on board ship for you. I would have left her safely at Barataria until we had you back, but she insisted on coming for she said you would need looking after.'

'And she is right as always,' Estelle said laughing up to him. He thought how beautiful she was and how brave. 'Are all your enemies vanquished now, Justin?'

'I have a little matter to settle in New Orleans,' he said grimly. 'I should have dealt with Frank Erskine before – and then we shall sail for England.'

'Does he matter?' Estelle asked. 'We shall not be returning to New Orleans for a long time, perhaps we never shall. He used Wolf against us, but he would not dare to try anything himself. Let's forget him. I want to leave all this behind us, to be with you – and to be happy.'

A boat had been launched from Justin's ship, the men pulling strongly for the shore.

'Shall we swim out to the sandbank?' he said. 'The sooner we are on the ship, the sooner you can be dry.'

177

'If I can,' she said and pulled a wry face. 'I am not sure how I got here.'

'The instinct for survival,' he told her, the corners of his mouth quirking. Yet it had not been amusing when he had seen her struggling against the current, knowing that she might be sucked under before he could reach her. 'You were very brave, my love, though for a foolish cause. Yet I shall not scold you. Come, you have me to help you now. I shall not let you drown, I promise.'

She nodded, took his hand, wading out with him until the water was too deep, and then letting herself go with him, finding it easier now that he was by her side, guiding her, telling her how to breathe, how to kick and move.

'I'll have you swimming like a dolphin,' he told her as they neared the sandbank, where the boat was waiting to take them on board. 'When we return to our island.'

She smiled for she had no breath to do more, and then strong hands were reaching down for her, lifting her into the boat, and a blanket was placed around her shoulders. Justin put his arms about her, hugging her and rubbing her arms and back as she shivered.

'It's into bed with you as soon as we're on board,' he said. 'I dare say Jessie already has it ready and a hot toddy to warm you.'

Estelle smiled at him but said nothing. She thought that she wanted him in her bed to warm her, but could not tell him so in the presence of his men.

Soon she was being helped up the rope ladder to the deck of the *Dark Angel*, and Jessie was waiting close by with another dry blanket to replace the one that had become wet.

'What you want to go swimming for, chile,' she scolded. 'This ain't summer. You lucky them sharks didn't get you.'

Estelle smiled and let the scolding words flow over her head. She was used to Jessie making a fuss, but her eyes sought Justin's, wanting him to understand her need of him. He smiled in return but turned away, giving orders to the crew. There was no more need for them to linger. Lafitte's men were in charge now; they would take Wolf's ship back to Grand Terre.

Estelle let herself be hustled away by Jessie. In the cabin she stripped off her bodice and sodden petticoats, drying herself

178

on the towel Jessie had waiting for her, and jumping into the bed, which had been warmed with a hot brick.

'Now you just drink this, chile,' Jessie said, giving her a tankard filled with a spicy hot drink. 'That will keep the chill off and then you won't take no harm.'

Estelle sipped the drink gratefully. She could feel its heat seeping into her body, warming her, easing the cramp in her legs, making her feel sleepy.

'Ah is goin' to leave you to sleep now,' Jessie said in a crooning tone. 'You'se safe now, chile. Captain St Arnaud, he gonna take care of you good.'

'Yes,' Estelle agreed, smiled and closed her eyes.

She awoke some hours later to find Justin sitting by her bed. He seemed to be watching her, and she stretched like a sleepy kitten, looking up at him, smiling. All the aches she had felt earlier had gone and she was suddenly wide awake.

'How long have you been here?'

'An hour or so I suppose.'

'You should have woken me.'

'You were sleeping like a baby. Besides, I like watching you.'

'Jessie gave me something. It made me sleepy.'

'Yes, I know. It was probably the best thing.'

'The best thing?' Estelle shook her head, her eyes dark, languorous, full of invitation. 'I can think of something much better.'

The look she gave him was so full of wickedness that he laughed.

'And what is that, my love?' he asked, pretending not to understand.

Estelle sat up, reached out and pulled him towards her, kissing his lips, invading them with the tip of her tongue. 'This,' she whispered as he reached out to hold her against him. 'And more . . .'

'You want more?' His eyes mocked and yet adored her, his hand moving down the side of her cheek, caressing her as he bent his head to kiss her again. He gave her little pecking kisses that made her laugh and arch towards him, her body aching for his touch, begging to be loved, but then he shook

179

his head and sat back, regarding her thoughtfully. 'We do not wish to shock poor Jessie. I think we must restrain ourselves until we are married, my love.'

'Do you truly wish to marry me?'

'Yes, I truly wish to marry you – but not until I have settled my business in England. After that, we shall be free to go wherever we want and do as we wish. The world will be ours, Estelle.'

'And until then you will not make love to me?'

She looked so disappointed that Justin laughed. 'A gentleman would not do so, Estelle, and a lady would not let him even if he tried.'

'Then you are no gentleman and I am no lady,' Estelle said and pouted at him. 'I do not want to wait so long, Justin – and whatever you do could not be wrong in Jessie's eyes. I think you have enslaved her with your charms.'

His laughter was warm, husky and joyous as he drew her to him, kissing her throat, moving slowly, tantalisingly, down to the sweet cleavage between her breasts, and then further, his tongue circling the nipples delicately so that they stood erect, sensitised to his caress. And then she was clinging to him, offering the warmth of her body to him, melting into his flesh as he stripped off his clothes and lay down beside her, holding her to him.

Silken thighs pressed against the harder thighs of the man, his downy with soft hair and slightly tanned, hers a pure cream of melting loveliness that opened eagerly to receive him. Their loving was tender, long and slow, each taking time to explore the other with searching hands and kisses, lingering in this sensuous dance of love, until at last they reached a wondrous place. Afterwards, they lay side by side, Justin's hands still caressing her, stroking the satin arch of her back, whispering words of love against her ear.

To Estelle it seemed all too soon that he told her regretfully that he must return to the deck. 'The ship does not sail itself, my love,' he said. 'And I must be there to watch over the men. Much as I might wish it, I cannot spend all day in your bed.'

'But you will spend your nights here?'

He laughed, his eyes dark with desire as he gazed down at

her lovely face. 'I shall spend as much of them here as I can,' he promised, 'and now I must leave you.'

Estelle lay where she was for some minutes after he had gone. Justin loved her, wanted her to be his wife, but would his love be strong enough to accept that she was merely a bastard? The child of her father's mistress – a free woman of colour.

He had promised to marry her, but perhaps it might be better if they were to continue as they were. She was his mistress and she was content to be so. She had not told him her secret, and now it hung heavy on her conscience. Justin had the blood of the English aristocracy in his veins. Would he want to take his place in their society when they reached England?

If that was his intention, then she must tell him the truth, for she was not the kind of wife he needed. They had been happy together on board his ship, and particularly on the island, but she did not think she could fit into the world to which he truly belonged.

The time was coming when she would be forced to tell him the truth, but not yet. For now she would take all the happiness that came her way for it might have to last her a lifetime.

Twelve

Estelle stood on board the ship looking towards the shore. The harbour at Bristol was a hive of activity, ships loading and unloading, people coming and going, shouting to each other and waving. Justin had gone on shore an hour earlier to make arrangements for their journey, but now she could see him on the harbour and it looked as if he was preparing to be rowed out to the ship.

Her heart beat wildly. It had been a voyage of some weeks, weeks that she had wished might go on forever. Justin had spent most of the day on deck, and she had spent some of her time there too, watching him or simply looking at the waves and enjoying the feel of the fresh air in her face. There was something truly thrilling about being at sea, watching the sails as they caught the wind, and feeling the ship move through the water. She sometimes thought that she could sail with Justin for the rest of her life and never want for more.

They had spent a few hours on shore at Kingston, but that was now a distant memory and for a long time the days had blurred into each other in an endless idyll of blue skies, sunshine and warm winds. Then, all at once, the weather had changed, becoming colder, the sky grey and the waves rough and treacherous as they battered themselves against the ship.

For the first time, Estelle found herself wishing that their voyage might end, and she had been relieved when they dropped anchor in this English harbour. Overhead the skies were dark and threatening, making her feel somehow uneasy. She did not think she liked this country they had come to. Now she had begun to feel nervous as she wondered what would happen once they went on shore.

Justin said he had some business at an estate some leagues inland.

'We shall go to Blechingfield House for a short visit,' Justin told her. 'I must speak with my uncle, and then we shall go on to London by carriage – I shall buy you many pretty gowns there, Estelle, and you shall have anything your heart desires.'

All her heart desired was to be with Justin, but she had merely smiled and said nothing, for she was afraid – afraid that the time was coming when she might lose him.

Justin's plans to visit the marquis had been laid carefully. He would take Sam with him to guard his back, for he was no green youth to fall into his uncle's trap this time. He had been thinking of this day for many years, and had prepared for it, having employed agents to purchase a house in London. It was there that he would take Estelle after his business here was finished. And then they would be married.

He intended a wedding trip to Paris, and then, according to her wishes, they would decide where their settled home would be. His fleet of ships was growing, and there was no necessity for Justin to sail the *Dark Angel* himself. He could if he wished leave that to another, and it was in his mind that while they stayed in Bristol, he might look for a good man to take over as captain. Sam was trustworthy, but he had no knowledge of charts or sextants, though he could chart a course by the stars as well as any man. Besides, he might wish to give up the sea if Justin was no longer his captain.

Vague plans for the future had formed in Justin's mind. He knew his own preferences, but believed that Estelle must decide. Although she had accepted all the hardships of these past months without complaint, she had been reared as a lady, and must long for a nice home and pretty clothes to wear. It would not be right for him to deny her those things, nor to force her to accept the life he would prefer.

He had secured lodgings for them in Bristol, for it was a journey of no more than an hour or so to his uncle's estate and he intended to return afterwards. He would visit the next day, taking Estelle, Jessie and Sam with him. His purpose was to discover why his uncle had conspired to have him beaten and abducted, but not to quarrel with him. Although the motive must have been that the marquis wished to be rid of his brother's bastard, Justin could not understand why his uncle had hated him so.

It no longer mattered that it had happened, for he had made his own life and a good one. He merely wished to know the reason why so that he might put it behind him.

Estelle caught her breath as the grand house came into view at last. It seemed ages since they had passed through the gates of the Blechingfield estate. Could all this land belong to one man? Her own father had been wealthy once, but he had never aspired to something like this. Her sense of unease was growing as the carriage came to a halt at the front of the house.

'Is this truly your uncle's house, Justin?'

'Yes, it belongs to the marquis,' Justin replied a little nerve twitching at the side of his temple. He nodded to Sam, who marched up to the door and rapped sharply with the heavy iron knocker. 'My father's younger brother.'

It was a moment or two before the impressive front door

183

was opened to reveal a small, elderly man dressed all in black. He stared at Sam in astonishment, clearly never having seen anyone like him before.

'Captain St Arnaud wishes to see his uncle the Marquis of Blechingfield,' Sam announced in a sonorous voice.

'Justin St Arnaud . . . my master's nephew that disappeared?' the old man said in a quavering voice. He looked beyond Sam to Justin, his gaze narrowing. 'Is it truly you, sir? We thought you must be dead long since. You went off so suddenly and no one knew why.'

'I believe someone knew why,' Justin said, coming forward as he recognised the man, who was much aged since they last met. 'I would like to see my uncle please, Henderson.'

'I fear that will not be possible,' the butler said with a sigh of regret. 'My master died ten days ago.'

'My uncle is dead?'

'Yes, sir, of a terrible wasting sickness that kept him to his bed for many months – and the lawyers have begun a search for you since you are the rightful owner of this estate.'

'What?' Justin was startled. 'How can this be? I am surely not my uncle's heir. There must be cousins – distant relations – someone to inherit the title.'

'As to that, sir, I cannot say. I know only that my master's lawyer came to the funeral four days ago. He told me that he had in his possession papers which proved that you were the legal owner – and that he was duty bound to begin a search for you.'

'Indeed?' Justin frowned. 'And where may this gentleman be found?'

'In London at his chambers I daresay. You had best come in, my lord,' the butler said. 'For Mr Barraclough left a letter here that I was to give you should you happen to call.'

'Yes, we shall come in,' Justin said. 'You may have the housekeeper bring us refreshments if you please, and I shall read this letter.' He turned to Estelle, who was looking at him with a mixture of what looked to be horror and disbelief. 'Come, my love,' he said, holding out his hand to her. 'This is not what I expected but a mystery yet to be solved.'

Estelle took his hand, allowing him to draw her into the house. The hall was very large, with a high-domed ceiling,

184

marble flooring and a grand staircase that wound its way in stately magnificence to the floor above. To her surprise the butler led them up those stairs and along the hall to a salon of huge proportions. A fire had been lit in the open hearth but it hardly took the chill from the room. She shivered, looking round with apprehension at the elegant furniture, the mirrors, pictures, exquisite chandeliers. It was too cold, too formal to be comfortable, and she stood in front of the fire, holding her hands to the flames.

'Yes, it is cold in here,' Justin remarked. 'I remember it always was, even in summer. However, there are other smaller rooms where we might be more comfortable. I shall order fires lit there for us.'

'Are we going to stay here?' She felt a sinking sensation inside. She did not like this house. She did not belong here!

'Perhaps it might be better than the inn at Bristol, at least for a few days. I had made other arrangements for I did not think we should be welcome here in this house, but it seems that things have changed.'

'I thought we were going to London?'

'We shall – when my business is finished here.' He glanced at the butler. 'You will bring me the letter? And ask the house-keeper to attend us here.'

'Of course, my lord.'

'I am not the marquis, Henderson. Captain will do well enough.'

'Yes, sir. As you wish.'

Justin glanced around the room as the butler withdrew. It had changed little in the last few years, the colours as sombre as they had been when he came here as a green youth. He had thought it dreary then and so it was, but it could be made comfortable he supposed.

'Would you like something to drink?' He examined the decanters ranged on the large silver charger on the sideboard. Each had an enamelled and gilt label, revealing their contents. 'It would appear there is port, sherry or brandy.' He turned to look at Estelle, who had a white, pinched look about her and was clearly ill at ease.

'No, thank you, nothing – perhaps some coffee?'

Justin grimaced. 'As I remember the English make terrible

coffee. I should ask for tea or chocolate if I were you – or perhaps some wine.'

'Something warm please.'

'I shall ask the housekeeper when she comes. You are missing the sunshine of New Orleans, Estelle, but tomorrow may be warmer. England has a strange climate. Never two days the same, which is just as well for otherwise the inhabitants would be left with little to say to one another. It is their main topic of conversation after all.'

She nodded but did not smile, though she knew he had intended to amuse her with his comment. Like her father, and most Frenchmen, Justin had little love for the English – or that had been her belief until now. She felt a sense of growing unease as she looked about her. If Justin had inherited all this he would naturally wish to take advantage of it and she was not sure that she could ever settle in this place.

The housekeeper came bustling in then, her manner eager and inquisitive. It was obvious that she believed her new master had come home and was anxious to please.

Justin ordered wine, cakes and hot chocolate for them, telling her that he would require the master suite prepared for them that night, and that fires should be lit in every reception room.

'My lady is cold for she is unused to this climate,' he said. 'We must make the house warm for her, madame.'

'Yes, certainly, Captain St Arnaud. I shall have fires lit in the master suite immediately and then in all the best reception rooms.' She looked curiously at Estelle before she curtsied and then went out.

'She is wondering who I am,' Estelle said.

'I shall let it be known that you are my fiancée,' Justin replied with a nod. 'The English are very proper about these things, we must not shock them too much.'

Again he was smiling, trying to amuse her with his sly comments. She nodded, but her face was pale, strained, and she said nothing. He began to realise that she was unusually quiet.

'Is something wrong?'

Estelle shook her head. Even if she had known how to explain her feelings she could not for the butler had returned.

He was carrying a silver salver on which lay a letter with

an important looking wax seal. His manner was so respectful towards Justin that Estelle knew a sudden desire to laugh. It was in such contrast to the way they lived on board the *Dark Angel*. Justin's men respected and admired him, but they met him on equal terms. He had always preferred it that way, for though he would order a man flogged for breaking the rules by which they all sailed, he bore no prejudices. Sometimes there had been squabbles amongst the crew, and occasionally a fight had broken out, but was usually quelled without much trouble. The men lived by mutual respect, and most obeyed the laws of the sea and the brotherhood. Those who broke them could find themselves severely punished.

Everything was different here. She felt stifled, unable to be herself. It was all so strange, so cold and unwelcoming that Estelle longed to be back on board the ship.

Justin took the letter, waved the servant away and broke the seal. He spent several minutes reading the letter, which consisted of two separate sheets, going back to the beginning and seeming to read it again, as if he could not quite comprehend it. Indeed, he was silent for so long that she broke the silence.

'What does it say? May I know?'

'Apparently, the estate of Blechingfield was not entailed on the next of kin as many English estates are. My father made his own fortune and bought this estate, his own inheritance from the former marquis a small place in the country, which was passed on to my uncle at his death.' Justin's expression was grim as he looked at her. 'My father left everything else to me but my uncle hid the will and claimed none had been made, therefore inheriting all that should have been mine. There is also a letter my father wrote to me shortly before his death. It was only when my uncle was on his deathbed that he revealed these things to Mr Barraclough and gave him the documents that make me the legal owner of this estate. It seems his misdeeds played on his conscience when he was ill and he revealed the documents, which for some reason known only to him he had not destroyed.'

Estelle stared at him, feeling shocked. How different Justin's life might have been if his uncle had not kept his inheritance from him.

'So it should always have been yours? Your uncle cheated you of your rights?'

'Yes, it would seem that way. It is clear to me now why he tried to get rid of me. He feared that somehow I would discover the truth, and take the estate away from him.'

'Your uncle tried to get rid of you?' Estelle stared at him in surprise for he had never told her this before.

'He paid men to beat me, abduct me and send me off to the West Indies, where he hoped I would die. Fortunately for me, the man they chose to sell me to as crew became a good friend to me. He had me nursed back to health, and then he took me under his wing, teaching me to read the charts and use a sextant. I learned my trade from Robbie and have been grateful for it.'

'Did you know that it was your uncle who had had you abducted?'

'Yes, for I heard something when I was lying in a semi-conscious state, and one of the men who abducted me told Robbie that the man who had paid them was rich and powerful. I suspected it must be my uncle for I hardly knew anyone else in England, but I never understood why he had done it.'

'He must have been a wicked man,' Estelle said, feeling horrified by the story. 'Why did you come here today? Was it for revenge?'

'No, merely to learn the truth,' Justin told her, a grim slant to his mouth. 'What happened that day has haunted me for years, though I had put it behind me. Yet still I needed to know, to understand why a man, who had seemed to welcome me to his home, hated me so much that he would pay to be rid of me.'

'And now that you know the truth – can you forgive?'

'Forgive?' Justin considered. 'No, I do not think that something like that can be forgiven, Estelle. He lied to me when I came here seeking my father. I wanted nothing from him. I needed only to know the truth of my birth, to understand why my mother had betrayed her husband with this English marquis. My uncle smiled and kissed me, told me that he had known of me and hoped to meet me one day, made me welcome in his house – and then betrayed me. I would have preferred honesty. Had he thrust me from his door, rejected me at once, then I could have accepted it – but his falseness made me distrustful of others. It blighted my life, and had I not been lucky enough to meet Robbie, I might have become bitter and twisted.'

There had been other reasons besides his uncle's betrayal that had taught him to distrust others, but Justin would not tell her that. It was something Estelle did not need to know, for she had wiped away the hurt that a green youth had experienced at the hands of a woman he had been foolish enough to believe he loved.

'Will you be able to forget?'

Justin saw the anxious look in her eyes and smiled, coming to her as she stood before the fire. A little colour had come back to her cheeks, and he thought again how lovely she was as he bent his head to kiss her.

'It is already forgotten,' he told her. 'We shall put the past behind us, my love, and look to the future – our future. I think we shall stay here a few days – no longer than a week – for there may be things I ought to investigate as master here. I owe it to my father to see that his estate is cared for in the manner he would wish, which may mean that I shall have to speak to agents and bailiffs. But then we shall go to London, where I already have a house, and we shall enjoy the season. I daresay I can find someone to introduce us into society so that you will have a chance to show off all the pretty gowns I intend to buy you, Estelle.'

It seemed that he had the future planned for them. Estelle knew that she must smile and appear to be pleased, for if not she must explain why she felt ill at ease, and she was not ready to do that just yet.

'It will be pleasant to spend some time on land again,' she said, forcing a smile. 'If the weather improves I should like to go walking. I glimpsed a park and a lake as we came here I think.'

'Oh yes, there is a lake,' Justin said. 'Do you ride, Estelle? My uncle kept a good stable and I am sure we could mount you.'

'A little,' she said uncertainly. 'As a child I rode often, but in later years I was more often driven in a carriage – unless I walked. Papa did not encourage me to walk out alone in New Orleans, but as you know, I often did so.'

189

'I remember well,' he said and smiled at her. 'It was seeing you in that part of the town that made me think you something you were not. Have you ever forgiven me for that, my love?'

'Yes,' she said. The mischief in his eyes made her want to throw her arms about him, but before she could follow her impulse, the door opened and the housekeeper returned with two maids. Each of them was carrying large trays, which they set upon small stands near the fire.

'A fire has been lit in your apartments, Captain,' the woman told them. 'I shall be happy to conduct ... your lady there myself when she is ready.'

'Ah yes,' Justin said. 'I do not know your name, madame?'

'Mrs Greene, sir.'

'Of course.' He smiled at her. 'Mademoiselle Lebrun is my betrothed. We intend to be married quite soon. We shall ring for you when we are ready. You may leave us now.'

The housekeeper bobbed a curtsey to them, glancing at Estelle once more before ushering the maids out of the room before her.

'Your servants think me a fallen woman and unworthy of you,' Estelle said. 'And it is true. I do not think we should marry, Justin. It is better than I remain your mistress.'

'What nonsense is this?'

'It is just what I think ...' She looked at him, seeing the glint of anger in his eyes. 'You are rich and powerful and I ...' Her voice failed her for she did not know how to continue. 'You should marry a lady from the English aristocracy.'

'I shall do no such thing,' he said. 'This is mere irritation of the nerves, Estelle. You are more upset by this climate than I thought. I want to hear no more of this nonsense. We shall be married as soon as I have finished my business here.'

Estelle busied herself with pouring a glass of wine for him, and a cup of chocolate for herself. He would see the sense of her reasoning when she told him the truth, but she was not quite ready to reveal her secret just yet.

Justin was determined that she should be able to ride properly as a lady should, and he had summoned a seamstress from Bristol to make her a riding habit.

'The woman is a French émigré,' he told Estelle. 'She is talented and will supply you with a few clothes for you to wear when we go to London. We shall buy more there, but you will need something to carry you through until then.'

Besides the fittings for all the new gowns Justin seemed to think she would want simply for their first few days in London, she was given riding lessons by a young man who had been recommended by one of Justin's neighbours. The news of his arrival had gone quickly around the area, and several invitations to dine at the houses of some important people had arrived almost at once.

Justin seemed always to be occupied with estate business these days, leaving Estelle much to her own company. He *had* introduced her to his agent, who was in charge of the day to day business, and the young man dined with them on their first evening at Blechingfield House. He was pleasant and treated Estelle with the deference due to her as Justin's future wife, as did her riding master. Yet sometimes she thought she caught a glimpse of contempt in the housekeeper's eyes.

Estelle was accustomed to entertaining her father's business friends, and entertaining Justin's agent or the neighbours who came to call was no different. Indeed, she thought it easier than being alone with Justin, for her secret weighed heavily on her mind. She must find a way of telling him why they could never marry.

The people who came to visit were friendly enough, but she sensed that they came out of curiosity, and that they whispered about her in private. She saw disapproval in the eyes of some of the ladies, and knew that they thought her shameless to live here with Justin without family or chaperone to protect her good name.

It did not matter that Justin introduced her as his betrothed, her situation was obvious, and when they understood that she had come from New Orleans in his ship with only her maid, they were shocked. She had broken all the conventions because she was unmarried, and for a single girl to become a man's mistress was social ruin. She saw condemnation, even disgust, in their eyes, but pride carried her through. She would not give these proud ladies the satisfaction of knowing she was hurt.

As the days passed and they met more and more of the people who would be their neighbours, Estelle became convinced that she would never feel at home here. She did not like these people with their cold, reserved manners and their long noses, down which they seemed to look at her with contempt.

She longed for the carefree time they had spent on Justin's ship, and sometimes at night when he was not with her, she wept into her pillow. It was no use. She could not marry him, and she must tell him so – but if she told him that these people made her feel uncomfortable he would merely laugh and say she must not be foolish. The only course open to her was to tell him the truth.

'Must we go to this dinner party this evening?' Estelle asked as Justin came into the bedroom towards the end of that week. They had separate rooms, as was the English custom, but he most often slept in her bed, leaving her before the servants were about in the morning. 'We seem not to have had a moment to ourselves since we got here.'

'It will not be long now,' he said with a little frown. 'Are you not happy here, Estelle?'

'I am happy with you,' she said. 'But I do not like this house. It is too big and too cold.'

'Yes, I know,' Justin said, and pulled a wry face. 'Yet I owe it to the people who live here to make sure that it continues to run properly in our absence. Be patient, my love. In only another day or so we shall be in London. I think you will prefer the house I bought there through my agents. It will be more what you were accustomed to in New Orleans, and you will make friends – particularly once we are married.'

Estelle turned away. She was fastening the clasp of her emerald necklace, but discovered her fingers were all thumbs. Justin came to assist her, fastening the little gold clasp and kissing the back of her neck.

'You look beautiful,' he said, looking at their reflection in the dressing mirror. 'Everyone will be envying me this evening.'

Estelle felt the prick of tears. He was so loving to her but she felt so unhappy. How could she risk losing him? She wanted to tell him again that it was impossible for them to

192

marry, but she forced a smile to her lips and picked up her shawl.

'Then I suppose we had better leave.'

If anything, the house at which they dined that evening was even colder than the one they had left to come here. Estelle looked about her, watching the men and women talking and laughing. Some of the men were wearing paint on their faces as were the women, and their manners left something to be desired in her opinion. The men often spoke with their mouths full, spitting food when they became excited and laughed out loud at some jest. Some of the ladies were little better – but they had an even worse fault in Estelle's opinion; it was their spiteful tongues. They seemed to delight in gossip and to enjoy tearing the reputations of their acquaintances to pieces.

The time Estelle dreaded was when the ladies were obliged to leave the gentlemen to their port and brandy. She knew that once they had removed to the drawing room most of the ladies would ignore her.

That evening she chose a seat by the window where she could gaze out at the garden. The one thing she had learned to admire in this country was the English garden, which could often be extremely beautiful.

'Do you like gardens?'

Estelle was surprised to hear the woman's voice and looked up. It was not often that the other ladies bothered to speak to her. This woman was perhaps ten or twelve years her senior but very beautiful, with blonde hair dressed high in curls on her head, leaving one ringlet to fall on her milk-white shoulders. Her jewels were magnificent, her gown an example of her dressmaker's finest art, and her eyes were a curious green, rather like a cat's and slanted at the corners. She wore a small black dot on her cheek, which was an artificial beauty spot and apparently much admired amongst society ladies.

'Yes, madame, very much. I have seen some lovely gardens since we came here.'

'The grounds at Blechingfield are very fine, though someone with knowledge of landscaping might improve them. My own have recently been much improved,' the woman told her and smiled as she sat down on the sofa next to Estelle. 'I do not think we have been introduced – I am Lady Helena Stockport. You are Mademoiselle Lebrun I am told, and your father was French, a gentleman of New Orleans.'

'Yes, madame, I mean Lady Helena.'

'Why not Helena?' the woman asked sweetly. 'I see no reason why we should not be friends, do you?'

'Not if you wish it,' Estelle said. It was the first time one of these proud ladies had tried to make friends with her.

'But of course,' Lady Helena said. 'I have been a regular visitor at Blechingfield for many years, and I would wish it to continue. When I was very young I met Captain St Arnaud and we became . . . friends. He was young himself then, and had no experience of the sea I think.'

'No, I believe you are right, madame,' Estelle said, for she did not wish to say anything that might reveal Justin's secrets.

'He has become quite famous as a merchant adventurer,' Lady Helena said and there was an odd smile on her lips. 'Some whisper that he was once a privateer and that he fought against us at the Battle of New Orleans along with that wicked pirate Lafitte, though I do not know if it be true. I was much amused when I learned that Blechingfield was rightfully Justin's inheritance.'

'Were you, madame?' Estelle looked at her, realising for the first time that her smile was rather sly. 'Why was that?'

'Oh . . .' Lady Helena gave a little shrug of her magnificent shoulders. 'There was a time when he was madly in love with me. He begged me to marry him, but I was unable to accept. I was recently widowed at the time and my husband had left me without sufficient money to live the life I preferred. I needed to marry a fortune, you see. And at that time poor Justin had nothing.'

Estelle felt the pain shaft through her. Justin had been in love with this lady. It was unlikely then that he could truly be in love with her.

'Had you known you might have married him, madame.'

'Yes, but that would have been a pity,' Lady Helena said, her eyes going to the doorway as the gentlemen began to come in. Justin stood for a moment on the threshold, his eyes searching the room. He was an impressive man, his figure

194

powerful beneath the elegant clothes he wore so easily. 'He was a boy then and unsophisticated. I think I prefer the man he has become.'

'It is a pity that you married again, madame.' Estelle's eyes glinted with anger. Now she understood why this woman had singled her out. It was not to make friends with her, but to let her know that Justin had once been madly in love with her.

'Oh, but that ended when my second husband died,' Lady Helena said with a little smile. 'I was left with sufficient funds the second time, you see, and I did not think it worth my while to marry a third time – of course one can always change one's mind.' She gave a false laugh, which made Estelle want to strike her.

The malice in her face told Estelle quite clearly that she meant to have Justin for herself. She had introduced herself that evening for the sole purpose of firing an opening shot. It seemed that in speaking so plainly, she had decided that Estelle was no danger to her and she was confident of making Justin fall in love with her once more.

'It has been pleasant talking to you, mademoiselle,' Lady Helena said and stood up. 'Please excuse me.'

Estelle watched as she glided across the room, waylaying Justin as he came to her, her hand touching his arm playfully, her smile wickedly enticing as she looked at him.

Justin hesitated for a moment, seeming surprised that she had spoken to him. He frowned, inclined his head, and then made some excuse to leave her, making his way unhurriedly towards Estelle.

'Has Lady Helena been talking to you?' he asked as he sat next to Estelle.

'Yes, for a few moments before you came.'

'What did she say to you?'

'Does it matter?'

'It might,' he said. 'Just remember that whatever happened is in the past, Estelle. All that is behind us and I have no wish to remember it.' Once that woman had shamed and humiliated a young man who believed himself in love. He had felt nothing for her this evening. Not even hatred.

'She is very beautiful, Justin.'

'I thought so once, yes,' he replied. 'The years have not

been kind to her. There are lines of malice about her eyes and mouth.'

'Do you really not admire her?'

'She is well enough – but I do not admire her or what she stands for, Estelle. There are some women who are cold at heart and can never be any different. I prefer the warmth of my New Orleans lady.'

'Truly?' She gazed anxiously into his eyes.

'Truly. Why will you not believe me?'

'Because you do not know the whole truth,' Estelle said. 'There is something I must tell you, Justin. It is the reason I can never marry you.'

'Nonsense! No reason on earth would prevent me from making you my wife, and the sooner the better. At least then I may be saved the flattery of mercenary predators like Lady Helena.'

Estelle laughed, her heart leaping for joy. He did not love that cold beauty, he loved her. Perhaps he even loved her enough to accept what she must tell him.

'I should like to leave,' she said. 'Would it seem rude if we went now? I think it is time I told you everything.'

'Your terrible secret?' Justin's eyes sparkled with mischief, but then, seeing her serious look, he stood up and taking her hand drew her to her feet. 'I came here this evening only for you, because I believed it might give you pleasure. If you are ready to leave we shall go.'

'Tell me then,' Justin said, as they stood together in her bedroom a little later. 'What is it that makes you look so stricken, my love? Why do you deny it when I say that we shall be married?'

'In New Orleans it would have been unlawful,' Estelle told him, her hands trembling so much that she gripped them behind her. 'It was for this reason that my father never married my mother, though he loved her until she died, and kept her memory sacred.'

'Your father was not married to your mother? Is that your secret, Estelle, that you are a bastard? You know that I have the same history. Why should that be an impediment to our union?'

'My father met Leah for the first time at a Quadroon Ball,'

Estelle went on, her face pale. 'I knew nothing of this until he lay dying. He loved Leah but he would not marry her for it would have broken the code by which he lived, and the laws which the Sieur De Bienville signed in the first years of the settlement. He married a French girl for he wanted an heir for his fortune, but she died and her child died with her. My mother died giving birth to me on the same day, and my father took me. He brought me up as the child of his wife, and no one knew of his secret – though after his death there were some whispers.'

Justin nodded, for he recalled something André de Varennes had said in his cups. 'Yes, I see that your father was in difficulty for he had as you say broken his own code, and had the secret been learned by his enemies it might have caused him some problems – but I do not see what any of this has to do with us.'

'But you must see that we cannot marry,' Estelle said, her voice catching with tears. 'I love you, Justin, and I know that you love me – but you cannot marry me. If this was to become known, it could be awkward for you in your new position. Everyone is ready to accept you into their society because of who and what you are – but to have a free woman of colour as your . . .'

'Damn it!' Justin pressed his fingers to her lips before she could continue. 'If I did not know how much this hurts you I should be angry,' he said, and his eyes glinted with sudden temper. 'I am insulted that you should imagine I would let such a slight thing weigh with me. Hurt that you hold my love so low that you think I could be swayed by the opinion of these people. To hell with them and their society. If they will not have you for what you are, they may go to the devil.'

'Justin . . .' Estelle stared at him. 'I pray you will not be angry with me. I thought only of you, of your wish to return to the society from which you came.'

'The society that cast me out because I was a bastard?' Justin glared at her. 'St Arnaud threw me out of his house after destroying my memory of my mother and inflicting a deep hurt that lived with me for a long time. I came here in search of my father – and it seems that he at least cared enough to make provision for his son – and my uncle tried to have me murdered. Do you imagine that I would give you up for any of this – that these people could mean more to me than you?'

'Oh, Justin . . .' Her throat tightened as she gazed up into his dark eyes, tears hovering on her lashes. 'Forgive me. I was wrong to deny you. I thought . . .'

'You thought me a fool who cared more for worldly treasures than the pure gold that comes from true loving.'

'No . . .' She tried to explain and could not, but then she saw that it did not matter. Justin understood and he loved her. Nothing could break this bond that bound them, and she knew that she was blessed beyond measure. 'So what do you want, Justin?'

'First I must go to London,' he told her. 'There are certain arrangements I must make concerning this estate. I wish to see Mr Barraclough and read my father's letter. Since I have no use for Blechingfield, it should go to the man who would have inherited it had it been entailed. There is it seems a distant cousin of my father's still living. I understand that he is a decent man, who will care for the people and the estate, and so he shall have it with my blessing.'

'You will give the estate away?' She stared at him in shock, for few men would give away so much to a man they did not even know.

'I have more than sufficient wealth for our needs,' Justin said and smiled at her. 'I intend that we shall be married in London, Estelle, and then I want to take you to France. We shall buy all the pretty things you need to make a home there – and then you must decide. Where would you wish to live? Shall we return to New Orleans or stay in France? England is too cold a climate for you, but you might be happier in France.'

'Is that your wish?'

'No, but it will suffice if you should wish for it.'

'May I tell you what I truly wish?'

'Yes, of course, my love. I want to make you happy. Tell me what you want and I shall try to give it to you.'

So she told him and Justin's laughter rang out long and joyfully, for it was exactly what he wanted himself.

Thirteen

'Have you enjoyed your stay in Paris?' Justin asked as they returned from the opera that evening. 'Has it pleased you to have all the young bucks running after you at every occasion?'

'It was pleasant enough,' Estelle said and laughed up at him. If she had been beautiful before their marriage she was dazzling now. When he looked at her, Justin felt such pride and love that he knew that this world could contain no greater happiness than sharing his life with her. She had given him back all that he had lost on the day of his mother's death, and that had been helped by his father's letter, which had explained the love affair with Madame St Arnaud. It seemed that it was indeed love, and that though they fought their feelings, they had conducted an affair, which lasted but six short months, though the love they felt for one another was lifelong. 'But there is not one of them could compare with you, Justin,' she said, bringing his thoughts back to the present.

'Now you flatter me,' he said and bent his head to kiss her lingeringly on the mouth. 'I daresay there are a hundred gentlemen that would prove you wrong if you cared to put them to the test.'

'For me there is only you,' she whispered, reaching up to tangle her arms about his neck. The perfume that was uniquely hers was so enticing that he swept her up in his arms, carrying her to their bed, where he began to kiss her in all the warm and tender places of her lovely body.

Afterwards, when they could think rationally again, Justin stroked the arch of her back, their bodies pressed close together.

'Are you ready to leave France?' he asked. 'I have two ships loaded with their cargoes, and they will go on ahead of us.

We shall follow in a few days – if you are sure it is what you want?'

'You know it is,' she snuggled up to him, nuzzling against his shoulder. 'Yes, I have enjoyed being here, Justin. The climate is warmer, and I have found the people more welcoming.' And perhaps that was because as the wife of a wealthy man all doors were opened to her. Here in France she had not been treated to the cold disdain that she had experienced in England. 'But you know what we want – what we both want.'

'To sail together aboard the *Dark Angel*,' Justin said. 'Sometimes we shall live at our house in New Orleans, just for a little while so that you can see those friends you still care for – but most of the time we shall live on our island. You are certain you would not rather stay here in France?'

'I have had a wonderful time here,' she said. 'And it will be nice to see Tante Rosemarie when we are in New Orleans, and perhaps a few others – but I am happiest on board the ship or on our island.'

'Then we shall build our house there,' Justin said. 'Lafitte has his own little kingdom on Grand Terre and we shall have ours. My ships will bring us cargoes and we shall trade with the Windward and Leeward Islands, and also Cartagena. People we like will be free to live on our island in houses they build for themselves – but we shall have no one there that we do not like, and everyone will live by the rules that govern us all or pay the consequences.'

'You speak as if you were a king,' she said teasing him. 'Indeed, I think you may become a despot given time and opportunity.'

'Not while I have you to bring me back to earth, Estelle,' he said and kissed her. 'So, the decision is made. We leave here in five days time. We sail first for New Orleans, and after that our island. Our men should have made a start on building us somewhere to shelter – though we shall not begin our grand house until we have secured the services of a master builder in New Orleans.'

'Do you intend a palace, Justin?' Her lips pouted at him, her dark eyes bright with mischief.

'A house that will make you happy,' he said. 'Not a cold,

draughty mansion like Blechingfield but a pretty sunlit house that will welcome us home when we return from a voyage.'

'We want it long and low,' Estelle said, 'with white plastered walls and windows that open to the sun.'

'And shutters so that we can keep it cool when necessary,' said the practical Justin. 'In New Orleans we shall find a master builder to draw it for us, my love, and then, if we can persuade him, he shall come with us and see it through to the end.'

'I am sure that you will find someone,' she said and kissed him. 'But before we leave I should like to go shopping one more time . . .'

'I thought that we should never meet again,' Tante Rosemarie said as she sipped her tea in the parlour of the house that had once belonged to Estelle's father. 'It is a pleasure to see you looking so well and happy again, my dear. Life on board ship clearly suits you, you are blooming. I have thought about you often, worried that you might be unhappy or alone.'

'And I have thought of you,' Estelle told her. 'And I have hit upon a plan that I think might appeal to you. As I told you, it is not our intention to live in New Orleans. We may visit for a few weeks now and then, if we have a cargo to sell here. As that would leave the house empty for long periods, I wondered if you would do us the favour of living here as our guest.'

'Live here?' Tante Rosemarie looked at her in surprise. 'I have always liked this house, and it would suit me better than living with my brother. I get on well enough with him – but Suzanne is difficult.'

'She has not improved in her temper since the birth of her child?'

'Unfortunately, she fell for another baby almost immediately,' Tante Rosemarie said, 'and she is carrying this one with more difficulty than the last. She is always in a mood and André has quite lost his patience with her.'

'I am sorry for it,' Estelle said. 'So may I tell Justin that you will grant us this favour?'

Tante Rosemarie laughed. 'I should be a fool to turn such an offer down, should I not? And I think the favour is yours to me, not mine to you, my dear. It is very generous of you.'

201

'We do not wish to sell the house, and if you are here it will always seem like a home when we come to visit. During my time of grief you became a good friend to me, dear Rosemarie.'

'Then of course I shall accept with pleasure.'

'I am so glad,' Estelle said. 'But you said there was something you wished to speak to Justin about. I am sorry he was not here to receive you, but he has an appointment with a master builder. We are trying to find someone who will build us a beautiful house on our island.'

'I came to warn Captain St Arnaud to be careful,' Tante Rosemarie said. 'My brother heard something when he was at his office the other day. It concerns Mr Erskine, my dear.'

'He would not try to abduct me again! Not now?' Estelle's face had turned pale, and for a moment she felt sick. The memory of that terrible night when she had been a prisoner on Wolf's ship had faded, but it still lingered in a corner of her mind to torment her.

'No, I do not imagine he dare try that now,' Tante Rosemarie said. 'For my brother would have something to say to that as would others in this community. You are married now, my dear, and must be treated with respect. However, Mr Erskine has not forgiven Justin for interfering in his business and he may try to harm him in some way.'

'You think Justin is in some danger?'

'I cannot be sure,' Tante Rosemarie said with a little frown. 'I know only that my brother heard a whisper. Erskine plans something, though I do not know what or where it may happen.'

'I thank you for warning us,' Estelle said. 'It was good of you to come and tell me.'

'My brother would have spoken to Justin himself, but he is very busy. Things have not gone too well for his business of late, and he is working very hard to put things right.'

'I am very sorry to hear that,' Estelle said. 'Is there anything we can do for him?'

'I am sure it is only temporary,' Tante Rosemarie said. 'I believe there has been some trouble on the waterfront. My brother's offices and the warehouse were attacked, and he thinks that some of the river traders have been warned against dealing with him.'

'But who would do such a thing?'

'My brother thinks it might be Frank Erskine,' Tante Rosemarie said, her brow furrowing with anxiety. 'André spoke out against Erskine at a public meeting, called him a liar and a cheat, and now these things have started to happen. It seems likely that they are connected.'

'Mr Erskine is a horrible man,' Estelle said with a little shiver. 'Your brother should be careful, Rosemarie. He might find that attacks on his warehouse are not the least of his worries.'

'Well, it cannot be helped,' Tante Rosemarie said as she stood up to leave. 'André was only saying what many people think. Erskine is not liked, Estelle – but most people are too frightened to say or do anything against him.'

'Yes, I can understand that,' Estelle said, and rose to kiss her on the cheek. 'Thank you again for coming, and I shall tell Justin what you say. We shall expect you to join us here when you are ready.'

'That will be very soon,' the older lady said. 'I shall not forget your kindness, my dear.'

'You must not worry about Erskine, my love,' Justin said when they spoke later that afternoon. 'I do not think he will dare to murder me, for I have friends, influential friends who might put two and two together. Nevertheless, you will do me the favour of not walking out alone, Estelle. Erskine knows that you are more important to me than anything else, and if he tried to strike at me, he would do it through you.'

'Yes, of course I shall obey you in this,' Estelle said and kissed him on the cheek. 'Now tell me, did you see our builder and what did he say?'

'We met as arranged,' Justin said, smiling at the eager light in her eyes. He had been less than truthful with her, for he knew that Erskine had sworn to be revenged on him, and would arrange an accident for Justin if he were careless. Because of that, he went nowhere without Sam or others of his crew to watch his back. 'He has agreed to draw something for us, and if we like it he will sail to the island with us when we leave and supervise the building for us.'

'Oh, Justin,' she cried, and threw her arms about him. 'How soon will it be ready? When can we leave?'

'It will take some days to draw up the plans,' he told her with a look of indulgence. 'And I have been negotiating a cargo of materials we shall need, which will be carried to the island by one of my ships.'

'So we must stay here for at least another week then?'

'Yes, if not longer,' Justin said and frowned, for he had guessed what lay behind her impatience. 'But you will not be bored, my love. Monsieur de Varennes has invited us to a party he is giving on Friday evening. I think we shall attend, for most of your old friends will be there.'

'Yes, Tante Rosemarie mentioned it, but did not deliver the invitation.'

'That is because her brother intended to do so himself,' Justin said. 'I believe he is a man we can do business with in the future. His son is a bit of a hothead, but I daresay he will grow out of it given time.'

'I think André is not happy in his marriage.'

'I have heard such rumours myself,' Justin said. 'But it would be as well if that young man learned to curb his tongue – otherwise he might end with a knife in his back one dark night.'

'Because he has made an enemy of Frank Erskine?' Estelle's eyes were dark with anxiety, for if André was at risk, then so was Justin. 'You will promise me to take care?'

'I am not likely to fall foul of Erskine's henchmen,' he told her. 'Forget this nonsense, Estelle, and tell me what you think of this material I have bought for you. Shall you have it made into curtains for our bedroom when the house is built?'

Estelle gave her attention to the bale of silk he had brought for her inspection. It was a jade green damask and shot through with silver lines. Very expensive, and very beautiful.

'I think it is lovely,' she said, knowing that he wanted to change the subject and allowing him to do so. 'You spoil me, Justin.'

'That is because I love you,' he said and kissed her. 'And now I am afraid I must leave you, Estelle. I have business this evening, and it will not wait.'

'Must you go out?' She looked at the window. It was a dark night and she was suddenly fearful. 'Would it not keep until tomorrow?'

'I believe not,' he said and frowned at her. 'Would you have me afraid of my own shadow?'

'Of course not.' She made an effort to put away her fears. 'I am foolish. Frank Erskine is more like to fear you than you him.'

'And perhaps he should,' Justin said and bent to kiss her cheek.

Monsieur de Varennes had come to him for help and his business was to see that more mischief was not done that night, mischief planned and paid for by Erskine. Interference in his business was bound to bring a sharp reaction from Erskine, but that was part of Justin's plan. There was only one way to deal with bullying cowards, and that was to face them down. By the time he had finished with the man he would not meddle so easily in the affairs of others.

The fight was short but bloody. Erskine's men had not been expecting to meet with opposition, and their plans to set fire to the warehouse of Monsieur de Varennes had gone awry.

Justin's men had been waiting for them in the darkness. The bullies that Erskine employed had not lingered when faced with men used to the cut and thrust of life at sea, men who had taken more prize ships than they could rightly remember, who relished the idea of a good fight after so many months of being merely merchant seamen.

After the first surprise, when some fought back and were cut down, the rest turned and fled into the night. Justin prevented his men from pursuing them and killing them. He wanted Erskine to learn of this night's work, to understand that he was no longer at liberty to use his cut-throats to terrorise other businessmen. De Varennes was not the only one to have suffered, and it must be ended before Erskine became too powerful.

'That was a good night's work,' Justin told his men. 'Go back to the ship now. It is safer not to drink on shore until this business is finished. The quartermaster will issue extra rations of rum, and there will be ten gold sovereigns for every man who took part in this tonight.'

'God bless you, Cap'n,' one of the men cried. 'We'll drink to your health, sir, and damnation to your enemies.'

205

'Erskine will go to Hell soon enough if the Cap'n has his way,' another said and the men went off laughing at the jest.

'And what of you, Cap'n?' Sam asked. 'You must watch more carefully now, for Erskine will not take kindly to your actions tonight. If he wished you dead before, he will do so twice as much by the time his men have reported what happened here.'

'Let us hope that he is angry,' Justin said with a smile. 'Angry men make mistakes. That is my only hope of trapping him into a duel.'

'So that's it,' Sam said. 'Well, I think you are risking a great deal, Cap'n, but you know your own mind on this.'

'To have him assassinated would bring me down to his level,' Justin said and stroked the scar on his cheek with the tip of his finger. 'Yet he is too dangerous to allow him to live. I want him dead, Sam, and if he gives me the chance, I shall see to it myself.'

'Do you like my gown?' Estelle did a little twirl for him. That evening she was wearing a dark emerald-green silk fashioned in the latest style with a high waist and a wide sash, which set off her colouring and figure to perfection. 'I had it made before we left Paris but kept it for a special occasion.'

'It is beautiful,' he said. 'I like it very much. Green is my favourite colour for you.'

She smiled, well pleased by his answer. She was looking forward to dining with the de Varennes family that evening, for she had been true to her word not to leave the house alone, and had remained in her parlour alone on those days when Justin had business without her.

'Yes, I know, that's why I chose it.'

'You look wonderful, my love,' he said. 'The gentlemen will all envy me this evening, and the ladies will drool over your gown.'

'When are we to leave New Orleans?' she asked, looking up at him. 'It is not that I am not happy here, but I long to see our island again.'

'My business keeps me here longer than I had imagined,' Justin said, not meeting her bright gaze. 'We shall go as soon as it is finished.'

With luck it might be in a way to being finished that evening.

Monsieur de Varennes had invited Frank Erskine to dine that evening, ostensibly to heal the breach between him and André. Would Erskine accept? He must know that de Varennes had approached Justin for help against his bullyboys, and that Justin was very likely to be present that evening. If he took the bait it would mean that his anger had grown to such proportions that he was willing to risk everything in a duel. He must know that if they were to meet in company Justin would find a way of challenging him, which he could not refuse unless he wished to be thought a coward and ostracised.

Erskine had not arrived when Tante Rosemarie welcomed them to the house, taking Estelle to sit with her in the drawing room as the gentlemen huddled together, apparently discussing some urgent business of their own. Estelle saw that Justin was frowning at something his host had to tell him, but her attempt to eavesdrop on the gentlemen's conversation was foiled as Suzanne came up to them. She was well into her second pregnancy, her body swollen and awkward, her lovely face sullen.

She sat on a small sofa opposite Estelle and looked at her, a flicker of jealousy in her eyes as she saw how slender and beautiful the other girl was. It had not escaped her notice that André could hardly take his eyes off the new Madame St Arnaud.

'So, you are not yet increasing,' Suzanne said, a note of spite in her voice. 'I should have thought you would have conceived a child by now.'

'No, it has not happened yet,' Estelle replied and felt a flicker of pain. She had found much happiness with Justin, but there was a little secret place in her mind that wondered why she had not managed to conceive before this.

'I had quite thought you must be.'

'No, unfortunately, that is not so,' she said. 'We cannot all be as fortunate as you, Suzanne.'

Suzanne gave a harsh laugh, her slight jealousy forgotten in favour of her other woes. 'I would not call myself fortunate, Estelle. I have had nothing but months of discomfort and illness. I wish that I might never have to go through this business again.'

'Suzanne,' Tante Rosemarie gave her a gentle reprimand,

glancing at André, who was gulping his wine as if it might be his last glass. 'I am sure you do not mean that, my dear. It is the duty of a loving wife to bear her husband's children.'

'If she had a loving husband perhaps,' Suzanne said and directed a resentful look at her husband. 'André never thinks of me. He drinks too much and . . .'

'Suzanne,' Tante Rosemarie warned. 'Not in company, my dear.'

Suzanne might have said more but a hush had fallen over the room, and turning her head, Estelle saw that Frank Erskine had entered. The colour drained from her face, and she felt sick. Had Justin known that he would be here this evening?

She half rose from her seat, but Tante Rosemarie caught her wrist and held it so tightly that Estelle stared at her. She had known this would happen. She had been expecting it, which was why she had chosen to sit beside Estelle.

'Justin mustn't . . .' Estelle whispered, but it was already too late. He had taken a few steps towards his enemy and his purpose was clear.

'It seems that you had the effrontery to accept our host's invitation,' Justin said in a loud clear voice that had several of the guests gasping. 'After your bullyboys tried to burn down his warehouse, ransacked his office and threatened his men, I did not expect it – but it is a most pleasant surprise. I am glad to see you here, sir, for it gives me the opportunity to do this.' He stepped forward and slapped Erskine across the face with a pair of grey gloves. He had not been wearing gloves and de Varennes must have given them to him. It was the correct procedure when challenging a man to a duel. 'You, sir, are a cheat, a liar, a murderer and a thief – and I think this world would be a better place without you.'

Erskine's face had gone from white to red, and now it was becoming a dark purple. His hands clenched at his sides as he struggled to control his rage, while saying nothing.

'Am I to add that you are also a coward?' Justin asked scornfully. 'Indeed, only a coward pays another man to abduct a defenceless woman.'

'Your whore is hardly a defenceless woman,' Erskine almost spat the words out, clearly unable to control his temper any longer. 'I accept your challenge, St Arnaud. You are no better

208

than a pirate but I shall show you that a gentleman does not run from your challenge.'

To the casual observer Justin's expression seemed not to alter, but Estelle saw the gleam in his eyes and knew that this was what he had always intended. This was the unfinished business that kept him here in New Orleans – that might rob him of his life and her of all that made life worth living. She longed to cry out, to beg them to stop, but it had gone beyond words. A challenge issued so publicly could not be taken back nor refused.

Her hand trembled, but Tante Rosemarie pressed it, giving her courage. The gentlemen were discussing weapons and seconds, as if it were all some party piece that they found rather intriguing. Her stomach churned as she realised that the duel was to take place at once. Monsieur de Varennes had produced two sets of duelling pistols, and Erskine was given the choice, for he had been challenged. He took the pistols out, weighed them in his hand, nodded as he accepted one set and gave them to his seconds to inspect, to see that all was well.

The decision made, the gentlemen left the room. Their manner was so correct, so punctilious, and so precise, that Estelle thought it would have been funny had it not been so serious. She tried to make eye contact with Justin, but he did not look at her.

As the door of the salon closed behind them she gave a little sob of despair. How could she bear it if anything were to happen to Justin?

'Why did they have to do it?' she asked of Tante Rosemarie.

'It was Captain St Arnaud's idea,' her friend told her. 'He said that it was the only way to bring Erskine to justice, and that all our lives were at risk until this thing was settled.'

'But if Erskine kills him . . .'

'He will not!' André was still standing by the sideboard, his wineglass in his hand. 'I give you my word that he will not, Estelle.'

'André!' Suzanne cried as he put the glass down and walked from the room, following the other men without glancing at his wife. 'There is no need for you to go . . .'

He ignored her and she rose to her feet, but one of the other ladies came to her, and took her arm, forcing her to sit down again. It was clear that everyone knew that this must happen, for otherwise Erskine's rule of terror would take over all their lives.

'I want to see,' Suzanne said. 'I want to see what happens.'

'That would be the worst thing you could do in your condition,' the lady who had stopped her from leaving the room said gently. 'A duel is not the place for us, my dear. We shall know the outcome soon enough.'

Estelle dug her nails into the palms of her hands. If it were not for Tante Rosemarie's gentle pressure on her arm she would have run from the room, but all she could do for the moment was sit and wait.

The duel was to take place in the courtyard behind the house, well away from any windows that the ladies might have been tempted to look out of in the hope of seeing what was going on. Both men were given a few minutes to make what preparations they would, adjustments to their clothing, last messages.

Erskine closed the collar of his dark coat and spoke briefly to one of his seconds. Justin did nothing. His affairs were in order, and he had no fear of facing any man's shot.

Monsieur de Varennes stuck carefully to the ritual of the gentleman's code in these things, each stage of the duel conducted in the same precise manner as had prevailed for many years.

'Are you ready gentlemen?' he asked, when the pistols had been primed, loaded and offered to first Erskine and then Justin. 'You will stand on the mark with your backs to each other and then take ten paces forward. After that, you may turn and fire at will. Is that understood?'

Erskine gave him a terse look. Justin smiled and inclined his head. The count began, and at the ninth step Erskine turned and fired at Justin's back. To his consternation, his shot went wide and in that very instant Justin turned and faced him. His face deadly white, Erskine spluttered, grabbed at his coat pocket and took out a gun, but it was not the single shot weapon that was traditionally used in such affairs as these. Instead, he had an evil-looking pistol of German origin that could fire about fifteen shots from its four barrels.

Justin raised his arm, his finger already on the trigger, but a mere second before he could fire a man standing to his right stepped forward.

'Damn you! By God, you won't do it,' André said and fired his own pistol at Erskine, who staggered from the shot, which had hit him in the shoulder. It was then that he made the biggest mistake of his life, for instead of shooting Justin, he swung round and aimed his pistol at André.

As André fell wounded, Justin called one word, 'Erskine!' and, as he jerked back, clutching at his shoulder, frantically preparing to fire again, Justin's shot rang out, and the ball entered the centre of Erskine's forehead. He fell like a stone, the neat round hole in his head showing hardly any blood, just a fringe of powder burns. His condition was not in doubt and he was attended only by his seconds as their duty demanded, but several of the gentlemen had gathered about André and were trying to decide whether he was dead or alive.

As Justin joined them, André's eyelids flickered.

'The young fool,' he murmured. 'But he may have saved my life. I suggest that André acted bravely to prevent murder. I don't know about the rest of you, but I consider him a hero.'

There were several cries of agreement. Erskine had not been liked, and the de Varennes' family was popular and well-respected. Besides, in producing that fearful pistol Erskine had broken all the laws of their code and they had no respect or pity for him.

'That is exactly what I saw,' one gentleman said. 'Erskine broke the code. He turned early, tried to murder St Arnaud and had another weapon concealed about his person. André acted swiftly, as was necessary, to save St Arnaud from being foully murdered.' There were murmurs of agreement from the other gentlemen.

Monsieur de Varennes inclined his head gratefully. With so many witnesses to testify that André had acted as he ought, he could not be accused of attempted murder – and in the end it had been Justin's ball that killed Erskine, which in the circumstances he had a perfect right to do.

'André makes an unlikely hero,' the father said with a little smile. 'But I accept the verdict of you all, gentlemen – and now perhaps we should join the ladies before they become too impatient.'

'You must send for a doctor,' Justin said, 'and there are certain formalities, but I can deal with them. Go in and join your guests, sir. I shall follow when I have made sure this business is properly finished.'

André was already being carried inside the house. Justin watched as the others trooped in behind. He smiled a little grimly as he imagined the tales that would be told to placate the ladies. Estelle would be on thorns, but before he could comfort her there were things that must be done. He organised one of de Varennes' servants to fetch the doctor, another to inform the Justice of what had taken place. Yet more were dispatched to carry Erskine's body into one of the lesser rooms at the back of the house, where it might be decently covered and left in peace until the formalities had been completed.

He was about to return to the house when he saw a woman emerge and come hurriedly towards him. He knew at once who it was and went to greet her, holding out his arms.

'Oh, Justin,' she said on a sob as he embraced her. 'Forgive me, I could not wait another moment. They told me that Erskine was dead and that you were not hurt – but I was afraid they were keeping the truth from me.'

'As you see, it was perfectly true. There were things to do, Estelle, and since this thing was done at my instigation, it was my responsibility to see it through.'

'André has been shot . . .'

'Erskine tried to murder me,' Justin said. 'He turned early and when his first shot went wide, he produced another weapon – some kind of devilish revolving pistol that fires several shots. He could have killed us all with it – and indeed, he did his best, but, fortunately for both André and myself, he was not a good shot.'

'That's why he fired early isn't it?'

'Yes. I expected that he might – but I knew that even with such an advantage he would probably only manage to wound me in the shoulder, and I was aware of what he was doing. I turned on the instant his shot went wide.'

'Only wound you!' she exclaimed. 'You nearly died the last time.'

212

'I think Sam's cure had as much to do with that as my wound,' Justin said and smiled wryly. 'And now, my love, we must return to the house. Everyone will be waiting to dine, and I cannot leave here until the formalities are complete.'

'I do not think I could eat a morsel!'

'I do not have a great appetite myself, but I shall manage enough for politeness and you must do the same, my love. It is important that we carry on as if everything were as it ought to be. When the Justice has been and everything signed and sealed according to the law, we shall take our leave.'

'Would it not be polite of me to go upstairs to comfort Suzanne?' Estelle asked. 'When the news of André came she collapsed and Tante Rosemarie had to assist her upstairs.'

'And you do not feel comfortable at sitting down to dinner,' Justin said with a smile. 'Very well, go up to your friend, Estelle. I daresay you may be of comfort to her. I shall tell you when I am ready to leave.'

Estelle smiled and thanked him for his understanding. She did not know how any of them could carry on as if nothing had happened, but she knew that they would do so.

Upstairs, Tante Rosemarie welcomed Estelle to Suzanne's bedroom, for her niece was in great distress.

'I am glad that you have come,' she said, smiling at Estelle. 'I should go to my nephew. The doctor may need help and I would wish to make sure that everything is in readiness for his arrival, but I could not leave Suzanne.'

'I am glad to be of help,' Estelle said. 'I could not go on with dinner as if everything were normal.'

'No, but it is necessary,' Tante Rosemarie told her. 'Unless we wish for a terrible scandal, this must be contained within our circle as much as possible. The duel itself was bad enough, but this other business – I pray that André will not be suspected of attempting to murder Mr Erskine.'

'Surely not?' Estelle said, and glanced towards the bed, where Suzanne lay with her lace kerchief pressed to her face. 'No, I am sure it will all go over quite easily.'

'We must pray for it,' Tante Rosemarie nodded towards the bed. 'Look after her, my dear.'

Estelle went over to the bed as the older woman left them. Suzanne opened her eyes and gave a little moan.

'What shall I do if he dies?' she said on a sob. 'Oh, I cannot bear it! Why did he have to get involved at all? It was not his quarrel.'

Estelle forbore to remind her that André had begun the breach with Erskine, contenting herself with a little shake of her head.

'Who knows why men will do these things?' she asked. 'Does your head ache, Suzanne? Would you like me to bathe it for you with water and lavender?'

'Thank you, but Tante Rosemarie has ordered a tisane.' She pushed up against the pile of silken pillows, wiping her face with a cologne-soaked kerchief. 'I daresay I shall be better in a moment. It was just the shock. I have been horrible to André of late, because I thought he no longer loved me – but I should not like him to die.'

'That would be tragic, for he acted bravely, Suzanne. Indeed, Mr Erskine had a fearful weapon that might have fired several shots and André's prompt action may have saved Justin's life. The gentlemen are calling him a hero.'

'Yes . . .' Suzanne looked struck by this. 'Yes, it was very brave of André, and clever of him to be prepared for treachery. I am glad that awful man has been killed – he used to say unpleasant things to me at times, and the servant girls were all afraid of him.' She looked brighter for a moment, and then her face crumpled and she gave a little sob. 'If only André doesn't die . . .'

The door opened at that moment to reveal Monsieur de Varennes. He stood at the threshold and looked in. 'May I come in a moment, daughter? I wanted to tell you that the doctor has arrived and he says that André's wound is fortunate. He may be confined to bed for some days but it was slight, and he will take no permanent harm.'

'Thank God for it,' Estelle said and gave Suzanne her own kerchief as she started to weep again. 'We are glad to hear your news, sir.'

'The Justice has also arrived, and things are in a way to be settled. Your husband will be ready in ten minutes, Madame St Arnaud. He tells me you wish to go home at once, and in truth I expect most of my guests to depart once it is all settled.'

'Thank you, sir. I shall come down in a few minutes.'

A maid arrived as Monsieur de Varennes departed. She was

carrying a tisane of lemon and honey with a few drops of brandy to help Suzanne sleep. She drank the small measure of brandy, sipped most of the tisane and then settled down to sleep.

'I think you may leave me now,' she said to Estelle. 'I was jealous of you because I thought that André liked you too much – but you have been very kind, and I know you love your husband.'

'As you love yours,' Estelle said. 'Perhaps if you told André how much you love him, you may feel a little happier.'

'Yes, I shall,' Suzanne said. 'Tomorrow, when I feel rested.'

Estelle left the room, closing the door softly behind her. Suzanne had a selfish nature and it was not likely that the shock she had received that evening would change it, but perhaps she had learned to be a little kinder to her husband.

Justin was waiting in the hall when she walked downstairs. He was talking to a man she had seen only once before, but whom she knew to be a Procurateur de Justice. As she approached, he shook hands with Justin, accepted his hat and gloves from one of the servants and took his leave.

'Is everything as it should be?' Estelle asked, looking at him anxiously.

'It could not be otherwise for there were a dozen witnesses to testify to Erskine's attempt to murder me, and André's prompt action can only be applauded.'

'Is that truly what happened?'

'Yes, of course,' Justin said and smiled. 'Erskine broke the rules. He knew that a duel would be the outcome of any meeting between us – and he cheated. The pistol he carried was a lethal weapon and might have killed any number of us. You should not let his death disturb you, my love. He was a man who lived by brutality and died a better death than he deserved. Had I not arranged this meeting, he would have been dealt with in a less honourable way.'

Estelle nodded. It was best to ask no more questions. Except one.

'Can we go home now, Justin?'

'We are leaving now.'

'I mean to our real home,' she said. 'I want to see our island again.'

215

'Yes, I know.' He smiled at her, tipping her face up to kiss her lips softly. 'That is what I want too, my love.'

Estelle stood at the helm of the ship, her hands on the wheel, Justin's arms about her as they saw the dark smudge of land on the horizon.

'We are nearly there,' he said, and kissed the back of her neck. 'Three of my ships are before us, and everything should be waiting for us – work can begin within days. All you have to do is decide where you want your house built, Estelle.'

'There are so many places . . .' she said, her heart beating faster as they saw the island begin to take shape. Suddenly it was there, looming before them in the sunlight, and she saw the perfect place: a little plateau that looked out across the sea to the west, but with an easy climb to the beach. 'Why not there?' She pointed towards the spot and Justin saw exactly what she meant.

'A good choice,' he approved, 'for we shall get the sea breezes and the evening sun. I had thought of the glade . . . but I think this is better. Yes, we shall build our house there.'

'We shall see our ships returning,' Estelle said. 'If you build a quay on the main beach they will be able to unload their cargoes and I shall be able to watch as you go about your business, but we shall also have our own private cove.'

'I see that you have it all thought out,' Justin teased. 'Time for me to take over now. We need to negotiate the rocks and currents, for they can be treacherous until you pass into the lagoon.'

Estelle moved away, watching as the men took soundings and called out to one another. She had been longing for this moment and now the excitement was rising inside her, but for a moment her thoughts were elsewhere.

Tante Rosemarie had cried a little as they parted, and Estelle had found it harder to part from her friend than she had expected.

'You will not forget us entirely I hope?'

'No, of course I shall not forget you,' Estelle told her and kissed her cheek. 'We shall come to New Orleans sometimes, as I promised you. Justin has decided that his ships will conduct much of their business through your brother, and he will not want to give up the sea entirely – though in time we may not wish to leave our home as often.'

'If you have children?'

'If we are lucky enough to have children, they will necessarily keep me on the island for a few months,' Estelle agreed. 'But sometimes I think that I never shall.'

'I am sure that you will,' Tante Rosemarie said and patted her cheek with her gloved hand. 'Suzanne fell quickly for her children, but some women have to wait a long time. A lady I know well was seven years before she had her first, Estelle. You should not despair just yet.'

'No, of course not,' Estelle said, but she could not help worrying that it might never happen. 'At least we shall have a doctor on the island if we need one, for Justin has found a man who wishes to leave New Orleans and make his home with us. Besides our crews, who will all have homes there to settle their families, several craftsmen have thrown in their lot with us.'

'Is it a large island then?'

'Oh yes, quite big enough to support a small settlement,' Estelle said happily. 'I daresay it would take more than a day to walk from one side to the other, and two to walk the length of it perhaps, though we have never tried. It is so beautiful and there is an abundance of fruit and birds. We shall supply ourselves with anything that cannot be produced on the island, but I believe a few sheep and pigs have already been established there.'

'It sounds very exciting,' Tante Rosemarie said with a smile. 'And of course you have the ships. You may leave whenever you wish.'

'My father thought the world was split into two places, New Orleans and Paris,' Estelle said with a fond smile. 'I am glad I have seen Paris. I enjoyed my stay there – but for me the island is more beautiful.'

'Then I can only wish you happiness, my dear.'

And now, she was almost sure that her happiness was complete. The suspicion that she was at last carrying Justin's child had begun to take root in her mind these past few days. She had hugged her secret to herself for she did not wish to speak too soon, and it would seal the happiness she felt bubbling up inside her if she kept her news until they were on the island.

They were negotiating the treacherous rocks that protected the island, Justin guiding his ship through the narrow passage that led into the lagoon. And then at last they had let down the anchor and the boats were being readied.

Justin came to help Estelle down into the first boat. She sat forward eagerly, straining to see all that was going on ashore. Already the beginnings of a quayside had sprung up and she saw that several men were working on various projects on the beach. Some of the greenery had been cleared away at one point of the beach, and it was there that huts had been built to shelter the craftsmen who had gone on before them. But the stretch of coastline that their house would look down on was untouched, and it would retain its natural beauty.

Some of the interior of the island would be used for homes and crops, but parts of it would remain wild, forbidden to all save for the pleasure of walking there.

Justin was truly king of his island, and already he had spoken of laws and ideals all those who wished to live there must abide by. Yet since they were fair, making all men equal, each receiving the same for their labour, and sharing the common produce for the common good, it seemed to bode well for the future of their community.

Once on shore there was much to see. A temporary home had been built for them, and Estelle found the plain but sturdy wooden building adequate for her immediate needs. Most of their belongings would remain in the chests and crates in which they had been transported to the island, but the bed was already erected and needed only the addition of linen and pillows.

They had a table and chairs, and a cupboard in which to store food, the same as the other dwellings that had been finished so far. The beautiful things they had bought in Paris would remain packed until their grand house was built over-looking the hilltops.

It was not until evening that Justin was free to come to her, and by then she had the house ready for them to live in, her sea chests making additional storage and filling up the empty spaces.

'You have worked hard,' Justin said as they ate the food Jessie had prepared for them. 'I was thinking we might take a walk after supper, but perhaps you are too tired?'

'No, I am not tired at all,' she said, her eyes glowing. 'I want to explore with you, Justin – to see our glade, to be certain that nothing has changed.'

'The men know that the glade is off limits other than for fruit gathering,' he said and held his hand out to her. 'It is our special place, Estelle, and always will be.'

'Yes,' she said and smiled as she took his hand.

He put his arm about her waist as they walked slowly up the beach and into the lush undergrowth of the interior. The path had been well trodden, some of the overhanging vegetation cleared to make it easier to walk, and they found the glade where they had declared their love for each other months ago without difficulty.

'I never dreamed that day that I should find such happiness,' Justin said as he looked down into her lovely face. 'I meant to take you back to New Orleans and from there to London and Paris – but I did not dare to hope that you would want to return here, Estelle.'

'But it is so beautiful, so peaceful,' she said. 'And I knew that you had plans for your island. I wanted to be a part of them, to share your life in every way.'

'You have made my life complete. There is nothing more I need,' he said and bent his head to kiss her softly on the lips.

'Nothing more?' Her eyes were bright with mischief as she gazed up at him. 'Are you sure there is nothing more you desire, Justin?'

'I am not sure what you mean?' He was clearly puzzled and her laughter rang out joyfully. 'Estelle?'

'Would you not like a son?' she asked. 'Every kingdom must have its prince, must it not?'

'Estelle . . .' His eyes glowed with a sudden fierce light and he let out a whoop of pure joy. 'We are to have a child? This is true? I had wondered . . .'

'As I had,' Estelle said. 'I feared I might be barren, that I might never give you a son – but now I am sure that I am with child.'

219

'My precious darling,' Justin said. 'How glad I am that Doctor John came with us, though I know that Jessie would have done most that is needful, but it is good to know that we have a doctor should you need him. I shall welcome the birth of our child, be it a daughter or a son – but you are my first concern.'

'We shall have a son,' Estelle told him confidently. 'Marietta once told me that I should have two sons, but I had begun to fear she was wrong. Of late I have felt that her spirit was with me. She says that we have passed through the storms into the light, and I am sure that in a few months I shall bear our first son.'

Justin lowered his head to kiss her, the look in his eyes gently teasing her. He traced the curve of her lovely cheek, feeling a new kind of peace enter his soul. It was as if all his life he had been searching for something, and now, at last, he held it in his hand.

'If Marietta has told you so, then I expect that is the way it will be,' he said, and then he laughed. In the trees overhead a bird flew from its perch, unsettled by the sound of his laughter, but then, around them, the silence settled into perfect peace once more.

They were truly in their own little paradise, and there they shall be left to make what they will of their lives.